Charlotte Hubbard

"Fans of Amish fiction will love Charlotte Hubbard's series *Seasons of the Heart*. Willow Ridge is a charming place, filled with unforgettable characters, and readers will want to visit again and again, finding new insights each time."
—Marta Perry, *Lydia's Hope, the Lost Sisters of Pleasant Valley*

"Fans will relish this tender tale of an *Englischer* finding her roots, as cultures collide while love blossoms in Missouri."
—Harriet Klausner

"This series and these very special books will sit proudly on my keeper shelf to visit again and again."
—Romance Reviews Today

Kelly Long

"Long creates storylines that captivate her readers . . ."
—*Romantic Times*

"Kelly Long writes with an intensity and passion that immediately draws the reader into her stories."
—Beth Wiseman

"Long's writing style is smooth and engaging, her characters sympathetic, well-rounded, and true to the period, yet timeless in their hopes and flaws and personal battles . . ."
—*USA Today* Books/HEA

Jennifer Beckstrand

"Readers will treasure this series and put the first outing on their keeper shelf."
—RT Book Reviews

"A delightful voice in Amish romance. Sweet and funny."
—Emma Miller

"A delightful cast of characters in a story that overflows with Amish love and laughter."
—Charlotte Hubbard

More Seasons of the Heart books by Charlotte Hubbard

Summer of Secrets
Autumn Winds
Winter of Wishes
Breath of Spring
An Amish Country Christmas

More Amish of Ice Mountain books by Kelly Long

The Amish Bride of Ice Mountain

More Huckleberry Hill books from Jennifer Beckstrand

Huckleberry Hill
Huckleberry Summer
Huckleberry Christmas

An AMISH CHRISTMAS QUILT

CHARLOTTE HUBBARD

KELLY LONG

JENNIFER BECKSTRAND

KENSINGTON BOOKS
www.kensingtonbooks.com

KENSINGTON BOOKS are published by

Kensington Publishing Corp.
119 West 40th Street
New York, NY 10018

All Kensington titles, imprints, and distributed lines are available at special quantity discounts for bulk purchases for sales promotion, premiums, fund-raising, and educational or institutional use.

Special book excerpts or customized printings can also be created to fit specific needs. For details, write or phone the office of the Kensington Special Sales Manager: Kensington Publishing Corp., 119 West 40th Street, New York, NY 10018. Attn. Special Sales Department. Phone: 1-800-221-2647.

ISBN-13: 978-1-61773-554-7
ISBN-10: 1-61773-554-X
First Kensington Trade Paperback Printing: November 2014

eISBN-13: 978-1-61773-555-4
eISBN-10: 1-61773-555- 8
First Kensington Electronic Edition: November 2014

10 9 8 7 6 5 4 3 2 1

Printed in the United States of America

CONTENTS

A WILLOW RIDGE CHRISTMAS PAGEANT

CHARLOTTE HUBBARD

CHAPTER 1

Mary Kauffman clutched herself as another contraction ripped through her insides. Fresh tears sprang to her eyes as she somehow kept from screaming—somehow kept the lines in her hand while the horse and buggy continued down the unfamiliar road. Was she anywhere near Willow Ridge and Aunt Miriam's? How much longer could she possibly keep driving, now that her water had broken?

"Are we there yet?" five-year-old Lucy whined from the back seat.

"Are we *lost*?" Sol asked in a testier voice. At seven, he was more acutely aware than Lucy of how their father's death was affecting their family—and more critical of Mary, as well. "I'm pretty sure we should've turned left onto that last blacktop we crossed."

Oh, but Mary wanted to scream—except Sol might be right. She was so frightened and in such excruciating pain, it was entirely possible that she'd forgotten which county road passed through Willow Ridge ... *because you've always been riding to Aunt Miriam's rather than driving ... always depended upon Dat or Elmer to get you where you needed to go.*

Lucy's two cats scuffled in the cardboard box on the seat beside

Mary, and then a ginger paw poked through a breathing hole in the top of the makeshift carrier. When one of them yowled, Rowdy, their border collie, let out a disciplinary *woof.*

Lucy begin sniffling again. "Can I *please* let the kitties out to—"

"No!" Mary snapped more vehemently than she intended. "We'll be at Aunt Miriam's in just a few—"

"I don't *ever* remember seeing those black and white cows before," Sol remarked tersely. "We need to turn around and—Rowdy, *no!* You can't get out and chase those cows!"

Mary's head pounded as the dog began to jump and lunge, barking frantically out the buggy's back window. Again, she peered down the gravel road, looking for signs of the Sweet Seasons Bakery Café, which belonged to her aunt. It was an unfortunate fact that most Plain houses were tall and white with additions on them, and that they sat back from gravel roads that looked so much alike. Or maybe the café was on a blacktop, and she really did need to turn back to—

Another hard contraction hit Mary so suddenly, she cried out before she could catch herself. All this way, she'd been so careful not to frighten the kids, not to let on that she'd gone into labor during the night, because she was determined to see them safely to Aunt Miriam's before the baby came. When they'd left Bowling Green in the wee hours this morning, Mary had bypassed her parents' place, sensing her mother would've made her stay. And maybe that was just one in a long line of stupid mistakes she'd made.

"Are you gonna have the baby *now,* Mamma?" Lucy wailed.

"She can't have it while we're out here on the road, silly! She's gotta be in a bed, like Mamm was when you were born," her brother replied. "I think I'd better drive—"

Again, Mary clutched herself as a keening cry rose from her throat. Somehow she steered the horse to the shoulder of the road and stopped it, even as her head began to spin and her mind filled with odd, rapid-fire images. She slumped against the wall of the buggy, caving in to another ripping pain as the blackness began closing in. Was she out of her head, or had Rowdy just jumped out the window? The kids' strident voices seemed so distant now . . .

* * *

Seth Brenneman propped open the door to his wood shop, allowing fresh air inside now that the final coat of varnish on his walnut table had dried. This dining room set—one of many orders he'd already received for pre-Christmas delivery—was complete, with its china hutch, ten chairs, and leaves for the table. He smiled as the natural light shimmered richly on the tabletop. It was only September 28, months ahead of Christmas, but already the holiday season promised to be the most profitable ever for the woodworking and construction business he and his two brothers ran. When Micah and Aaron returned from an installation, they would deliver this set to its new owners in Bloomingdale, so Seth began piling furniture pads near the door.

Loud, strident barking made him stick his head outside. The racket came from a black and white border collie—and when it caught sight of Seth, it bounded toward him, barking even more insistently. Nobody around Willow Ridge owned a dog like this; he wondered if someone had dumped it on the roadside. The last thing he needed was a noisy, bothersome dog to feed, so he removed the chunk of wood from beneath the door to close it—

But the dog shot toward him, fixing him with an intense brown-eyed gaze that refused to be ignored. It charged at him, nipping his pant leg, still barking frantically as it pivoted to dash back toward the road. When the dog saw that Seth wasn't following, it came at him again, barking even louder and faster as it circled him.

"Hey! What're you—don't nip *me*, you ornery—" As Seth dodged the dog's next attack, he noticed a surrey on the road with a small horse trailer behind it. At first sight he thought nothing of it, because in Willow Ridge, Missouri, double-sized buggies were an everyday thing. But when the border collie headed in that direction again, barking at him over its shoulder, Seth noticed the surrey wasn't moving. As he loped toward the road, he heard a little girl crying her heart out. Then another young voice rose over the caterwauling.

"*Wake up*! You'd better not die and leave us here—not like our *real mamm* did!"

Seth broke into a run, his thoughts racing. The dog was circling the rig and the Belgian hitched to it began to toss its head nervously. A shrill whinny came from the trailer. Before his visions of a runaway buggy could become reality, Seth took hold of the harness. "Whoa, now," he crooned to the draft horse. "No need to rush off, fella."

The horse stomped its massive front hoof and shook its head—understandable, considering the racket the dog was making.

"You! Enough!" Seth commanded, pointing at the border collie. "Sit!"

The dog obeyed, planting itself close enough to lunge at him if he made any threatening moves—and Seth respected the border collie's protective instincts. He slowly opened the front door of the double rig and peered inside. "What's the trouble? My name's—"

Words left him. A young woman dressed in black slumped against the opposite side of the rig, her face pallid and slack beneath her black *kapp*. Beside her, a cardboard box shifted on the seat as mewling noises came from inside it. When he lifted the box, the little girl and boy in the back seat grabbed each other and gaped fearfully at him. Worn suitcases and taped boxes were piled around them, leaving just enough room for the dog to ride on the floor between the two back bench seats.

When the woman moaned, Seth thrust the thumping box toward the kids. "Here—you'd better take this while I see to your *mamm*."

After the little girl snatched the box, clutching it in her lap, he got a better look at the young woman who'd been driving. She appeared to be still in her teens, awfully thin—yet her arm was curved around a bulging belly. Whether or not she seemed old enough or strong enough, her baby was trying to be born. When she writhed in pain again, Seth hopped into the rig.

"We've got a clinic just up the road," he explained to the kids as he grabbed the lines. "Hang on. We'll be there in a few."

The Belgian surged forward and the border collie again began to circle and bark, but Seth barely noticed the racket. He wanted to rouse the young woman—to stroke the strawberry-blond hair back from her pale, sweaty face and tell her where he was taking her. But he thought better of it, considering how scared of him the kids looked.

What have I gotten myself into? Why would this girl be on the road when her baby is so close to—and where's the man of this family? Why does everyone look so . . . pinched?

It struck him then that perhaps the young woman wore a black *kapp* because she was in mourning . . . even more of a hardship for the kids, if their birth mother had apparently died, as well. As the Belgian stepped briskly down the road, Seth glanced into the back seat, where the towheaded brother and sister still clung to each other.

"It'll be all right," he assured them, touched by the way their eyes filled their faces. "We've got a real *gut* fella here who's delivered lots of babies. Where were ya goin' when your *mamm* passed out?"

The boy frowned. "Our *mamm*'s in Heaven. This is our—"

"Take us to Aunt Miriam's," the little girl interrupted in a tiny voice.

Seth approached the intersection, watching for oncoming traffic. "Miriam Lantz? And her name's Miriam Hooley now?" he asked as he steered the Belgian onto the county blacktop. Countless Plain women were named Miriam, after all.

The girl's face went blank. Either she didn't know Miriam's last name or she was too scared to recall it. "I want to see if my kitties are okay," she whined.

"No!" her brother said as he grabbed for the box in her lap. "You can't let them—"

When the box shifted with the kids' scuffle, a ginger-colored cat sprang out of the loose top, followed by a striped one. As the kids tried to catch them, squealing, and the cats scrambled around the boxes to avoid being caught, Seth was *very* glad to be pulling into the lot of the Willow Ridge Clinic. "You've got to corral those cats while I help your *mamm*," Seth told them more brusquely than he intended to. "Don't run out into the road! Get them back in their box and then come inside!"

Pandemonium had erupted in the back seat. Seth suspected both kids were getting clawed as they tried to grab the cats, but his main concern was the young woman slumped against the opposite side of the buggy. Her loosened hair clung damply to a face that resembled white candle wax. Her breathing was ragged and shallow—and when he grasped her shoulder, she didn't respond.

Out cold. Only one thing to do, he thought as he opened his door. "I'm taking her inside," he told the kids, "so you'll have to look after yourselves until I get back. Better yet, come into the clinic—but not with the cats!"

Scooping the petite woman into his arms, Seth eased her across the seat and then stepped to the ground. Even in her advanced pregnancy, he doubted she weighed a hundred pounds. As her head lolled against his shoulder and her mouth dropped open, Seth hoped he wasn't hurting her—wasn't moving her the wrong way—but he didn't know what else to do. He hurried to the clinic door and then kicked repeatedly on it.

"Open up!" he called out. The girl was dead weight in his arms, limp and helpless with her distended belly. While Seth wasn't a man who prayed over every little thing, he found himself petitioning for this young mother's welfare. "Open the door—hurry!" he cried, desperately hoping their local nurse, Andy Leitner, or his assistant, Rebecca, was at the front desk.

Lord, please help us along here. Please don't let her lose this baby on account of how I don't know what I'm doing.

She stirred in his arms and for a few seconds her eyes opened . . . deep green eyes, like an evergreen windbreak, they were. When she met his gaze, Seth's heartbeat stilled. He saw her need, her yearning, her pain—her absolute trust—and it scared him half to death. He was so drawn in, unable to look away, that he was only vaguely aware of the clinic door opening.

"Oh, my! Come in, Seth," Rebecca said breathlessly. "Andy's with a patient, but I'll get him right away! Put her on the table in there."

With utmost care, Seth entered the small exam room and eased the woman onto the padded table. "It's going to be all right," he murmured, hoping he was correct. "You're in *gut* hands here—"

The young woman's eyes rolled back as her belly and hips undulated with a powerful contraction. Seth reminded himself that he'd assisted several mares and cows with birthings over the years.

He tried to keep his thoughts on this level—livestock bearing their young, competently and naturally, and usually without complications—because the thought of being present when this woman's baby came out made him gaze anxiously toward the hallway. Delivery was another matter altogether when a woman was involved, because every now and again they didn't survive the ordeal. This girl looked so fragile and—

"Who do we have here?" Andy Leitner asked as he stepped into the room. His dark eyes never left the young woman as he washed his hands at the sink.

"I don't have any idea," Seth replied, "but I'm mighty glad you're with her. She's got a couple of little kids out in a buggy, along with two cats that got loose and some sort of horse in a trailer, and a border collie whipping them all into a frenzy." He paused . . . didn't hear the dog barking anymore. "I'd better go check on them. It seems awfully quiet out there."

And what'll you do with them? Probably not a gut *idea for them to sit in the waiting room while their* mamm *cries out with her contractions. And if the cats jumped out of the buggy and ran off—*

Seth stepped outside and stopped in his tracks. Despite not being tied, the Belgian stood obediently at the hitching post. No distressed whinnies came from the trailer. At one side of the surrey, the boy and his sister were gazing at him, each of them holding a cat, under the watchful eye of the black and white dog. He'd heard border collies were herders and organizers, and he was now a believer. A very grateful believer.

He smiled at the kids, stooping to their level. "Does the Aunt Miriam you know own a bakery?" he asked on a hunch.

Their eyes lit up. "*Jah!*" the little girl said with a squeal. "I want a snickerdoodle!"

"And she makes really *gut* chocolate pie, too—that's what I had at her wedding," the boy replied. Then his brow furrowed. "Is this Willow Ridge?"

Bingo! Thank You, Lord! Seth thought as his smile widened. "It is, and Miriam's café is right down the road. Shall we go there, so she'll know you and your *mamm* are in town?"

"She's not our—"

"Button it up, Sol!" his sister blurted as she scrambled back into the buggy. "You didn't even know we was in the right town! And I'm too starvin' to care!"

After the kids put the cats back into their box, Seth slipped into the driver's seat. He was relieved to be delivering these kids to someone who'd know who they were . . . and what to do with them. Sol coaxed the dog into the back, and as they rolled onto the blacktop, the *clip-clop, clip-clop* of the Belgian's sturdy hooves steadied Seth's pulse. He could settle the kids at a table, let Miriam fuss over them, leave money for their lunch, and then be on his way back to the shop. By now, Aaron and Micah were probably wondering where he was and why he'd left the shop door wide open.

Seth soon realized his plan wasn't going to work out that way. When the kids burst through the door of the Sweet Seasons and spotted Miriam pouring coffee, they were oblivious to the lunch crowd.

"Aunt Miriam!" the little girl cried as she rushed between the tables.

When Miriam looked up, her eyes widened. "Lucy and Sol! I wasn't expectin' you kids so soon—and where's your *mamm*?" She set down her carafe and slipped her arms around them.

Seth squeezed between the tables as quickly as he could, nodding at the folks he knew as they ate their dinner. "She's at the clinic, havin' her baby," he said in a low voice. "I found their buggy stopped alongside the road and—"

"Well, I'd better get myself right down there! Will ya drive me?" Miriam bustled toward the counter to set down her order pad. "Naomi, I'm off to help my niece from Bowling Green— Mose's girl, the one I told ya was comin'?"

From the cookstove in the kitchen, Seth's mother waved her off. "We'll be just fine, dearie. You go see to her—and you're takin' her, son?"

There was no way out of it now, was there? "*Jah*, tell Aaron and Micah that's where I am if they come in askin'," Seth replied.

"But I want pie!" Sol piped up. "Chocolate pie!"

"I'm starvin'! " Lucy joined in as both kids gazed up at Miriam. "We left so early we didn't hardly have nothin' to eat."

Seth smiled. Miriam Hooley considered it her mission to feed everyone she met, and her expression said she wasn't about to ignore these pleading children.

"Truth be told, it might be best if you kids had your lunch while I see how that baby's comin' along," Miriam responded as she glanced at Seth over their heads.

He nodded, even as he suspected what was coming next.

"Let's sit ya right here at this table," she said, leading them toward an empty one near the kitchen doorway. "Seth can have his lunch with ya, and then ya can find Ben and get settled in at our place. By then I'm thinkin' you'll have a baby sister or brother."

"*Please*, not another girl," Sol said with a roll of his eyes.

Seth chuckled as he pulled out a chair for Lucy. "I felt the same way when my little sister Hannah was born," he said. "We had three boys who were getting along just fine, and then everything changed with a sister. But she turned out to be the best sister ever," he added as he smiled at Lucy.

Sol considered what Seth had said, but didn't comment as he took his place at the table. Instead, the boy looked at Miriam. "So, how long do we have to stay here with *him*?" he asked as he pointed at Seth. "We've got our cats and Rowdy in the rig, and our miniature pony, Clarabelle, in the trailer."

"*Jah*, we couldn't leave 'em at the farm all by theirselves," Lucy said with an emphatic nod.

Seth took his seat. He wasn't sure how to respond to Sol, who had a chip on his shoulder about the size of his head. When Miriam glanced at Seth, as though asking if there was a problem she hadn't yet heard about, he shrugged. "I think Rowdy'll keep watch over the cats while we eat, and the horses'll be fine," he replied as he reached for a laminated menu.

"You'll have to ask Ben about makin' a place in the barn for the pets," Miriam said, as though she hadn't expected such a menagerie to arrive with this family. "I'll go check on your *mamm* now, and when I get back—"

"She's not our *mamm*," Sol muttered. "I wish people would stop—"

Before Sol could utter another word, Miriam clapped her hands on either side of his face. The boy had no choice but to look her in the eye.

"*You*, young fella, had better change your tune," Miriam said in a low, no-nonsense tone. "I know ya miss your *dat*, and I know you've been missin' your *mamm* even longer. But God's made sure ya had another parent to take care of ya—not to mention bringin' Seth to your rig to look after ya today," she added with a rise of her eyebrows. "You're gonna be stayin' with Ben and me, and at our house we have an attitude of gratitude. I'll be askin' Seth how ya behaved while I was gone, and I'll hear a *gut* report, ain't so?"

Sol nodded reluctantly. When Miriam released him, he looked down at his lap.

"Order anything ya want for lunch," Miriam said in a lighter tone, smiling gently at Lucy. "You kids've had a long trip today. Ya must be real tired. I'll see ya at the house—and before I go to the clinic, I'll tell Ben you're here."

The kids watched Miriam stop in the kitchen to talk with Naomi for a moment before she went out the back kitchen door. When they looked at Seth again, he smiled and pointed to the menu. "They make really *gut* hamburgers here, or ya could have grilled cheese—or we can see what's on the buffet," he said, pointing toward the steam table.

Sol and Lucy seemed frozen in place, looking at him as though they'd forgotten how to talk. It was the same expression they'd worn in the rig when he'd first gotten in. Was he really so scary? Or were these kids just tired and shy?

Takes ya back a few years, doesn't it? At their age, you were too bashful to say boo to a stranger, too. So now what'll you do?

Seth hoped Ben Hooley would come sooner rather than later, or he and these two kids might be sitting here for a long, long while. Miriam's daughter, Rhoda, was waiting tables and seemed to sense his desperation—and by the time she'd coaxed the kids' orders from them, Ben showed up. He was a fellow who could talk to anybody, and as he engaged Lucy and Sol in chatter about their animals, relief washed over Seth. He really should be getting back to the shop. . . .

And yet, something compelled him to stop by the clinic on his way back to work. Perhaps it was the memory of the young woman's dead weight in his arms, her utter helplessness as she slumped unconscious in the rig while her kids and their pets had no idea where they were or what to do. When he entered the clinic, Seth was glad no one was sitting in the lobby, for the heart-rending cries coming from the exam room made the hairs on his neck prickle. How could one slender, weak body endure such wrenching pain?

He didn't realize he was staring at the doorway when Miriam peeked out of it. "Seth!" she said in an urgent whisper. "Come hold her shoulders—"

Before he could refuse, Miriam was gripping his hand, leading him into the little room.

"Mary's havin' trouble—too weak to push much. If you'll prop her up from behind, I think we can get this wee one born."

Seth's objections and fear stuck in his throat. It was highly improper for him, an unmarried man, to be in this room while someone else's wife was having a baby, but when Andy Leitner tented a sheet over the girl's bent knees, he didn't argue.

"Wash your hands, and then if you'll sit behind her—hold her at a better angle," Andy instructed, "maybe we won't have to use forceps or do a C-section. This is Mary's first child, and she's awfully small."

Mary. Her name is Mary and she's having her first child.

Seth quickly did as he was told. He mounted the table so he could straddle it, and when the young woman was settled against his chest, he again wondered what he'd gotten himself into. Mary was conscious but weak, exhausted from the stress of the day's drive, so the least he could do was sit behind her and put his height and bulk to use. She felt so tiny, like his sister Hannah when she'd been a kid—

Jah, keep it on that level, like she's a sister and not some other fella's widow.

Mary sucked in her breath, seeming to gather herself for another effort. Her shoulders fit easily between Seth's and with her head angled to one side, she seemed to be offering up her neck for him to kiss it, or—

Oh, don't go there!

"Give a good push now, Mary," Andy instructed in a calm voice. "The baby's head's right here and—"

"*Jah*, we're waitin' to catch this wee one," Miriam encouraged her. "Give us a *gut*, big push—harder now—"

Seth found himself mentally pushing with Mary, gently grasping her forearms as her body tensed with an effort he could only imagine. It was a good thing God had made childbearing a female function, because he was quite certain he couldn't endure what this waif was going through.

With a gasp, Mary strained and pushed back against his chest. Andy and Miriam were intent on whatever was happening on their side of the sheet, and then a startled little wail filled the room.

"And here he is, a beautiful little boy!" Andy exclaimed. "While Miriam bathes him, I'll stitch you up, Mary, and then you can hold him. You did a fine job."

But Mary had gone limp in Seth's arms. Considering the size of the blood-smeared infant Miriam was carrying to the countertop, he wondered how the baby had made its way through such a slender young woman. Until now he hadn't realized what a harrowing experience giving birth must be—especially for a first-time mother.

Seth sat patiently, silently coaxing Mary to breathe with him . . . holding her while Andy repaired the damage done to her body. But who would fix the other things that had obviously gone wrong in this poor woman's life? If Lucy and Sol's *dat* had died, how was Mary going to support this little family?

Don't go there. Just let those thoughts roll on by like the water down at the mill—

"What do you think?" Miriam asked as she walked up beside him. "He looks to be a fine, healthy little fella, and there's no doubt he's Elmer Kauffman's boy. Got his *dat*'s long face and square chin."

Seth's breath caught. The baby was the ugliest thing he'd ever seen, with a wrinkled face and red skin—*but that's all right, because he's Elmer Kauffman's boy. Nobody you have to be concerned about.*

And yet Seth's heart thumped in his chest. "He looks fat and sassy. A lot better than his poor *mamm* does." His voice sounded funny and tight, and he couldn't seem to look away from the little balled fists and the tiny rosebud mouth that opened and shut.

"Mary'll come around," Miriam said softly. "She's my brother Mose's daughter, from Bowling Green. Lost her Elmer to a fire in his sawmill a month ago, and was wantin' a change of scenery, plus folks to help when the baby came," she explained. "Her parents weren't wild about Mary leavin' town, in her condition—just like they weren't wild about her hitchin' up with Elmer and his two kids so soon after Elmer's wife passed."

"Ah. Family squabbles," Seth murmured.

"*Jah*, you said it. Mose bein' a preacher, he gets a little overbearin' when other folks don't do things the way he wants. Especially after those things don't go quite right." Miriam touched the tip of the baby's nose with her finger, grinning. "But it's all turnin' out just fine now. God got Mary on the road with the kids somehow, and when they ran into trouble, He convinced you to check on her, Seth. *Denki* for that."

Seth chuckled. "Their border collie was mighty insistent."

"But Rowdy did what needed to be done. That's all the Lord asks of anybody."

Seth tried not to read too much into what Miriam had said. She—and his mother, Naomi, her partner at the Sweet Seasons—dropped plenty of hints about him being twenty-four and single. He'd joined the church, and he'd established a successful woodworking business with his brothers. With several of his buddies getting married recently, that made him one of Willow Ridge's most eligible bachelors.

Not that he was in a hurry to change his status. Because he and his youngest brother, Aaron, still lived at home, they could handle the livestock chores and other work their wheelchair-bound father wasn't up to, so it seemed a comfortable arrangement. Nothing worth changing for any of the girls he'd ever dated, anyway.

And witnessing this baby's birth didn't make him feel any more inclined to get romantically involved, either.

So when Andy told him he could let Mary rest on the exam table, Seth eased out from under her, said his good-byes, and returned to the shop. It was a sunny September day, and he had satisfying work awaiting him. Mary and her kids were in good hands and a welcoming home. He'd simply helped her the way any fellow would've done, and he could return to his routine without a backward glance or a second thought.

Well, almost.

CHAPTER 2

The Saturday after Emmanuel was born, Miriam's kitchen bustled with local women who'd come to a frolic to make diapers and baby clothes. Mary resigned herself to acting cheerful and grateful, although in truth she felt overwhelmed, still sore, and totally drained. How had her aunt put in a full day at the Sweet Seasons, and then welcomed her friends into her home for this spur-of-the-moment sewing party?

All Mary had done since the baby's birth was sit with him, nap with him, and nurse him—and given the chance, she would be hiding away in her room rather than socializing this afternoon.

"Emmanuel, what a *gut* boy you are, smilin' even though you're the only fella amongst us hens," Naomi Brenneman cooed.

Mary put on a smile as her cousins, Rachel and Rhoda, gathered around her rocking chair with Seth's mother. Her other cousin Rebecca, who'd assisted her at the clinic—and who wore jeans and a T-shirt, as she'd been living among *Englisch* until she'd reunited with Miriam's family a year ago—joined them, as well. "He *should* be smiling, because you ladies have all come over to sew for him," Mary replied. "You must think I'm horribly unprepared to be a mother—"

"Don't go puttin' yourself down, Mary," Naomi insisted kindly. "What with takin' on another man's kids and hardly havin' time to adjust to bein' a wife before ya lost your husband, you've had more on your plate than any of us could digest by ourselves. Sewin' up some diapers, blankets, and clothes is the least we can do for ya."

"*Jah*, and it's a nice excuse to spend an afternoon visitin', too," Rhoda spoke up. "This is Andy's daughter, Taylor, and she's been lookin' forward to playin' with Lucy today."

Mary smiled at the little girl, who resembled her father—the nurse who ran the Willow Ridge Clinic. "If you go on back to the *dawdi haus*, I bet Lucy would be glad to meet you. She's shy around crowds. You could go to the barn to see her two kitties and Clarabelle, her miniature pony, too."

Taylor's eyes lit up and she hurried out of the kitchen.

"So how's Andy coming along with his instruction, and with learning *Deitsch* so he can join the Old Order?" Mary asked.

Rhoda beamed. "He's gettin' a handle on the language. And he's doin' real well at the clinic and with his medical wagon," she replied. "It's all *gut*! Just a matter of time until all the pieces fall into place so Andy and I can marry."

Mary was amazed at the faith and patience required on Rhoda's part, waiting for a man who'd left his *Englisch* life behind to become Amish, for *her*. Mary also hoped that one day she would be as comfortable with Elmer's children as Rhoda was with Andy's kids, Taylor and Brett—who were the same ages as Sol and Lucy.

"I'm certainly grateful to your Andy for helping me birth Emmanuel," Mary said. "He's a wonderful-*gut* man."

"*Jah*, he's that," Rhoda said, her blue eyes a-sparkle. Then she tweaked Emmanuel's cheek and rested her hand on Mary's shoulder. "One of these days life'll look better to ya, cuz," she murmured. "We all have our peaks and valleys—and we have our faith to see us through the low spots until we can rise above them."

Doesn't that sound like something Aunt Miriam would say? Ever the optimists, these women.

"So this is the new wee one? And his name's Emmanuel?" A plump woman Mary hadn't yet met was bustling toward them, her *kapp* strings a-flutter and her smile bright. "Why, with a name like that, every day'll be Christmas! *O come, o come, E-maaa-nyew-elle!*"

Mary wanted to laugh out loud, but that would be rude. The woman who'd just burst into song appeared to be about thirty, with thick glasses and dark hair and eyebrows—and cheeks that had shimmied while she'd been singing.

"I'm Alberta Zook—cousin to Henry, the storekeeper—and I'm also the teacher at the Willow Ridge school," she added. "Did I hear correctly that you've got a boy in second grade?"

"*Jah*, Solomon—he goes by Sol—is seven," Mary replied. "We'll be sure he gets to the schoolhouse, come Monday morning. He's not said as much, but he's missing his friends—and he's ready to spend his days at something other than watching me tend the baby."

"We'll put him to work! And he'll have Henry's two boys to buddy up with," Alberta declared gleefully. Then she shook her head. "As I look toward the Christmas Eve program this year, I'm wondering how we'll cobble one together. All of our older scholars graduated from eighth grade last spring, which leaves me with only Cyrus and Levi Zook and their little sister, Amelia—and now Sol."

"Oh, my!" Mary blurted. "How did *that* happen, that you have so few scholars?"

Alberta shrugged. "Willow Ridge is a small district and we've hit one of those transitional times—the kids who just finished school will soon be courting and marrying, and we've got babies being born, but right now we've got a gap. With the Knepp twins to join us next September, and Andy Leitner's kids coming whenever he and Rhoda get hitched, we'll be on the rise again."

"And Lucy will start school next year," Mary remarked as she continued to rock the baby.

"So you're going to stay here? Praise be!" Alberta exclaimed. "As you can imagine, I'm having an *interesting* year, what with only my three young cousins in my classroom. Sol will be a welcome addition."

Mary smiled, but she felt as though Teacher Alberta had just proclaimed the Kauffman clan's future. She hadn't intended to imply that she'd be sticking around in Willow Ridge. She had a farm to return to, and parents who'd be insisting that she and the kids live with them, and—well, the list of responsibilities went on and on.

A fresh start is exactly what you need. Look at how these women are welcoming you, so eager to help you and the kids.

Mary blinked. It seemed very selfish to consider living in Willow Ridge just because she *wanted* to. After all, Elmer's brothers had offered to take her in, and Sol and Lucy were their blood kin. Her parents had finally come around to accepting Sol and Lucy—and they were eager to welcome Emmanuel. . . .

You feel so stifled there. You'll be facing up to everyone else's expectations rather than living your own life.

Those were dangerous thoughts for a young Amish widow. Conformity and community paved the path to a life of Plain faith, and if she severed her ties in Bowling Green, she might as well spit in her preacher father's face.

He and Mamm will find you a new husband—one they believe more suitable than Elmer was—and you'll be all set. Is that such a bad thing?

The women who'd gathered at Miriam's long kitchen table to make diapers were chatting merrily as they began their afternoon—time they were devoting to *her* and her little family. And what examples they were! Aunt Miriam had started her bakery café when she'd been widowed—and she'd reunited with her daughter, Rebecca, whom everyone believed had died in a flood, when after nineteen years, she'd returned to Willow Ridge. Meanwhile, Rhoda Lantz was in love with a divorced *Englisch* fellow who was taking his instruction to join the Old Order so he could marry her. Naomi Brenneman had partnered with Miriam to bring in additional income after her husband suffered a construction accident and became wheelchair-bound. The whole district was recovering nicely from the misadventures of their former bishop, Hiram Knepp, who'd been excommunicated and had then started up a new colony under very dubious circumstances.

If these people could pull together after such ordeals, to move in new directions, why couldn't she do the same? While she'd lived her entire life in Bowling Green, Willow Ridge vibrated with a vitality she found refreshing and uplifting.

Mary placed Emmanuel in his carrier and then very carefully—so as not to strain her stitches, which still hurt—she headed toward the table. It was time to join these wonderful, generous women. It was time to thread her needle and stitch up a new life for herself.

Several days later, Seth held another post in place and then drove in the long screws with his pneumatic screwdriver—*zzzt, zzzt, zzzt*—building a small addition to the front of Ben Hooley's barn. While Ben hadn't said as much, Seth suspected that Rowdy and the Kauffmans' two cats were creating havoc among the Hooleys' driving and draft horses—not to mention Miriam's chickens.

When he finished this afternoon, Clarabelle would have her own stall, and there would be an open area filled with straw for the border collie and the cats to sleep in, along with a dog door. It was an expense that a lot of Amish men wouldn't have considered . . . and to Seth, it also suggested that the Kauffmans might be staying in Willow Ridge longer than Mary's recovery would require.

Grinning at that notion, Seth drove the screws that would secure the stall railings. *Zzzt, zzzt, zzzt*—

"What're *you* doin'?" a small voice demanded.

Seth looked over to see Sol standing a few feet away, his brow furrowed as he ran his hand over Rowdy's black ears. How was it that every word from this kid's mouth sounded judgmental? Had the youngster taken on such an attitude after his *dat* died, or had he always had such an edge to him? Seth reached for more long screws, considering his answer. "Your Uncle Ben is havin' me build a stable for Clarabelle, Rowdy, and your cats," he replied. "He wants you and Lucy to be able to play with them, and feed them, without possibly gettin' trampled by his big horses."

"Why's he doin' *that*?" Sol demanded. "We'll be goin' back to Bowling Green any time now. We've got a farm there—and Clarabelle *likes* her stall there. It's our *home*."

Seth's eyebrows rose, but he didn't answer immediately. In the week since Mary and her little brood had come to town, he'd not seen them or heard anything more of their plans. What should he believe? Their immediate departure might be wishful thinking on Sol's part.

"We all need a safe, warm place to call home," Seth mused aloud. "My brothers and I built this barn, along with Miriam and Ben's house, ya know. We built the Sweet Seasons and the furniture in it, too, and some of the other newer buildings hereabouts."

"Oh, *jah*?" Sol retorted. "Well, my *dat* ran a sawmill. How do ya suppose you'll be gettin' any more lumber, now that it's burnt down?"

Seth gritted his teeth. He'd heard about Elmer Kauffman's fatal fire, and he felt bad that this family had lost their anchor to such a tragic accident. He also understood how a seven-year-old's world-view would center around his father's workplace to the exclusion of other sawmills. It was beside the point that the Kauffman mill had produced wooden pallets rather than lumber that went into cabinetry or residential construction.

Should he correct the youngster? Set him straight about his attitude, just as Miriam had the other day? Or should he be more tolerant and patient, knowing how Sol's world had been turned upside down when his *dat* had died? Since Sol was shooting questions at him, maybe he should do the same . . . to take the edge off the conversation and gather a little information in a roundabout way. "I'm really sorry about your *dat* dyin' in that fire, Sol," Seth said in a low voice. Then, before the boy could get huffy again, he said, "How's your baby brother doin'?"

The boy grimaced. "Emmanuel? He spends most of his time sleepin' or cryin' or stinkin' up our room."

Emmanuel. A strong, stalwart name—one a boy can grow into.

Seth chuckled as he rummaged in his sack for more long screws. "He'll get past that. We all started out the same way, ya know."

"Mary's up at all hours of the night with him, too," Sol groused. "I hardly get any sleep. Nodded off at school today, and Teacher Alberta screeched at me."

And what of poor Mary? She must be exhausted, even with Miriam's help . . .

Seth held his comments, both about the boy calling his step-*mamm* by her first name and about his constant complaining. Sol was a very good reason not to let his thoughts wax romantic when it came to Mary Kauffman. "And how's it goin' in your new school?" he asked, thinking that was a safer subject. "I bet you're makin' lots of new friends."

"Puh! Cyrus and Levi Zook are the only other scholars—unless ya count their little sister, Amelia." A sly smile flickered on the boy's face. "We boys're keepin' the teacher busy. She says she's got eyes in the back of her head, so she sees every little thing we're doin', but most times—even with her big ol' glasses—Teacher Alberta's as blind as a bat."

Seth stifled a laugh. More than one fellow in Willow Ridge had noticed how, with her black-rimmed glasses, her large nose, and her thick eyebrows, Alberta Zook looked like she was wearing one of those gag masks Henry sold in the toy aisle of his market.

"You'd best behave yourselves," he warned. "If Ben and the Zooks' *dat* get word you're causin' her trouble, they'll be payin' ya a visit in class—and givin' ya extra chores after school to work some of that mischief out of ya."

Sol shrugged. "We'll be goin' home soon. I don't know *why* you and Ben think we need this new stable."

As the boy turned and found a stick to throw for his dog, Seth considered what he'd just heard. He'd had no idea that the Willow Ridge school had so few scholars this term. Had he not been paying attention to the affairs of his hometown? Or had his woodworking projects kept him so busy he just hadn't thought about the school and its students? He and his brothers spent a lot of time on the road, installing cabinets and delivering the furniture they built in their shop . . . and as bachelors, he and Aaron had no direct connection to the school these days.

Better change your tune if you're thinkin' a woman like Mary will be interested. She needs a solid, invested type of fellow, not somebody who can't see the forest beyond his own little trees.

And where had *that* thought come from? Mary Kauffman was attractive, for sure, but her roots were in Bowling Green. Maybe Sol had it right—maybe he and his sibs and Mary would soon be heading back to her family, so it would be a waste of time to culti-vate any interest in her. If Ben had gone to the expense of adding an annex to his barn, that was *his* miscalculation, wasn't it?

Seth laughed, at himself mostly. It seemed the birth of Em-manuel had set the world spinning in a whole new direction—just as it had centuries ago.

CHAPTER 3

Mary gazed at her baby as he fed at her breast. At six weeks, he looked plump and happy, with dewy skin and crystal-blue eyes that watched her intently as he suckled. Sometimes it was a comfort, seeing this boy's resemblance to his *dat*, and at other times it tore out her heart. While she and Sol and Lucy had found a haven here in the Hooleys' *dawdi haus*, they still had to deal with their life in Bowling Green. Someday soon, she would be able to return to the farm—Elmer's place, half a mile down the road from her parents' home and surrounded by other members of the Kauffman family—and she would have to make a life for herself and three children.

But how would that happen? Now that she had more kids than hands, no income, and no one to tend the farm or the livestock, how would she get her little family through the winter, much less the years ahead?

It's Elmer's family, she reminded herself. *His kids, his farm . . . and he left me behind to tend them all.*

"You, I can handle, Emmanuel," Mary murmured in a choked voice. "But how long can I live off the generosity of the Hooleys? I *hate* to think of moving back to Mamm and Dat's . . . or moving in with one of Elmer's brothers, but I see no other—"

"Uh-oh."

Mary raised her head, listening. With Sol going to school during the day, and Miriam and Ben working at their shops across the road, she and Lucy were alone here at the house with the baby. The gurgling of the toilet told her the little girl had used the bathroom—again. Or was she playing in there?

"Lucy?" Mary called over her shoulder. "Is everything all right?"

No answer.

"Lucy?" Mary repeated more insistently. While the little girl was quiet and well-behaved, she also knew that while Emmanuel nursed, Mary wouldn't be moving from the rocking chair. Lucy had a tendency to explore other parts of Ben and Miriam's house then—natural curiosity for a five-year-old without any playmates. Or was it?

Did all girls that age slink around like cats? Had Lucy been so removed and secretive with her own mother, or had losing one parent and then the other made her more withdrawn? Children were such a mystery. Mary had done her best to embrace Elmer's grieving son and daughter after she'd married him, but she'd been the youngest in her family and she'd had so little experience around kids.

Maybe Mamm and Dat were right. Maybe I should've looked before I leaped, thought twice about hitching up with an older fellow whose kids needed a keeper.

Mary glanced up as Lucy entered the bedroom. "I asked you a question," she said as the girl skirted the rocking chair and avoided eye contact. "What happened in the bathroom that made you say *uh-oh?*"

Lucy stopped but didn't turn around. Her little shoulders rose as though she anticipated a scolding. "Nothin'," she insisted. "I was helpin' you. Washin' diapers."

What might the rest of the story be? Lucy was an earnest helper and seemed especially fascinated as she watched Mary empty and rinse Emmanuel's cloth diapers in the toilet before soaking them in the diaper pail. "*And?*" she asked in a purposeful voice.

Lucy remained in place, still facing the opposite wall. "It went down. With the poop."

Mary's pulse accelerated. "The diaper went down the toilet? Lucy, how did—"

But the little girl's shoulders were shuddering and she began to wail—which seemed to be her response when anything went wrong, maybe because her *dat* had turned into a cream puff at the first sign of her tears?

"Oh, Lucy, I'm not mad," Mary murmured with a sigh. "I'm just—"

Helpless. Clueless. Restless. Lost. Even more the outsider now that Elmer's gone.

But such a downward spiral of depressing thoughts would only make her cry right along with Lucy. It had been inevitable that something would go wrong while she and the kids stayed with Miriam and Ben, so there was nothing to do but face up to it. Mary dabbed at Emmanuel's lips, desperately wishing she could be drifting off into a sated, blissful sleep, the way he was. When she'd laid him in his crib, she went into the bathroom.

There was no sign of a diaper in the toilet. Had Lucy really flushed one down by accident? How had the whole diaper gone down, as large as it was? Or . . . was Lucy fibbing again? Mary had caught the little girl in a few whoppers, so it was possible that Lucy had made up this story to get attention while her baby brother nursed.

There was only one way to find out.

Mary held down the flush lever. The water whirled in the bowl but it didn't go down.

Oh, this isn't gut, she thought. But if there *was* a diaper down in the pipes, maybe one more flush would wash it along . . . before other waste could get caught in it and clog the pipe completely. Mary recalled seeing a plunger in the hall closet, so she fetched it. After she pumped it up and down vigorously, she flushed again.

The water rose to the top of the bowl and began spilling over onto the floor.

"Oh! Oh, no, this is—" Grabbing towels from the linen cabinet, Mary dropped them to the floor to sop up the water, once again aware that the men in her life had always dealt with these emergencies. When the toilet had stopped overflowing, she pondered her options. She didn't dare leave Lucy here with Emmanuel while she called Miriam from the phone in the barn . . . and by the time she went that far, she might as well go across the road to the café.

"Let's get our coats on," she told Lucy. "We have to tell Aunt Miriam or Uncle Ben about the toilet so they can get it fixed."

Lucy's eyes widened and she began to cry more loudly. Mary badly wanted to join her, but that wouldn't solve their problem, would it? She tucked Emmanuel into his padded carrier basket, and by the time the three of them were at the door where the coats were hung, he was wailing, too. He'd been sleeping so soundly— the day had been going so *well* until Lucy had—

Lord, don't let me hold this against her. She was trying to help . . . I think. Truth be told, I'm so tired from Emmanuel's wee-hour feedings, I'm not sure I can think anymore. . . .

They made a woeful little parade as they crossed the county highway, and it didn't help Mary's mood that little snowflakes floated in the November air. When they entered the Sweet Seasons, Mary spotted Aunt Miriam cutting pies at the back kitchen counter. She kept her head down as she went through the crowded, noisy dining room full of people she didn't know, gripping the handles of Emmanuel's basket. When she got to the kitchen, she saw that Lucy had stopped in an aisle to gawk at one of the men who was eating his dinner.

"Lucy!" Mary said in a loud whisper. "Get *in* here before I—"

"And what brings ya here amongst us, honey-bugs?" Miriam asked as she bustled over. "It's *gut* to see ya gettin' outta the house. Let me get ya some of this hamburger soup we're servin' for lunch—"

"The toilet's clogged. I'm so sorry," Mary blurted. "I've sopped up the water, but Lucy says she flushed a diaper and—"

Mary nipped her lip, watching Miriam's expression. At forty-something, her aunt radiated a perpetual acceptance, a cheerfulness that probably accounted for her crow's-feet, from smiling so much. As she grasped Mary's shoulders, Miriam remained calm and unruffled.

"Ya came to the right place at the right time," Miriam said with a chuckle. "Just so happens the Brenneman boys, who built our house and installed the plumbing, are eatin' their dinner. I'll go talk to them."

"*Jah*, my Seth went to plumber school before he joined the Old Order," said Naomi as she lifted a sizzling skillet of sausage from the stove. "He knows the pipes and drains around Willow Ridge like the back of his hand."

Seth Brenneman. Every time Mary heard that fellow's name, it was spoken in a tone that suggested he was above and beyond the average man. Aunt Miriam had recounted how Seth had driven their rig to the clinic, and then he'd sat behind her while she was delivering Emmanuel. Mary didn't remember any of those details. She dreaded the Sunday when the baby would be old enough to appear in church, for she would surely need to thank this stranger for his kindness. Sol and Lucy had gone on and on about how tall Seth was, and how strong—and how he'd gotten Rowdy to behave with a single command.

When she saw the burly blond rising from his chair in the dining room—coming toward the kitchen—Mary swallowed hard. He was a bear of a man, yet his smile suggested a boyish, fun-loving mischief as he leaned against the door frame.

"It's *gut* to see ya up and around, Mary, lookin' a lot more chipper than when we first met," he said in a mellow baritone voice. "Shall we go over and see about that troublesome toilet?"

Mary nearly fainted. Seth Brenneman was easygoing and pleasant and muscular and cute and—

Everything Elmer was not.

Mary chided herself for such an uncharitable thought. Her husband had been a fine, upstanding man of the faith. A good provider, until he'd died in a fire at his sawmill. She braced herself against Seth's friendliness as she gripped the handles of Emmanuel's basket. "*Jah. Denki.*"

"I'll be right over, soon as I fetch my tools."

Mary steered Lucy toward the back door of the café's kitchen, so she wouldn't have to wait for Seth to move from the other doorway. "See you later, Aunt Miriam," she said. "We've got a mess to clean up."

And it's you that's in a mess, Mary's thoughts raced. *How embarrassing, to finally meet this man while he has to do such a nasty job.*

But maybe that was for the best, Mary reasoned. If Seth was

occupied with unclogging a toilet, he couldn't pay any attention to *her*.

Half an hour later, Seth tugged carefully on the drain snake he'd coiled down Miriam's toilet. The diaper hadn't gone too far into the pipe, so he was able to snag it and ease it back up the way it had gone down. From across the small bathroom, Lucy watched him with wide eyes. She was clutching a faceless Amish doll as though it might protect her from him.

"I was rinsin' Emmanuel's poopy diaper," she confessed in a tiny voice. "I flushed too quick and the potty *ate* it."

Seth stopped tugging for a moment to smile at her. Lucy appeared to be doing well now—her blond hair was coiled into neat braids that joined at the back of her head, and she wore a cheerful blue dress. "When I was a kid, I dropped all kinds of stuff down the toilet," he replied. "Not because I was helpin', either—I was just playin'. That's probably why I went to school to be a plumber."

Lucy screwed up her face. "You played in the potty? *Ewwww*."

"*Jah*, boys are pretty dumb sometimes." Seth grasped the edge of the diaper and pulled steadily on it as he brought up the end of the snake. He dropped the snake on the towels that covered the floor, wrung out the diaper, and then went to the sink to wash up. "I've got ya all fixed up now, Lucy. No harm done."

The little girl watched him as he recoiled the snake and gathered his tools. He felt more at ease with her today . . . found it gratifying that she had watched him work, even if she'd stayed as far away from him as the bathroom walls allowed.

"So your brother's in school?" he asked.

Lucy nodded.

"And your kitties and Rowdy are doin' all right?"

A grin twitched her lips. "Rowdy herds Aunt Miriam's chickens. They don't like it much," she added matter-of-factly. "When Ben gets home, I'm gonna ride Clarabelle. She's our pony."

When Lucy raised her hand to indicate Clarabelle's height, Seth nodded. "A miniature pony, is she? I guess you don't want *me* to ride her, then."

Lucy's stricken expression made Seth wish he hadn't made that joke. He sighed. While it was easier today to make small talk with this wee blonde while her judgmental brother wasn't here, Seth really wanted to ask how the girl's mother was getting along. The rhythmic sound of a rocking chair on the sitting room's hardwood floor suggested Mary was looking after the baby—

Emmanuel, which means God with us. A gut, sturdy name for a little fella who has a long row to hoe.

As the words to an old carol about Emmanuel filled his head, Seth concentrated on gathering the wet towels, leaving the bathroom in better shape than he'd found it. This being mid-November, he had several Christmas furniture orders to keep up with—no time for lollygagging, letting his thoughts wander, or getting caught up in Mary's green-eyed gaze. Lucy had gone into the other room with her *mamm,* and when Seth stepped out of the bathroom, he stopped, speechless.

What a picture Mary made, cradling her newborn to her shoulder, slowly rocking him as she, too, looked ready to nap. She had draped a quilt over them, a design featuring deep red poinsettias over green stars that formed the leaves. With her eyes closed and the hint of a smile on her lips, she looked pretty and peaceful . . . draped in festive colors that covered her black dress. Seth's mind whirled with questions he longed to ask her, but it was just as well that Mary was occupied with a much more important little man. What would he accomplish, getting friendly with her? She had three kids and was grieving a deceased husband. She was in good hands here, with Miriam and Ben, and nothing he could say or do would improve her lot—or his.

Very quietly, Seth slipped away from the *dawdi haus* with his toolbox.

"How much do we owe you?" Mary called after him.

Seth closed his eyes against the funny things her voice did to him. When he opened them again, Mary was standing in the doorway holding her baby in one arm as she grasped the edges of the quilt to keep it wrapped around them. "Only took me ten minutes. No charge," he replied.

"But you took time out of your day to help us," she protested.

Seth considered his answer. Mary had no money to spare for such minor emergencies, yet her earnest expression told him she'd feel beholden if he refused payment. He decided to ease his way out of this situation by changing the subject. "That's a mighty nice Christmas quilt. I like the bold reds and greens."

Mary's expression wilted. "I . . . I made it for my first Christmas as a Kauffman, and gave it to Elmer last year, but—well, I don't guess he'll be using it again. Probably too early to be getting it out, but—"

"Better to enjoy it yourself than to hide it away. And staying cuddly and warm is always in season, what with a few flakes in the air these days." Seth sighed. It seemed he had a talent for starting uncomfortable conversations. "I'll leave you to your rocking now. Didn't mean to disturb you and the baby."

"Ya can't disturb me any more than I already am."

Seth had been turning to leave, but he stopped. Took a closer look at Mary Kauffman, whose troubles surely stacked up a lot higher than his did. "I'm sorry for your loss, Mary," he murmured. "I can't imagine—"

"So don't," she interrupted emphatically. "Don't go thinkin' about my loss, or how to fix what's wrong in my life, or how to win over the kids to get my attention, because I'll have none of that. It is what it is, Elmer's death. I'll get by."

As Mary returned to her rocking chair, Seth stood stock-still. She'd clearly told him to go fly a kite, yet beneath her independent, stoic tone he'd heard longing and loneliness. She was tougher than she looked, yet at her age—with three little kids—she was dooming herself to a life of scraping by, depending upon the charity of her parents—

But listen to her. Don't go fallin' for those green, green eyes or that glossy red-blond hair or the way you could scoop her up with just one arm. Just go, before ya say somethin' else that'll get sticky.

CHAPTER 4

"That's gonna be a real pretty quilt," Miriam remarked as she looked over Mary's shoulder. "I've seen a lot of Star of Bethlehem patterns, but this one's a real eye-catcher in just red, cream, and two shades of green."

Mary carefully rolled her circular blade over a stack of fabric, around the four sides of her template. "I chose this one because it's the simplest," she replied. "It's made with bigger house-shaped pieces and diamonds, instead of dozens of itty-bitty diamonds. It just looks . . . stronger. No-nonsense."

If Miriam asked, Mary was going to tell her that this quilt had seemed like the perfect therapy—a nice pastime while Emmanuel still slept a lot. She was toying with the idea of giving it to Seth Brenneman as payment for all of his kindnesses . . . not the least of which was rescuing her and Sol and Lucy the day she'd passed out on the road. But if she changed her mind—if she decided Seth would get *ideas* from such a gift—she could always tell Lucy it would be hers someday.

"And that means a lot fewer seams to sew and edges to tuck," her aunt remarked with a grin. "Will ya have enough fabric, or shall I get some more? The quilt shop's got a nice sale on this poly-cotton now."

rou've done too much for us already," Mary protested. "I've got a little cash laid by—"

"No such thing as doing *too much* for you and your kids, Mary," Miriam insisted. "It's a blessing to me, spendin' time with Lucy and Sol and seein' how Emmanuel's growing like a little weed. Such a happy boy, he is."

Did she dare tell her aunt what she'd been thinking about as she cut and sewed the blocks for this quilt? Mary gathered her courage and decided that now, while no one else was within earshot, was a good time to sound out her idea. "*Jah*, the baby's happy, and I've been happy here, too, Aunt Miriam, so—so I'm thinking of selling Elmer's farm in Bowling Green. Maybe finding a little house in Willow Ridge."

Miriam landed on the bench beside her with an *oof* and leaned her elbows on the table. "And what's put *that* bee in your bonnet, child? Your family's all in Bowling—"

"My family wants to breathe down my neck every minute, thinking I can't manage for myself—and telling me every little thing I should do," Mary retorted. "And while Elmer's kin mean well, they're the same way. And besides, *you* are my family, too, Aunt Miriam. I don't intend to live in your *dawdi haus* forever, but these past two months have given me time to think for myself. And you know how Dat feels about a woman doing that. Especially when she's only twenty."

Miriam chuckled richly. "Mose gets smothery sometimes," she agreed. Then a slow smile spread across her face. "Ya wouldn't be leanin' this way on account of a certain plumber here in town—"

"Absolutely not!" Mary declared. "I told Seth to keep his eyes and ideas to himself because I'm not interested in him or any other fella. You can ask him."

"I just might." With a knowing smile, Miriam rose from the table. "We've got church at the Brenneman place tomorrow, and I hope you'll come along, Mary. With Emmanuel bein' two months old now, folks are expectin' him—and you—to start circulatin'. And if you're thinkin' to stay in Willow Ridge, goin' to church'll be the best way to meet folks and figure out if this is really where ya want to live."

Mary couldn't argue with her aunt's logic. It would be a big mistake to rush into another major life change, just to escape the close confines of her parents' plans for her future. After all, she'd decided to marry Elmer partly to defy them, and only *after* she'd become his wife had she realized what a challenge it was to step into another woman's shoes when two young children were involved. She loved Sol and Lucy dearly, but she hadn't anticipated their resistance to her . . . hadn't figured on losing her husband before they'd been married a year, either.

You had no idea what it meant to be a wife—to submit to Elmer's wishes and opinions about every little thing. If every man's like he was, why would you want to hitch up again?

Mary sighed. Such thoughts had played tug-of-war in her mind ever since Elmer had died, and when she dwelled on them, she only got more depressed. It wasn't as though her husband had ever raised his voice or his hand to her. Elmer had been levelheaded and a good money manager. In retrospect, she suspected she'd been too young and naïve—with a head full of romantic notions—to understand the family dynamics she'd married into. Their difficult relationship had been as much her fault as his . . . but those times were behind her now.

Mary placed her diamond template over the stack of fabric to cut more pieces. "You're right," she told Miriam. "It's time the four of us Kauffmans went to church. Sol shouldn't be the only one who's out amongst other folks."

"Glad to hear it. And what with it bein' the first Sunday of Advent, we'll be lookin' to find the Savior," Miriam remarked in a thoughtful tone. "Before ya know it, we'll start bakin' cookies and bringin' in evergreen branches and puttin' out the Nativity scenes. It's my favorite time of the year."

It used to be mine, too, Mary thought as Miriam rose from the table. *But this year? Not so much.*

The key would be to stay so busy she had no time for caving in to crying jags—which was the main reason she'd started this Star of Bethlehem quilt. Or so she told herself.

As she cut more pieces, Mary mentally prepared for attending church tomorrow at the Brenneman place. If she focused on meeting the other women, who would be fussing over Emmanuel and getting acquainted with Lucy and Sol, she wouldn't have to work at avoiding Seth. She could keep busy putting out the common meal after the service. She'd met the bishop, Tom Hostetler, at Miriam and Ben's wedding, and Ben's older sisters, Jerusalem and Nazareth, had already come to see her, just as Miriam's girls, Rachel, Rhoda, and Rebecca, had.

If she concentrated on expanding this little circle of friends and family, it would fill her day with talk of food and kids. She'd have no time to be riveted by a winsome male smile or two eyes that seemed to peer into her soul, so she'd have no concerns about a fellow who'd seen her at her very worst and most defenseless.

So there you have it. Plan your work and work your plan.

Seth smiled as he peered out the front window. He'd watched for Mary Kauffman the last two church Sundays and had been disappointed, but this morning she was coming up the porch steps with Miriam and Lucy! It was tradition for the women to enter through the kitchen while the men came in the front room, but what fun would life be if he always followed tradition? Ben was steering Sol toward where the men were congregating, so Seth headed for the kitchen to enjoy a few moments of Mary's company without the boy's negativity clouding their conversation.

Ignoring the surprised expressions on the women's faces, Seth made his way among them to the door. His heart was thumping, and he hoped he wouldn't make a fool of himself. He was just being pleasant and polite, welcoming this young woman to his home for the first time, after all. "*Gut* morning to you, Miriam— and to you, too, Mary and Lucy!" he said as he opened the door for them. "It's *gut* to see you out on this sunny December day."

Miriam's expression suggested that she knew what he was up to, but Seth didn't care. What safer place to get better acquainted with Mary than here in his mother's kitchen, among all these clucking hens? He tried not to notice how bashful Lucy looked, and how she clung to her *mamm*'s skirts as she gawked at him and all the strangers in the kitchen.

"We're happy to be here," Mary replied—and then she passed Emmanuel to him. "Hang on to my son while I take off my coat. I figured his carrier would be too bulky in this crowd."

Seth sucked in his breath as he grasped the blanketed baby.

What if he dropped him? What if Emmanuel started bawling at the top of his lungs? The women around him would get a good laugh out of that. Handling an infant was second nature to them, whereas *he* couldn't recall the last time he'd held one. With everyone jostling him to get a look at Mary's boy, Seth tucked Emmanuel against his side, along the length of his left forearm. He cradled the baby's wee head in his hand.

"Oh, would you look at this fine little fella!"

"What a lot of hair he has!"

"And he's bein' so *gut* and quiet in this crowded room, too."

"That's because Emmanuel knows he's in solid, strong hands." Miriam smiled up at Seth, and then she *winked!*

Seth took that as a high compliment—just as Mary's trust in him was nothing short of amazing. As he began swaying slightly from side to side, Emmanuel made cooing sounds and began to wiggle. Then his smile came out like the sun on this December day.

Seth couldn't breathe, couldn't stop gazing at the tiny boy who was so raptly looking back at him. The voices around them faded, and he drank in the baby's rosy skin and shining eyes. Emmanuel looked a lot cuter and more animated than when he'd first been born.

The baby seemed alert and aware of him, but Seth didn't feel the need to talk. Communication flowed between them on a different level, and Seth suddenly felt enthralled—downright ecstatic. When he held out his finger and Emmanuel grabbed hold of it, complete and utter love flooded Seth's soul. *Tidings of comfort and joy, comfort and joy . . .*

"What's a man got to do to see his grandson?" A booming voice filled the kitchen. "Two months old he is, and I have yet to lay eyes on him."

All thoughts of Christmas carols vanished as Miriam's brother, Preacher Moses Miller, entered the kitchen with his wife, Lovinia, as well as Miriam's two other sisters from Bowling Green, and their husbands. Judging from Mary's stricken expression, they hadn't told her they were coming. Seth's arm instinctively tightened around Emmanuel as the ladies who'd been standing around him stepped away—

Except for Miriam. Her brown eyes took on a determined shine as she stood taller beside Seth. "So when did *you* folks arrive?" she asked in a strained voice. "And why didn't ya tell us ya were comin', so ya could've stayed at our place?"

"It seems we're not the *only* ones who haven't picked up the phone or dropped a line lately," Preacher Mose replied as he gazed sternly at his daughter. "Leah and Dan made us welcome at their place."

Leah Kanagy, Miriam's sister, slipped in the kitchen door behind her siblings and in-laws as though it hadn't been *her* idea to keep Mose's visit a secret.

Seth now understood why Miriam had referred to Mary's *dat* as overbearing. Mose Miller wasn't a tall man, but his chiseled face, broad shoulders, and barrel chest gave him a daunting air. While he kept a congregation awake with his dramatic sermons, Mose was showing a side Seth hadn't noticed when he'd preached at Ben and Miriam's wedding ceremony. Miriam's brother didn't seem very patient or forgiving—and what a shame that he'd chosen to cause a scene this morning, just when Mary was getting out among other people.

"We should be preparin' our hearts to worship the Lord—and we shouldn't keep Bishop Tom and the others waitin'," Seth said as he continued to sway with Emmanuel. "Let's resume this discussion after the service."

Seth had no idea what had prompted him to make such a statement—to challenge a preacher, no less. The words had come to him out of the blue, or maybe from divine inspiration, and he maintained his eye contact even as Preacher Mose glared at him.

"And who are *you* to interfere in this family matter—while you hold my grandson?" Mary's *dat* demanded.

"Seth Brenneman," he replied as he extended his hand. "And while you're a guest in my home, Mose, I'd appreciate it if you'd lower your voice. Emmanuel's not used to folks squabblin'. I suspect he's gonna cry—"

Indeed, the boy's wail filled the kitchen like a fire siren as his face turned a distressed shade of red. Mary stepped up and cradled Emmanuel against her shoulder. She looked ready to cry, too, as she comforted her son with baby talk.

"I think Seth said it just right," Miriam agreed as she looked at the women gathered in the kitchen. "It's time for church. Let's take our places."

Just then, the bishop poked his head through the kitchen door. "Mose Miller! Thought I heard your voice," he said cheerfully. "It's a privilege to have ya amongst us, and we'd like ya to join us up front today."

Seth relaxed when Preacher Mose accepted Tom's invitation. As Mose's two brothers-in-law followed him into the front room, the ladies in the kitchen let out a collective sigh of relief. Mary's mother, Lovinia, stepped closer to gaze at her new grandson with an expression of joy tinged with regret.

"It's so *gut* to see you and this precious wee one," she murmured to Mary. "I tried to tell your *dat* we had no call to come bustin' in here on the sly—"

"It's okay, Mama," Mary replied, glancing at her two visiting aunts. "It's not like he said anything untrue, because I—I *haven't* called you. Let's go in for church, and you can all visit with Emmanuel during the service."

Mary's visiting aunts, Deborah and Mattie, smiled brightly and then followed Miriam into the front room. Mary gestured for her *mamm* to precede her. Then she turned to Seth.

"*Denki* for looking after Emmanuel and for the way you handled Dat," she murmured.

"Maybe some of your family issues will get settled today," Seth suggested gently. "It's hard on ya, feelin' pulled in different directions and not knowin' which path to take."

The past few moments had revealed a lot about the Millers and the way they handled life-altering conflicts. Seth felt blessed that his family had made the best of his father's construction accident: while his *dat* was still frustrated about being in a wheelchair, he'd taken a hospital job and Mamm had found an outlet for her cooking talents—and a way to bring in additional income—by partnering with Miriam in the café. The Brennemans had known their struggles, but they'd supported each other with patience and love. As Seth took his place on the pew bench with his brothers, he hoped that if Moses Miller was preaching one of this morning's sermons, he wouldn't air his grievances about his daughter. Preachers did that sometimes.

After the first hymn, the four leaders took their seats in front of the crowd and Bishop Tom greeted them with a smile. "We welcome Leah and Miriam's brother, Preacher Mose Miller from Bowling Green—and we appreciate him servin' as our deacon today while Reuben Riehl's out with the flu."

Denki, Lord, Seth thought as he settled in for the service. Perhaps the next three hours would ease Mose Miller's testiness and give Mary a chance to prepare answers for the questions he was certain to ask later. Seth saw that young Sol was seated between his two visiting uncles, while across the room Mary and Lucy sat with Miriam and her sisters, who took turns holding Emmanuel. Their smiles suggested that some of the tensions had already been eased. In his way, little Emmanuel was like the Savior, a prince of peace in a troubled family.

While Seth reminded himself that it wasn't a good idea to fall for Mary—or to get crosswise with her father—he believed some good would come from today's difficult visit. Maybe he could make a positive difference.

Or you could hold Emmanuel again. Wouldn't that be something?

CHAPTER 5

As the men began setting up the front room for the common meal, Mary felt she'd mended some fences with the women in her family. They'd passed Emmanuel from aunt to aunt and to his grandmother during church, and he'd won them over with his smiles and gurgles. She'd prayed for ways to ease the tension between her and Dat, as well, although Mary doubted he'd ever change his authoritarian ways. She stayed out of his way by remaining in the kitchen, helping Naomi and Miriam unwrap food the other women had brought to share.

As everyone was seated, Teacher Alberta stood up to address them. "What with only three young Zooks and Sol Kauffman being our current scholars, the traditional Christmas Eve skits and recitations at the schoolhouse aren't going to work," she said as she fidgeted with the strings of her *kapp*. "I'd welcome your ideas, as it's time to plan our program for that evening."

A buzz filled the room as folks realized the importance of what Teacher Alberta had said. Taylor Leitner waved her hand excitedly, as though waiting to be called upon in class.

"I know!" she cried. "We could have a Willow Ridge Christmas pageant, with Brett and me joining in, along with the preschool kids—like the four Knepps and Lucy Kauffman. We could dress up like angels and the three kings and—"

"That's too *Englisch*," Mary's father declared. "As I understand it, your father's not yet been accepted into the Amish church."

Mary sighed, noticing how Rhoda—who hoped to become Taylor's new *mamm*—looked disappointed about her *dat's* strict, Old Order ideas. While it was quite common for Amish scholars to reenact the story of Mary, Joseph, and the birth of Jesus, her father had rejected the idea. Teacher Alberta resumed her seat, as though realizing she would receive no further help.

"What about a living Nativity?" Brett Leitner asked eagerly. "We could have one of Bishop Tom's cows, and a sheep or two from Dan Kanagy's flock—"

"And our Clarabelle's sorta like a donkey!" Sol blurted.

"And your *mamm's* name is Mary, and she's got a baby called Emmanuel!" ten-year-old Levi Zook chimed in. "How perfect is *that*?"

"And Seth's a carpenter! He could be Joseph!" Taylor said, clapping her hands together.

Mary's cheeks prickled. It was fine when the kids had called out their ideas about using animals, but sitting outside on a December night with Emmanuel was another thing altogether. And even though such an event would last only a few hours, the thought of Seth standing with her as though he were the baby's father . . .

Would it be all that bad? If the animals got out of hand he'd know what to do. And just as Joseph was patient and wise and kind, so is Seth.

When Mary looked up, Seth was staring at her from a nearby table. His wide-eyed expression suggested he was terrified by the living Nativity idea. Why? she wondered. She had a hard time imagining that the man who'd rescued her in the buggy and then assisted with Emmanuel's delivery—and who'd stood up to her *dat* this morning—could be afraid of anything.

But her father once again quashed the whole notion of putting on an untraditional public show, so the subject was dropped. Folks caught up with their visiting, as they always did during the common meal. The women and girls talked of baking their favorite cookies—

"And will ya come home for Christmas, Mary?" her mother asked softly.

Home for Christmas. The phrase caught Mary by surprise, for she'd never before had to think about it. Had her *dat* asked the same thing, her defenses would've gone up, yet when it was Mama pleading so gently, so desperately, the words melted her heart like butter.

"I don't know," Mary rasped. "The kids and I have been doing so well in Willow Ridge. We're moving beyond Elmer's death in ways we couldn't if we still lived on the farm."

The loneliness in her mother's eyes made Mary feel lower than dirt. After she and the kids had come here for Emmanuel's birth, the Miller home had no doubt become a place where Mama walked on eggshells—

And would that change if you moved back? Dat would still tell you what to do—not accepting any of your ideas because they're not his ideas.

"And speaking of the farm," her father said as he squeezed between the crowded tables, "how will you keep the pipes from freezing this winter? What if the propane tank runs out? And what of the horses and chickens you left behind?" His voice rang through the crowded room as he stood beside Mary. "Your irresponsible handling of Elmer's property makes it quite clear that having a baby hasn't improved your ability to make *gut* decisions."

The room got quiet. Once again, Mary's face flared—and from across the room, Seth's frown told her he was growing more incensed by the moment.

And suddenly, *she* grew angry, too. "I can see *you've* not been by the farm to check on things," Mary retorted, "or you'd know that the animals are with Elmer's brother, Emery, and that he's winterized the toilets and pipes, like I asked him to. He's also refilled the propane tank."

Those were the wrong things to say and the wrong way to say them—in front of everyone in Willow Ridge, no less. Mary waited for her *dat* to slap her. Mama slipped protective arms around her and Emmanuel, as though she, too, expected her husband to react badly. But Mary had only stated the facts and corrected her father's assumptions. Was that so wrong?

"Mose," Miriam said from across the table, "you're takin' this too far. You'd catch more flies with honey instead of pourin' so much vinegar on this situation—on *every* situation—"

"I didn't ask you, Miriam."

Mary's eyes widened—and she saw her future as though someone had written it with a black crayon on the Brennemans' white wall. Lucy's chin was quivering. From his seat beside Uncle Wilmer, Sol was gaping at his grandfather as though he didn't know the man— and didn't want to. None one had *ever* spoken to Aunt Miriam in such a tone.

Mary blinked back tears. "Truth be told, Emery's interested in Elmer's land," she said in the strongest voice she could muster. "He'll give me a fair price, and I'm going to build a little place here in Willow Ridge with the money. My mind's made up. It seems like the best thing to do for the kids and for me, as well."

Beside her, Mama let out a little sob, but she was patting Mary's hand, understanding her predicament.

Her father, however, shook his head as though Mary had once again made a stupid, ill-considered decision. "*Fine.* I hope the Lord looks after you, Mary," he declared, "because I'm washing my hands of this whole situation. Never mind that you've broken your mother's heart."

Mary pressed her forehead to Mama's, clutching her shoulders. "I'm so sorry, Mama," she rasped as tears flowed down her cheeks.

"I am, too," her *mamm* whispered. "But I—I don't blame ya one bit. I'll write and call when I can."

"I will, too, Mama. I promise."

When her father signaled to her uncles, they rose from the table. Mary clung to Emmanuel, her head bowed. Aunt Deborah and Aunt Mattie squeezed her shoulder as they made their way to the kitchen for their wraps. Her mother followed them, of course, and within minutes the three couples were headed back to Bowling Green.

Had there ever been a moment so low—so humiliating? Surely

everyone here wondered what sort of trouble Mary would bring into their midst, now that she intended to live in Willow Ridge. She'd remained sequestered at Aunt Miriam's, so she didn't really know a lot of them, beyond making their acquaintance at Miriam and Ben's wedding. Now they had a horrible impression of her. No doubt this angry discussion with her *dat*—the way she'd sassed him, in front of her children—would be the topic of gossip for weeks to come. They probably thought she was an unfit mother. . . .

Bishop Tom stood up. "I think this unfortunate incident deserves a moment of prayer," he said quietly. "We should lift Mary up as she decides on her family's future, and we should ask the Lord to be present with Mose and Lovinia Miller—to work out His purpose, and to be with all of us as we await the Savior. We need Him as badly today as the folks centuries ago did, when Jesus was born."

Mary bowed her head, nuzzling Emmanuel's sweet-smelling neck. While it was dangerous to draw too many parallels between her son and the Christ Child, this baby had given her the strength to see her life in a new light . . . the fortitude to speak up for her beliefs. Because she had Emmanuel to raise, she had dared to move beyond others' assumptions. He was saving her from herself and her old fears.

If I'm out of line, Lord, show me a better way. Walk with Mama, and with Dat. If it's Your will, help us find peace and forgiveness for each other. Thank You for the way Aunt Miriam and—and Seth—are standing with me as I consider a new home. A new life.

When the people around her resumed their meal and conversations, Mary felt refreshed. Bishop Tom was such a dear man—so different from her *dat*. It seemed everyone ate quickly, probably because the confrontation between her and Dat had made them uneasy. As Mary looked for someone to hold Emmanuel so she could help clear the tables, Miriam slipped an arm around her shoulders.

"The apple didn't fall far from the tree, honey-bug," her aunt murmured. "Mose picked up on the same personality our *dat*—your grandfather—was known for. After my Jesse had been around them while we were engaged, it was an easy decision for us to move away."

"But you newlyweds weren't running *from* something, so much as Uncle Jesse was looking for affordable land where his smithy would do well," Mary pointed out ruefully. "It's no secret why I'm selling Elmer's land. So now everyone thinks I can't get along with my family, and in the eyes of the church, that's just *wrong*."

Miriam considered this. "You made your choice based on your heart, not your head," she murmured. "Your *dat* considers that impractical, but sometimes it's the only way we women can have a life. It's not like you've left your husband, after all. Every woman here understands that you'll be a better parent if you've not constantly got your back up."

As Mary glanced around the room, where Rhoda, Naomi, and the other women were picking up dirty dishes, their smiles confirmed what Aunt Miriam had just said. Her shoulders relaxed. It occurred to her that over the years, the women in the Bowling Green district had shown the same support for her *mamm*—not speaking out directly against their preacher, but finding lots of ways to encourage Mama when she seemed down. And wasn't that the same sense of community and sisterhood Mary felt here, in this very room?

The men were taking down the tables, and when Ben saw Mary and Miriam conferring, he joined them. "We're standin' with you and your kids, Mary," he said gently. "Long as ya need it, you've got a home in our *dawdi haus*. And when your farm sells, we just happen to know some brothers who'll build ya a sturdy little home."

Tears filled her eyes. Mary's heart overflowed with the love her aunt and uncle were showing her. Across the crowded room, she saw Seth shaking his head, holding up his palms in protest as Teacher Alberta pleaded with him. From the snatch of conversation that carried across the crowd, Mary concluded that he wanted nothing to do with a Christmas pageant or a live Nativity scene, no matter how excited the kids were about the idea.

And that suited her just fine. Sitting out in the cold with a new baby sounded uncomfortable and risky, especially if it was windy or snowing on Christmas Eve. Now that her parents had left in a huff—and now that she'd made her poor mother cry—Mary already felt as though she'd set herself out in the cold.

But you honored an important decision, instead of backing down. You have the support of these compassionate people, and they won't let you fail. What's a little cold weather on Christmas Eve, compared to the difficulties you've already weathered? Keep an open mind and an open heart. It's the season for miracles. . . .

CHAPTER 6

Thursday of that week, Mary completed the final squares of the Star of Bethlehem quilt top. Miriam and Ben were working, Sol was at school, and Emmanuel and Lucy were napping, so she stayed at her aunt's treadle machine, stitching the large squares into rows with strips of an evergreen cotton print between them. In the center of each square, an eight-point star made of bold red and green diamonds was encircled by dark green house-shaped pieces and diamonds in a lighter shade of green. With a red triangle in each corner of a square, the design looked cheerful yet masculine.

By the time Emmanuel stirred in his crib, Mary was attaching the last row. It felt so satisfying to complete one major part of her project. The Christmas quilt had been good therapy after Emmanuel's birth and in the aftermath of Sunday's confrontation with Dat.

"Knock, knock!" came a voice from the doorway.

Mary looked up and smiled. "Rhoda and Taylor! Come and see what I've been making—and tell me how I should do the quilting."

At the sound of voices, Lucy roused from her nap. Her face lit up when she saw seven-year-old Taylor, whose lavender Plain-style dress matched her own. "Can we get cookies in the kitchen?" she asked hopefully.

"*Jah*—but save some for when Sol gets home," Mary replied. It did her heart good to watch the two little girls becoming friends, just as she was pleased that Rhoda had come to visit at such an opportune time.

"Oh, what a pretty piece," Rhoda said as Mary smoothed the finished quilt top over the bed. "You've been a busy bee since your boy was born."

"*Jah*, I figured I'd best take advantage of this time at Miriam and Ben's," Mary replied. "Once I hear from Elmer's brother about settling up for the farm in Bowling Green, we'll *really* be busy."

When Mary stood back from the bed, she couldn't help but smile. It was one thing to piece each square of a quilt, and something else altogether to see them stitched into the final design.

"It would detract from that nice, simple pattern if ya quilted the usual loops or swirls over it," Rhoda remarked in a thoughtful tone. "Why not stitch just inside the house shapes, and inside the red corner triangles, and then tie the center of each star? And if ya ask me—who's not so *gut* at gettin' my stitches perfect and even—I'd do that quiltin' on the machine. But that's just me."

Mary could easily visualize the way Rhoda's suggestion would look. "What a wonderful-*gut* idea," she replied. "And it would save me dragging out Miriam's quilting frame—not to mention saving me a lot of time. I could probably finish it by Christmas if I machine quilted it."

"For somebody special?" Rhoda asked with a sly grin.

Was she that transparent? Or did Rhoda have a matchmaker's heart, the same as most of the ladies here in Willow Ridge? They'd watched her hand Emmanuel over to Seth on Sunday morning, after all—a gesture that had implied a great deal of trust. "Not really," Mary hedged. "It would just be *gut* to finish this Christmas project before we move on to our new life and a new year."

"We're all glad you've decided to stay in Willow Ridge, Mary," Rhoda said as a smile lit her face. "My Brett and your Sol seem to be buddyin' up the way the two girls are. What with Andy's kids bein' betwixt and between—not yet Plain but no longer livin' their *Englisch* life—they're happy to be makin' friends with other kids who're new in town."

That was a blessing Mary hadn't foreseen.

"Truth be told, you're my inspiration, Rhoda," she murmured. "Seeing the way Andy's kids have taken to you gives me hope that someday Lucy and Sol will consider me more as their *mamm* than their *dat*'s second wife, you know? We've had some rough moments, especially between Sol and me."

"Can't be easy, takin' up where their birth mother left off—and then losin' the man who glued your family together." Rhoda slung her arm around Mary's shoulders. "I think a fresh start away from all those memories—and your *dat*'s criticism—is the best thing ya could possibly do.

"Matter of fact," Rhoda continued in a lighter voice, "Taylor and I came to ask if you and the kids wanted to see our Nativity set. Bishop Tom carved it, ya know. And with all the talk last Sunday about puttin' on a Christmas pageant, we thought your kids would enjoy it."

"How nice of you to ask!" Mary glanced at the clock. "Sol will be walking home from the schoolhouse soon, and with the sun so bright and warm today, it would do us all *gut* to get some fresh air. Let me get our jackets and Emmanuel's basket!"

As they walked, Mary lifted her face to the sun ... watched Lucy and Taylor skip along the side of the road with Rowdy bounding ahead of them and then circling back. As she looked out over Willow Ridge, where the white homes and cardinal-red barns shone in the afternoon light, Mary felt more lighthearted than she had in a long, long time. "We're having a really mild winter so far," she remarked as she and Rhoda followed the girls.

"*Jah*, ya just never know how December'll play out. It's like they say—if ya don't like Missouri weather right now, wait a day," Rhoda replied. "Jacket weather suits me fine, even if snow would be pretty for Christmas."

Mary waved high above her head when she saw Sol coming down the intersecting gravel road, and he waved back. As Lucy and Taylor called Sol's name, Rowdy raced ahead, barking ecstatically as the boy ran to meet them. A buggy was also coming down the gravel road, and Brett leaned out of its window to call out to the other kids. It made quite a picture, watching Sol, Lucy, Taylor—and Rowdy—jump into the rig when it came to a stop.

"Brett went over to tell Tom we were settin' up his Nativity," Rhoda explained. "Looks like he convinced the bishop to take a break and join us for a few."

"I should've brought some of our cookies," Mary said. "This is turning out to be a little Advent party."

Once they arrived at the Leitners' home, which was inside the clinic building, everyone gathered around the most unique Nativity set Mary had ever seen. The carved figures were Amish men and women, wearing broad-brimmed black hats and Plain dresses. They were faceless but they certainly didn't lack for personality.

"Look at this!" Mary said as she leaned down to study the set. "The wise men are carrying an ear of corn, a bucket of milk, and a chicken!"

"Bringin' their homegrown gifts to the Baby Jesus," Rhoda explained.

Taylor giggled, elbowing her brother. "Brett used to call them the *three wise guys*, but we've fixed his thinking."

"And the little quilts on the animals and in the manger are so detailed—and the star's got a quilt pattern, too," Mary marveled. She smiled at Bishop Tom, who was watching the Leitner kids show their favorite pieces to Sol and Lucy. "Did you do the carving *and* the painting, Bishop? This is a quite a labor of love."

"*Jah*, it is, and the tourists snap up every last Nativity I can display at Zook's Market," he remarked with a humble shrug. "Makin' these sets keeps me busy on winter days. They're intended for *Englisch* more than for us Plain folks—lots of districts don't allow them, as the Nativity figures could be considered graven images."

"*Jah*, Dat and the leaders of his church are set against them," Mary agreed.

Bishop Tom smiled at Rhoda then. "But since you bought this for Taylor and Brett before they started down the path to becomin' Plain, I'm happy you've gotten it out," he said. "Watchin' these kids share Jesus's birth brings new life to the story, even for us older folks who've known it since we were kids ourselves."

Mary had to agree. Lucy and Sol looked enthralled as Taylor and Brett handed them each carved, painted piece. Then they discussed where the figures ought to be placed beneath the star-topped manger, so humans and animals alike were gazing at the baby. The wooly sheep, the humble donkey, and the contented cow conveyed a feeling of peace, and even without facial features, Mary and Joseph expressed wonder and adoration. It was a treat to hear the four kids tell how each character played a part in the first Christmas as she gazed at the little baby on His quilt, in a hay manger.

When Rowdy barked at something outside, Taylor's eyes lit up. "Bishop Tom, you should carve a border collie for this set—to keep the sheep from wandering off, you know?"

"*Jah*, Rowdy's real *gut* about watchin' Emmanuel. Real gentle and quiet," Sol chimed in. "And if sheep and cows and a donkey were around, he'd make sure they wouldn't hurt our little brother."

Our little brother. The words were music to Mary's ears, for Sol hadn't shown much inclination to hold or talk to Emmanuel.

Tom chuckled. "A border collie, eh? It makes perfect sense, I suppose." He smiled at the kids then, as though he had a secret to share. "I've given a lot of thought to puttin' on a living Nativity, like you kids were so excited about last Sunday. I think we should give it a go."

When Taylor and the other kids jumped up and down, clapping their hands, Bishop Tom grinned. "It would solve Teacher Alberta's predicament about puttin' on the Christmas Eve program," he explained. "And since it would include our younger kids, as well as a few local folks' animals, I think it's a worthwhile community effort. As long as we keep Jesus's birth and the Holy Spirit first and foremost, we're still tellin' the greatest story on earth."

The bishop focused on Mary then, his expression softening as he stroked Emmanuel's cheek. "Of course, it's really up to *you*, Mary," he continued in a lower voice. "If you're not inclined to sit outside with this wee boy on a December night, everyone would understand. I suppose we could wrap up somebody's doll baby—"

"That wouldn't be the same!" Taylor protested. "If we're going to have lambs and Lucy's little pony and—"

"Ah-ah! Watch your tongue," Rhoda warned with a shake of

her finger. "It's Mary's choice. If she doesn't want to risk Emmanuel catchin' his death of cold, we'll respect her decision."

A look of contrition stole over Taylor's face. "*Jah*, you're right," she agreed. "Who knows but what we might have snow or ice that night? Nobody would want to be outside in that sort of weather."

Mary's thoughts were racing. Was she willing to take part in such an event because her father had so vehemently spoken out against it, or because the idea of reenacting Jesus's birth stirred something deep inside her? She'd often portrayed Mary in the Christmas Eve skits when she'd been a scholar, but giving birth to her firstborn son had put the story into a new perspective for her.

"Where do you suppose we should have it?" Mary asked. "A living Nativity won't require anyone to memorize parts, but we still have to plan it out—"

"Seth built that new room for Clarabelle and Rowdy and the kitties!" Lucy exclaimed.

"*Jah*!" Sol looked more enthusiastic than Mary had ever seen him. "Clarabelle—or even a cow— could use her stall," he said. "We could stack hay bales for you to sit on. And if we're there at Ben and Miriam's, you can take Emmanuel back to the house if he gets too cold."

"That little stable would shield ya from the wind, too," Bishop Tom remarked as he stroked his silver-shot beard. "Ben could probably borrow some lights or space heaters from the Schrocks. Lots of our Mennonite friends will probably come that night, if we let them know what we're doin'."

"Rebecca!" Taylor blurted. "She's not Plain, so she can post notices on her computer, and print up posters for store bulletin boards all around here. I bet *bunches* of people will come! This is going to be *so cool*!"

"I think so, too!" Mary said. As she hugged Emmanuel, the whole idea blossomed in her imagination and in her heart. It was so good to see Lucy and Sol wanting to participate with the Leitner kids, who'd originally had the idea. "We'll need a cow and some sheep—"

"I can talk Dan Kanagy into sharin' a ewe and a lamb or two. I'll bring an older cow from my dairy herd—and I've got a trailer to bring them all down the road," Tom said with a nod. "The Knepp kids and the Zooks'll be tickled to take part, so the only challenge will be gettin' Joseph to cooperate." The bishop looked at Mary as though he had information from a Higher Source about the nature of her relationship with Seth Brenneman.

Mary let out a laugh. "Last I heard, Seth was telling Teacher Alberta he wanted no part of any play-acting."

"It's not like anybody'll need to talk. Everyone can sing carols and just enjoy seein' who all comes," Tom said. "Doesn't have to be Seth who plays Joseph, either. Invite whoever ya want, Mary. Ben would probably help out."

As they discussed a few more ideas, Mary felt a surge of happiness and Christmas spirit. What a wonderful sensation—all from being invited to see the Leitners' Nativity set, and visiting with a bishop who was open to new ideas. Didn't this afternoon's surprises suggest that she'd made the right decision, selling Elmer's farm to start fresh in Willow Ridge?

As she and the kids prepared to leave, Mary felt a tug on her sleeve. It was Taylor, smiling up at her. "I didn't mean to sound bossy about you and the baby being in an outdoor Nativity," she said in a low voice.

"Oh, I know that, sweetheart," Mary replied. "You're just excited—and so am I! You've made my whole Christmas season shine a lot brighter, you know it?"

Taylor's face lit up, and then she grinned furtively. "I'm not telling you who to pick for Joseph, either," she murmured. "But it just *fits* that Seth is a carpenter, like Joseph was. And anybody can see how he cares for you and Emmanuel."

Can they, now? Mary wondered. In the last few minutes, a bishop and a seven-year-old girl had pointed this out to her as though the whole world already knew she and Seth should be together. It was too soon to go along with such a match—or to assume Seth would want to—but Mary smiled as she put on her jacket. She couldn't imagine any twenty-something man wanting to court a widow with three kids, but thoughts of spending time with Seth certainly put her in a better mood than mourning Elmer did.

"And besides, he's so nice. And *cute*," Taylor added with a decisive nod.

"I won't go telling him that—even though I agree with you," Mary replied. It wasn't the Plain way to value good looks over a man's other qualities. "And don't you tell Seth I said so, either!"

Taylor drew her fingers across her lips, as though closing a zipper. Then she giggled. "I hope it's not snowy and cold on Christmas Eve. This is going to be so *fabulous*!"

CHAPTER 7

When the bell above the shop door jangled, Seth looked up from the shelf he was restocking. Was he imagining things, or was that Mary Kauffman peering into his showroom? "Come on in!" he called out. "I just got a new shipment of wooden toys. They're on consignment from crafters in other Amish towns."

"Aunt Miriam told me you might have something for Lucy and Sol," Mary replied as she walked toward him. "She's baking cookies with them, so this is a *gut* time to find their Christmas gifts."

Seth paused to watch her. What a picture she made! Her strawberry-blond hair glimmered beneath her crisp *kapp*, and even though Mary still wore black, she seemed so much healthier—and happier—than she had on that fateful day when he'd found her passed out in her surrey. From his basket carrier, Emmanuel gurgled happily. Was it Seth's imagination again, or did the wee boy kick his feet and wiggle when their gazes met?

Better keep your mind on business, he reminded himself. *Letting your imagination run free can only lead to trouble.*

And yet, how could anything bad come from getting better acquainted with Mary Kauffman, now that she'd committed to staying in Willow Ridge? It was a rare treat, seeing her here without

Lucy and Sol . . . even if the tilt of her brows suggested she might have something on her mind besides shopping.

"These wooden yo-yos are a big hit with the boys," Seth remarked as he held one up. "And we have wooden pull-carts and checker games, along with doll cradles and kid-sized rocking chairs. Look around all you want. It's *gut* to see you."

Mary smiled up at him. "If I can't find something here, either I'm too picky or Lucy and Sol already have too many toys," she remarked. She placed her hand on the head of a rocking horse with yarn fringe for a mane and tail, smiling as it swung forward and back . . . forward and back. "I'd be fibbing if I didn't tell you why I really came to see you, though."

Seth's heart turned a couple of flip-flops. His mind raced over several enticing possibilities. "*Jah*, and why would that be?"

"Yesterday afternoon, Bishop Tom agreed that a living Nativity would be a *gut* idea, weather permitting. The Leitner kids and my two are *so* excited, and Ben's going to fix up that new addition to the barn you built for us, so—" Mary fixed her deep green eyes on him. "All we need is Joseph. I'm hoping you'll join us, Seth."

The smile dropped from his face. "It's not that I don't like the Nativity idea," he insisted, "but Christmas Eve programs were the bane of my existence when I was a kid in school. I'm sorry, Mary, but—"

"But you won't have to say *one word*," Mary said persuasively. "I could ask Ben, but . . . well, after the way you helped me when Emmanuel was born, and how you seemed so—so solid and strong—when Dat fussed at me last Sunday, I was hoping . . ."

Seth really, really hated to disappoint Mary. She didn't impress him as the type to be constantly pecking at a fellow, asking for favors to get his attention, either. And he couldn't deny how the shine in her eyes and her melodious voice affected him as they stood in silence . . . a silence she was probably using to make him give in.

"I have a hard time believing you're *afraid* to be in front of people, Seth. And you've known most of the folks who'll be there all your life, *jah*?"

He let out a harsh sigh. There was no getting out of this conversation, so he'd better get his objections out in the open. "It's not that I'm afraid so much as I get frustrated," he replied in a thin voice. "Whenever folks are watchin' me, expectin' me to do this or that, I invariably mess up and do something really stupid. To this day, my two brothers tease me about the Christmas Eve I fell backwards off the platform during the skits at the schoolhouse."

"But I'm not your two brothers. I wouldn't dream of making fun of you, Seth," Mary said quietly. "I . . . I *like* you. And I know you'll keep the animals under control—and Emmanuel trusts you, too. See?"

Mary took the baby from his carrier and offered him to Seth. Of *course*, he set down his box of toys to hold the little guy, even as he suspected Mary was using the baby to get her way about the Nativity on Christmas Eve. "I like you, too, Mary, but bein' in the spotlight's just not my cup of tea."

"I admire humility in a man."

Once more Seth wanted to turn cartwheels. This pretty young mother was saying things he'd always longed to hear, and he wanted to believe them, but . . .

"All right, so I've told ya why I'm not wild about bein' in the Nativity play," Seth said, holding her gaze. "Surely you have something that frustrates you, too, Mary."

Mary's expression got more serious. She watched Emmanuel pat the side of Seth's face with his little hand. "I do," she replied in a tight voice. "I get so tired of being told—mostly by the men in my family and Elmer's—that I'm too impulsive and gullible. I know all about feeling *stupid*, Seth, along with being made to feel that my opinions and decisions can't be taken seriously. And I detest being talked about as though I'm not in the room and my feelings don't matter." ·

Seth's jaw dropped. "Why would anyone say *you* were stupid or gullible, Mary?" he countered. "From what I've seen, you've made the best of a lot of bad situations. You're movin' forward after a year that would've rattled *anybody*," he insisted. "Why, I don't know another soul who could've handled so many problems the way you have. And yet here ya stand, smilin' at me as though life's treatin' ya real *gut*."

Mary sighed softly. "Actually, from the moment I told Dat I was selling Elmer's farm, all the pieces seemed to fall into place. Emery and I have settled on a *gut* price for that land in Bowling Green . . . so if you don't want to talk about the living Nativity, maybe we could discuss building me a house?" Her eyebrows rose expressively. "I have no idea how to go about planning a place, or what it might cost, or if I'll have enough money from selling the farm to make it work. I don't even know where I might find a piece of land to put it on. But I want *you* to help me with it, Seth. *Please?*"

Seth couldn't breathe. Couldn't think. Couldn't for the life of him recall what day it was or what he'd eaten for dinner. Mary's sweet face—her earnest expression, and the trust she was placing in him—compelled him to gaze back at her even though he was scared half out of his mind. Was she figuring to share that house with *him* someday? Did she have ulterior motives about latching on to him because she had three little kids to raise and no means of support? He had a sudden vision of a sturdy little white house with a porch and a swing, and he was sitting beside Mary in the evening breeze as they glided forward and back . . .

But then, that was his imagination kicking in again, wasn't it?

"I don't know what land sells for in Bowling Green," he said in a low voice, "but my brothers and I are experienced at stretchin' a dollar without cuttin' any corners, far as the construction goes. I might even know of a plot of land—"

When Mary's eyes lit up, Seth kicked himself. Why did he think the dogleg of property between his *mamm's* garden and the Lantz place would make a good setting for Mary's house? And why had he mentioned it, especially without consulting his father first?

"Well, *anyway*," Seth hurried on, "if ya tell me what all you'd like in your house—how many bedrooms and how big ya want the kitchen and such—I could sketch something up and give ya an estimate. We could adjust from there, once ya knew where ya wanted to build."

Mary pressed her palms together, looking as delighted as a child . . . a very pretty, persuasive child. "Oh, Seth, *denki* so much! Just seeing the plans on paper would be making a dream come true. I—I've never had any say about the houses I've lived in."

Seth blinked. It had never occurred to him that most Plain women didn't get a chance to design a home. They accepted whatever their husbands decided upon, perhaps getting to choose the kitchen appliances, at most. "Well, then! Get your ideas together, and if anything ya suggest won't work, I can steer ya toward something that will. Micah and Aaron and I are real *gut* at makin' the most out of a little space."

Mary's ecstatic expression made him feel inexplicably happy. And he'd gotten her off the subject of the Nativity, too! She bought one of the rocking horses for Lucy and a sturdy wooden wagon for Sol, and then asked if he'd keep her purchases here at the shop until Ben could pick them up.

As Mary flashed him a final smile and left the shop with Emmanuel, Seth stood amazed at what had taken place in the space of twenty minutes. He was flattered that she wanted him to build her future home here in Willow Ridge. And the way his heart was banging against his rib cage suggested that he was secretly hoping to play a long-term role in Mary's life, even though it was way too early to be considering such a thing.

For his next trick, he'd have to approach Dat about that plot of land. He went to the back workroom, where china hutches and bedroom sets were in various stages of completion, to look out the window. Nobody knew why the Lantz place, where Miriam had lived with her first husband, and the Brenneman land had been interlocked like puzzle pieces in the survey, or why the two families hadn't ever evened up the property between them. It was only a few acres—not nearly enough to farm—and the only access to a road would be along the Brennemans' lane, which ran past the shop, or down the Lantzes' lane, which met the county highway alongside the Sweet Seasons. No man would even consider it—

But Mary's not a man. Her needs are different, and so's her way of looking at life and—and everything that matters.

Once again, Seth's train of thought was chugging along faster than he cared to consider, but he'd agreed to go along for the ride. There was no backing out now—and why would he want to? Mary hadn't asked him to do anything he hadn't done dozens of times before.

CHAPTER 8

Mary sat at Miriam's sewing machine the afternoon of Monday, December 20, working on costumes with Rhoda and Rebecca. Because Plain folks didn't believe in wearing clothing that attracted attention, it was a big deal for the kids to have the bishop's permission to wear *wings* and kingly cloaks and shepherds' robes . . . even if a lot of the costumes' grandeur depended upon the wearers' imaginations.

"You say your church in New Haven was getting rid of these little white choir robes?" Mary asked Rebecca. "They're making our job so much easier, because I can just hem them to make them fit each angel."

"They look shimmery, too!" Rhoda remarked as she leaned over Mary's shoulder. "And the girls can wear them right over the top of their dresses. I'm just glad ya brought us the wings, sister, because designin' those had me stumped. Guess I haven't spent enough time around angels to know how they work!"

The three of them laughed. Strains of "The First Noel" drifted in from the kitchen, where Teacher Alberta was working with all the children so they'd be ready to sing on Saturday night. She was showing great patience, as nearly half of the eleven kids weren't old enough to be in school.

"While I was talking to the youth choir director, she said they'd gotten new Christmas pageant costumes this year," Rebecca explained. "It was lucky timing that I could latch on to their cast-offs."

"*Jah*, I was thinking we'd have to redesign some of our old dresses for the wise men's robes," Mary said as she focused on the hem she was stitching. "I can't think the two Zook boys or Sol would be any too happy wearing dresses!"

"It's *gut* that the Zooks brought along several pairs of long johns, too," Rebecca remarked. "The kids'll need something warm under their costumes so they won't have to wear coats. The weather report for Christmas Eve looks really good, though. In the fifties during the day!"

"And with the Schrocks bringing over the space heaters and big lights they use in their auctioneerin' business, the whole stable area should stay fairly warm," Rhoda said. And we'll be able to see if the kids—or *you*, Mary—are lookin' chilled."

"Those stretchy gloves Rebecca found, along with the thermal underwear, should keep us all comfy," Mary said as she removed the slick fabric from beneath the sewing machine's needle. "There! The four angel robes are ready. Let's write the girls' names inside the back plackets—Taylor and Amelia Zook will wear the longer ones, and Lucy and Sara Knepp need the short ones. And they each have a set of those silvery wings, *jah*?"

"They do," Rebecca replied as she checked the hangers they were preparing for each child. "And I'll look over the halos to be sure they're all in good shape."

"Let's have the four shepherds come in next," Mary suggested. "I've picked out all the solid-colored tunics and robes but we'll need to use one of the striped ones, unless we sew something up real quick."

Rhoda held up each wrap-around robe to be sure they were in good repair. "Well, Brett's not Amish, so let's give him this red and tan striped piece. It looks to be the right length—and again, it's *gut* the boys can wear these over their pants and shirts. With the long johns, three layers should be plenty warm enough."

When Rebecca brought the four shepherds in from the kitchen, Mary chuckled. Each of the boys tentatively slipped into the heavy cotton robes, allowing her and Rhoda to tie their belts and check the lengths. Next came the rectangular headpieces, which hung down over the boys' shoulders and were held on with stretchy bands.

"Brett, it's awfully nice of you to be a shepherd so Sol can play one of the wise men," Mary remarked. "He'll be a lot less bashful that way, being with Cyrus and Levi like he is at school."

Brett draped his arms around Josh and Joey, the Knepp twins. "These guys and Timmy are already my buddies," he said. "We'll be good shepherds together, with those lambs Bishop Tom's bringing."

"And I just happened to find something for *you*, Timmy!" Rebecca said as she reached into her sack of accessories. "The Schrock ladies use this for their Easter decorations in the quilt shop. They said you could carry it, if you want."

Little Timmy Knepp, not yet four, lit up like a Christmas candle as Rebecca handed him a fleecy stuffed lamb. The toy was nearly as big as he was, and the smile on his face was priceless.

"You boys look mighty fine!" Rhoda proclaimed. She knelt in front of Timmy to pin up the bottom edge of his robe. "You guys are *gut* to go. Your singin' sounded real nice, too. When ya get back to the kitchen, have the wise men come back here."

As Rhoda and Rebecca put the other shepherds' costumes on hangers, Mary sat down at the sewing machine to hem Timmy's robe. She heard Cyrus and Levi Zook come in with Sol, sounding bold and ready to look kingly—until both of the Zook boys sounded off at once.

"You think we're gonna wear *that* sort of getup?" Levi demanded.

"Those are *dresses*!" Cyrus said. "My friends would laugh their butts off if they saw me—"

"Cyrus! Enough of your mouth!" Rhoda scolded. "You'll be wearin' your pants and shirt underneath the tunic, so it's not like—"

"Oh, no I won't!"

"Me, neither," his brother chimed in.

"So have you ever seen a *king*, a wise man from the East, wearing tri-blend trousers and suspenders, then?" Rebecca challenged them. "Here—look at these illustrations of people in Bible times. Real men—even Jesus—wore flowing tunics. And to be sure no one mistakes you for a girl—"

Mary turned around to watch this little confrontation. Her son's eyes were wide, as though he didn't really want to wear a flowing robe, either, but he had sense enough not to protest—not in front of *her*, anyway.

Rebecca held up a dark, wavy hairpiece, and then slipped it over Sol's head before he could back away. "Beards!" she said as she tucked the wiglet around his chin. "And we have cool crowns for you to choose from, and some awesome pots to hold your gold and frankincense and myrrh. But if you're not man enough to do a good job, like the other kids, then we'll have Ben and Bishop Tom and Andy Leitner play your parts. They're the wisest men I know."

"*Jah*, and they'll be mighty disappointed that they gave us special permission to put on this living Nativity, and then you oldest boys set such a bad example for the younger ones," Rhoda said sternly. She planted her fist on her hip. "So how's it going to be, Cyrus and Levi? We're not fittin' ya for your costumes unless we know you're gonna show up Saturday night. With the right attitude."

"It's too late to cancel," Rebecca stated. "The posters are all out and I advertised this pageant on the Sweet Seasons website. So— with you or without you—the show will go on."

Mary nipped her lip. While the Zook boys carried on a silent but meaningful exchange of gazes, Sol chose a cloak of deep purple and slipped into it. Next he settled the largest crown on his head, and chose the most ostentatious of the three boxes. "How's this?" he asked, looking to Mary for her reaction.

She walked around him, checking the cloak's length. "Seems to me the wisdom of Solomon is shining through," she said in a low voice. "Your *dat* would be so pleased that you're a willing participant, and a leader, Sol—even though you're the youngest of the kings."

Cyrus was watching Sol with an appraising eye. He chose a tunic of rich green velveteen, dropped it over his head, and then put on a gold stole. Rebecca was ready with a reddish-brown beard, and they completed the costume with a turban-style hat and an elegant brass decanter. On impulse, Mary went to her closet and came out with a full-length mirror that usually hung on the back of the door. When the two costumed boys saw themselves, their delight filled the room.

"Whoa, *Bessy!*" Cyrus exclaimed as he turned this way and that.

"And you're sure some other district's bishop's not gonna tell us this is all wrong?" Sol asked cautiously. "What if . . . what if Grandfather sees us this way and—"

"Bishop Tom and Ben will be right there, and so will Seth and I," Mary assured him. It saddened her that Sol was intimidated by her father's brusque personality, but perhaps this would be a time for some risk-taking . . . some teachable moments in their faith. "I can't think God's going to punish us for presenting the story of Jesus's birth, if we all act with respect and humility."

She turned then, to see Levi dressed in a stately tunic of cranberry red with a coordinating red and gold crown. In a black beard, holding a box made to resemble carved ivory, he stepped between his kingly companions at the mirror.

Mary kept her chuckle to her herself. Levi wasn't saying anything, but his flicker of a grin—and the way he stood taller, with his shoulders squared—suggested that he was secretly pleased with his appearance. Approaching footsteps announced that the other children had finished their singing session with Teacher Alberta, and when they burst into the kitchen they all stopped and gaped at the wise men.

"Ooooh," said little Sara Knepp, her eyes widening.

"You guys look *awesome*," Taylor stated.

That cinched it. Mary could see by the Zook boys' faces that Taylor's opinion carried weight even though she wasn't officially Plain yet. And when Teacher Alberta entered the kitchen, she pushed up her thick glasses to get a clearer look at the three kings.

"My *stars*," she said as she circled them. "Oh, this pageant will be so much better thanks to all you've done for us, Rebecca. And as long as we follow the one Star, to worship and remember the Jesus who was born to die for us, we'll recall this Christmas Eve as one of the finest of our lives."

Mary smiled. She couldn't have said that better herself.

* * *

As Seth worked alongside Ben on Friday, preparing the space where the living Nativity would take place, he felt a rising excitement—a floating sensation, which he'd felt ever since he'd told Mary that he'd participate in the pageant. He drove a few bolts into the upright support Ben was holding, which connected crossbars that would serve as a temporary pen for the sheep. Sol was tossing a ball for Rowdy, then racing the agile dog across the lot to retrieve it.

"Looks like Mary's sewed up your costume and hers, Joseph," Ben remarked as they completed the pen. "She seems mighty pleased that this whole Nativity scenario has worked out so well."

"It has," Seth agreed. "From the sounds of the forecast, we'll be fine—especially with the lights and the space heater and the generator the Schrocks are loanin' us. I heard the kids practicin' their carols, and I think everybody who comes will be pleased and inspired—even if it's only the parents and the locals."

"Hard to know what sort of crowd we might draw. Let's get these hay bales arranged, so you and Mary have a place to sit when ya want to," Ben suggested as they began that task. "The bales can hide the heater and the lights, too, along with the cords goin' to the generator in the barn, so it looks a little more realistic to the folks who're watchin'."

Seth and Ben had just placed a double row of bales in a small semicircle, and then another layer of bales on top of the back ones, when Rowdy bounded up onto them. The dog was barking with his ball in his mouth, springing from bale to bale. Sol was right behind him, laughing and jumping onto the bales, as well.

"All right, guys, we can't have this tearin' around," Seth said. He snapped his fingers to get Rowdy's attention, and then pointed to the ground. "Rowdy, *down*. Right now."

The border collie's ears rose and his alert eyes held Seth's gaze for a moment. Then he hopped off the bales and sat on the ground.

Sol frowned. "We were just playin'—"

"And if Rowdy thinks he can carouse in here, he'll do the same tomorrow night," Seth explained. "We can't have him roughhousin', knockin' over little angels and shepherds, or agitatin' the sheep and the cow."

Sol immediately looked to Ben for support. "So how come *he* can tell us what to do when it's your barnyard, Uncle Ben?" he asked shrilly. "And Rowdy's *my* dog, not his!"

"Seth's watchin' out for you and the other kids," Ben replied, as he, too, gestured for Sol to climb down. "This is where your *mamm'll* be sittin' with Emmanuel, and she doesn't need Rowdy upsettin' the baby. The whole idea of this Nativity is to worship Jesus, like we're in church. If Rowdy doesn't behave, we'll have to put him in the barn."

Storm clouds passed across the boy's forehead. "But he's just bein' a dog. If Seth's gonna keep bossin' him around—"

Ben grasped the boy's shoulders and set him firmly on the ground. "It's your job to listen and do what adults tell ya," he pointed out. "Rowdy's smart and his instincts are *gut*. He knows to obey Seth because he *trusts* him—just like when he ran to Seth for help that first day ya came to Willow Ridge. But we don't want him learnin' bad habits."

When Sol opened his mouth to protest again, Ben grew stern. "Go inside and change your *attitude*, young fella," he said. "If you're playin' the part of a wise man—and named for one of the great kings of the Old Testament—it's time ya grew into those roles."

Heaving a theatrical sigh, Sol turned.

As the boy trudged toward the house, Seth wondered once again if he should curb his feelings for Mary before he got too attached to her. "I wish I knew what to do about that kid," he murmured as the two of them resumed their work. "Mary's asked me to draw up plans for a house, and she's actin' interested in *me*—but Sol's quick to let me know he's none too happy about Mary and me gettin' friendly."

"He's moody," Ben agreed as they assessed the placement of the bales. "Some of that's just him protectin' his territory as the man of the family. But Elmer let him get away with more than I would have—maybe because Sol was so depressed after his mother passed."

"*Jah*, those kids have had a tough couple of years. I try to keep that in mind, knowin' I'm lucky to have both of my parents still alive." Seth picked up his tools and surveyed the area to be sure he'd collected all of them. "But I don't think we're doin' Sol any favors if we let him whine and carry on—"

"Ya got that right," Ben agreed.

"—and I *won't* tolerate his backtalk," Seth continued firmly. "But then, maybe I've been a single man too long, and I'm not the best judge of how to handle Sol, either. Maybe his attitude is God's way of tellin' me to think again, where seein' Mary is concerned."

Ben let out a short laugh. "If you're gonna let that boy determine the path your relationship with Mary'll take, it's already headin' down a dead end. I sure hope ya won't let that happen, Seth. From what I can see, the two of ya are as well suited as Miriam and I are."

Seth's eyes widened. Since Ben Hooley had come here from Lancaster County, no one had ever questioned that he and Miriam made the perfect pair. It had been easy for them to court because Miriam's girls were grown . . . but Seth doubted that young children would have dissuaded Ben. He was the kind of man who determined what he wanted—what God intended for him to pursue—and let nothing stand in his way. Willow Ridge was truly blessed to have Ben as one of its new preachers.

A *woof* made Seth glance at Rowdy, who was still sitting obediently nearby. When the border collie eagerly lifted a paw, Seth couldn't resist the dog's invitation. He sat on a bale and shook hands, admiring the dog's intelligence. "You're a *gut* dog, Rowdy," he said.

Rowdy woofed again, thumping his tail to confirm Seth's assessment.

Seth chuckled. Maybe he'd do well to assume some of the dog's confidence. "Do ya think we can bring Sol around?" he asked, still grasping Rowdy's paw. "He needs somebody to guide him—to *herd* him—and he's not keen on listenin' to me. But if *you* steer Sol away from trouble, and maybe make him laugh more," Seth continued in a pensive tone, "maybe I can take him from there, ya think?"

Despite the complicated nature of the conversation, Seth sensed that Rowdy had followed along and knew exactly what he was supposed to do. *Woof! Woof!* he replied as he held Seth's gaze.

"All right, then, we'll work on it. You and me," Seth said.

"*Woof!*"

When Seth released him, Rowdy circled the bales and then ran toward the house.

"Looks like you two're gonna be a team," Ben said, clapping Seth on the shoulder. "Sol's bad attitude doesn't stand a chance. We all do better believin' we're loved and needed. Rowdy knows that; now it's just a matter of convincin' our boy."

We all do better believin' we're loved and needed. It was a tall order, winning Sol to his side. Yet now that Ben had stated the goal so clearly, Seth felt he had a better chance of reaching it.

Later that night, when the Brenneman house had settled into a deep December sleep, Seth lay awake. He told himself that the afternoon's incident with Sol was a natural part of the package when it came to falling for a widow with kids, yet the boy's continual backtalk and bad attitude grated on him. As he considered the long-term picture, multiplying and magnifying Sol's retorts and protests and moods in the silence of the night, Seth became restless and agitated. He replayed the incidents of Sol's defiance, seeing the kid's belligerent frowns and hearing his rising whine, again and again, until he got out of bed to pace. How stupid had he been, talking to a dog? Believing that he and Rowdy could reverse Sol's attitude?

He'd made a big mistake, falling for Mary. The best thing would be to go out to the phone shanty and call her *right now*—leave a message saying he couldn't participate in the Christmas Eve program, nor should she get her hopes up or continue to be interested in him. Seth didn't want to hurt Mary, but deep in his heart he knew he wasn't cut out to be Sol's next *dat.* It would never work. *Never.*

Yet when he reached the kitchen, he waffled. He saw Mary's flawless face in his mind as he took a sugar cookie from a plate on the counter and washed it down with a glass of milk. Only a heartless coward would leave a phone message. Mary deserved his explanation face-to-face, even if such a conversation scared him nearly as much as the prospect of raising Sol did. He didn't have much time before the pageant to inform her—but surely Ben or

Andy Leitner could wear his costume. Either man would be a better Joseph, and they wouldn't break her heart. It was the only decent thing to do.

When Seth went back to bed, he dropped off to sleep almost immediately. In his dream, he was in the back workroom of the cabinet shop, sanding the top of a table, when a bright light came through the window. The glare and intensity were so strong that he dropped his sander to shield his eyes, wondering if there'd been some sort of explosion and if he should take cover. Then he sensed a presence.

Peering between his fingers into the light, Seth thought he could make out a mighty set of wings that nearly filled the room. The being's face was so compelling and ethereal, yet so powerful that he dared not look directly at it. "Who are you?" he rasped. "What have I done that—are you . . . taking me away from this life? I'm not nearly ready—"

Fear not.

While the presence didn't seem to move its lips, Seth heard the words as plainly as if one of his brothers had spoken them—not that Micah or Aaron would use such archaic language. It occurred to his dream-immersed mind that anyone in the Bible who'd been visited by an angel had heard these exact words—people like the Virgin Mary and John the Baptist's father, and the shepherds keeping watch over their flocks by night.

Fear not to take unto thee Mary thy wife . . .

Seth sat bolt upright in his bed. He was breathing rapidly, his heart racing in his chest. As the familiar shadows of his bedroom furniture became apparent to him, he realized that he was alone and unharmed. He took stock of what he'd just experienced. Those words he'd heard, *Fear not to take unto thee Mary thy wife,* had been spoken by an angel of the Lord to Joseph, who was considering what to do after his fiancée, Mary, had revealed she was pregnant.

Seth let out the breath he'd been holding. While the dream had felt so *real,* it was merely his imagination again. The words had surely come to him from Christmas sermons and evening devotional readings of the Decembers in his lifetime—nothing more.

His mind was just going into overdrive the way it had when he'd fixated on Sol's misbehavior. He should just let it go—forget the dream and get back to sleep.

Yet Seth lay awake, still feeling the powerful glow and the impact of his vision. *What if it really was an angel of the Lord, coming to you? The Bible's full of such visitations, yet we tend to think they don't happen to ordinary folks in this day and age.*

And why wouldn't they? another part of his mind challenged.

Who am I, that an angel of the Lord would visit me? Seth reasoned. And yet . . . hadn't every person in the Bible been going along his or her way, unaware of the miracles that would come to pass and the part he or she would play in them, when the angel appeared?

As such questions and counter-questions filled his thoughts, Seth knew it was useless to try to sleep any more. What if he was going crazy? Should he tell someone about this dream—and to whom could he possibly entrust such a vision? It wasn't as though he were engaged to Mary Kauffman, and she wasn't pregnant, so the details didn't really add up. He was making way too much of a figment of his imagination.

Maybe he should confide in Bishop Tom . . . or Ben Hooley. Those men would know better how to interpret his dream, or they could counsel him about how to react to it. Or maybe they would gently tell him that angels tended to be phantoms of *women's* imaginations—

Why do you need any affirmation? Why can't you believe that God still speaks to us today, and that too often we're just not listening—or we dismiss His message because we don't want to hear it, or to be bothered with it?

Seth considered that option. The safer, saner thing would be to keep the dream to himself . . . to see how things worked out with Mary. What would it hurt to play Joseph in the living Nativity? It was just for a few hours on Christmas Eve, after all. It would make Mary happy, and if nothing else, it would validate her confidence in him. Perhaps the evening would be a chance for him and Sol to spend some positive time together. And maybe playing Joseph would help him overcome his apparent jinx when it came to being in front of an audience. He'd be standing on solid ground instead of on a platform in the schoolhouse . . . and he would be showing Sol that dependable men honored their commitments.

Seth smiled in the darkness. He knew what he would do now—the answer was as clear as Mary's beautiful green eyes. He *had* seen an angel. He was sure of it.

Long into the wee hours, Seth pondered these things in his heart.

CHAPTER 9

As she walked to the barn with angel Lucy and wise man Sol on Christmas Eve, Mary felt as though hundreds of butterflies fluttered in her stomach. She wore a soft ivory scarf over her head and a loose blue gown tied around her dress—along with a set of long underwear and stretchy little gloves. It was a perfect evening for their living Nativity. The night sky was a canopy of indigo velvet, dotted with diamond stars. A ewe and two lambs stood in a pen to one side of the hay bales, while a black-and-white cow, tethered to a post along with Clarabelle, munched hay from a manger on the other side. Rowdy trotted up to greet them, sniffing their costumes and gazing at them as though he, too, understood the significance of this event.

Rebecca was making her last-minute preparations, and when she flipped the switch on the light pole, Mary and Lucy let out an "ohh!" The area around the hay bales and pens took on a soft glow, because Rebecca had covered the light with pearlescent fabric to mute the glare.

"Are we ready? I think our Nativity's going to be a huge success, with such a heavenly little angel and a regal king," Rebecca said as she grinned at each of the kids. "And how's our main attraction?"

Emmanuel, cradled in Mary's arms, wiggled when Rebecca smiled down at him.

"He's been fed and changed, so he's ready," Mary replied. She smiled at the little parade walking up the Hooleys' lane. "And here come our shepherds and the other wise men and angels. Everybody looks really *gut*, Rebecca. We couldn't have done this without your help."

As Rebecca murmured something in reply, Mary lost track of it. A tall, broad-shouldered man in a flowing brick-red tunic was striding up the lane toward her, and while she couldn't see his eyes, she sensed Seth was looking right at her . . . just as she was gazing at him. *Thank you for this night, Lord, as we celebrate the birth of Your son and the beginning of our new life in Willow Ridge,* Mary prayed quickly. *Help me be your faithful handmaiden, as the Virgin Mary was so long ago.*

"Let's hope this works the way I envisioned it," Rebecca said as other folks began to gather from around town.

Mary turned just in time to see a star-shaped balloon rise into the air, on a long ribbon tied to the light post—and when Rebecca turned on the second lantern, which was aimed skyward, the star glowed and sparkled. Miriam, Ben, Bishop Tom, and the Zook family all let out a delighted *oh!*

"Folks will be able to see that from quite a ways off!" Tom said. His face shone with boyish wonder as he gazed raptly at the shimmering star above them.

Rebecca clasped her hands ecstatically, gazing upward with everyone else. "I took the liberty of using some spray glitter and gold sequins," she explained. "Not very Plain, but maybe folks out driving tonight will see it and stop to visit us."

"Just like the star guided the wise men to the stable," Teacher Alberta murmured. Then she looked around at the crowd. "Children, let's all walk slowly around the animals so they get accustomed to us. When Mary, Joseph, and Emmanuel are in place, we'll all sing 'Away in a Manger,' while you shepherds and wise men wait behind the bales, like we talked about. Then the shepherds can come out, and we'll sing 'Silent Night,' and then 'We Three Kings' as the wise men enter." Then, for the benefit of the adults who'd come, she added, "And all of your families can help us sing,"

Mary's heart fluttered as she sat down on the center hay bale, cradling Emmanuel in her arms. As Seth came to stand beside her, his expression made her hold her breath.

"It's quite a night," he murmured. "Even better than I dared to imagine."

"*Jah*, it is," Mary replied. "I—I'm so glad you're here."

As the four little angels stood beside them and began to sing, Mary's heart overflowed. Was there anything sweeter than little children's voices rising on "Away in a Manger"? Taylor was singing out, holding Amelia and Sara's hands as their wings fluttered gently. Lucy, clasping Sara's hand, looked totally enthralled... downright angelic as she sang her heart out. The parents and neighbors kept their voices low, watching the four angels in their white robes and wings. More than a few were swiping at their eyes.

Emmanuel smiled and cooed as though he enjoyed the music. As the shepherds approached, Mary held him up against her so he could see what was going on. Brett Leitner and the three Knepp boys came around from behind the bales and then fell on their knees, gazing at the baby. Little Timmy clutched his stuffed lamb and stuck his thumb in his mouth, looking a bit intimidated but adorable.

As everyone began to sing "Silent Night," Mary glanced up at Seth, who had joined in with his low, baritone voice.

"... all is calm, all is bright..." he sang, almost as though he were addressing her alone.

Did Jesus's mother feel such a sense of wonder? Mary pondered as she held Seth's gaze. *Did she feel heavenly love surrounding her— or was she young and scared about birthing her first child in a strange, dirty place among the animals? I can't imagine her precarious situation. Jesus might have been born alongside the road, just as Emmanuel nearly was... but for the grace of God and a gut man.*

Having a strong, dependable Joseph by her side made all the difference. Mary felt so at ease with Seth, yet so tingly in her awareness of him. The glow on his face made her heart dance as she tried to maintain a worshipful attitude—

A squawk rose from behind them, and a familiar little voice cried, "Ma-maaa, I falled in *cow poop!*"

"Oh, Lucy," Mary murmured as her daughter's wail rose above the singing. Rowdy jumped to his feet and began barking, which made the lambs start to bleat as the cow anxiously stomped its hooves.

Before Mary could stand up, Seth was striding around the shepherds and the sheep to rescue her daughter. As he scooped Lucy from the ground, murmuring gentle consolations—and silencing the dog—Aunt Miriam met him and carried her little girl to the house to clean her up. Quiet laughter came from the crowd—and *what* a crowd it was! In the soft light, Mary recognized several families from Willow Ridge, but they were making way for people she'd never seen, coming up from the road in clusters.

The expressions on their faces amazed her. Probably twenty *Englisch* strangers had gathered to look at the angels, the animals, and the shepherds—but it was Emmanuel their gazes lingered on. Mary smiled up at them with more confidence than she felt, remembering how Jesus' mother had greeted unexpected visitors on that holy night long ago.

As Teacher Alberta struck up "We Three Kings," Cyrus, Levi, and Sol entered from behind the hay bales. One by one, in a stately cadence, they appeared and then knelt before Mary and Emmanuel, offering their gifts. Mary fought a giggle when she recalled the fuss the Zook boys had made earlier in the week. Now, their earnest bearded expressions and their clear voices conveyed their sincere wishes to worship the King they celebrated on this night.

As the carol ended, Mary noticed a police officer standing next to Ben and Bishop Tom. Her heart clutched, yet the officer's smile reassured her. "I saw all the cars down this way, and then I saw the *star!*" he said as he gazed up at it. "Just had to see what you folks were doing this evening."

"And we're glad ya stopped by to share our Christmas Eve, Officer McClatchey," Aunt Miriam said as she stepped up beside the men. Lucy was in her arms, munching a cookie and looking restored to angelic happiness. "Looks like ya brought lots of folks with ya. My word, the cars are parked along the road for as far as I can see!"

The policeman gave Mary a little wave and she smiled back at him. Who could have foreseen such a crowd? Once again, it was Rebecca's gift for getting the word out that had brought so many people to Willow Ridge to share their living Nativity.

"I don't see many reminders of true Christmas spirit on my job," Officer McClatchey remarked as he continued to gaze at the children. "You folks've given me quite a gift tonight. God bless you—and Merry Christmas," he added as he shook the men's hands.

"Christmas blessings to you and your family, as well," Bishop Tom replied.

"Merry Christmas, and God bless ya in the comin' year!" Miriam called after him. When she set Lucy on the ground, the little angel rejoined the other children—and then decided to sit on the hay beside Mary.

Mary leaned close to her. "You all right now, sweetie?" she whispered.

"It was Christmas poop, so it was special," Lucy replied as she wiped frosting from her mouth. "Aunt Miriam said so."

Stifling a laugh, Mary hugged her daughter and flashed her aunt a smile. Teacher Alberta struck up "The First Noel," and when the crowd joined in, the music rose in a rich, full swell that surely rivaled the heavenly chorus of that first Christmas. Mary stood up, singing along with Seth as she held the baby to her shoulder so folks in the back could see him. Emmanuel let out joyful squawks, laughing as he flapped his arms. The shepherds and kings and angels stood up, singing more earnestly, and it seemed the whole world was in tune . . . in harmony with the precious gift God had given so long ago when he'd sent His Son to earth in such humble surroundings.

The people near the front looked startled and then parted to make way—and when Mary saw her father's glowering face, the next notes of the carol stuck in her throat. Seth moved closer to her, singing louder, as though his music would keep her *dat* from causing a scene. As her father headed toward Bishop Tom, Mary's *mamm* paused on the front row to beam at them all, a loving glow on her face as she gazed at her grandson.

"Why did I figure you liberals in Willow Ridge would put on this brazen *spectacle*?" Dat's voice rose over the last line of the song. "Despite how the *Ordnung* clearly forbids us to attract attention with such unseemly—"

"*Gut* evening, Mose," Ben spoke out. "And a blessed merry Christmas to ya!"

"What a fine surprise that ya came all the way from Bowling Green to celebrate the Lord's birth with us," Bishop Tom chimed in. "Mighty glad to have ya!"

The crowd shifted, craning to see the man who'd interrupted their blissful Nativity scene. Mary was wishing a hole would open up in the ground and swallow her, but in the next moment's silence, it was her mother who reclaimed the evening's essence.

"Have you ever seen such a wondrous sight?" Mama asked with awe in her voice. "All my life I've heard the story of Christ's birth, but *this*—this live rendition—has made the miracle real for me so I can truly believe as never before." She paused to look over at Mary's *dat.* "If just this once you'd be *silent*, Moses Miller, to behold this gift of God come down to Earth on this holiest of nights—"

Teacher Alberta began to sing "O Come, All Ye Faithful." The children joined in, their voices strong and pure. They circled around to face Mary, Seth, and Emmanuel as the crowd joined in their singing. Mary beheld the innocent, winged angels in white . . . the humble, earnest shepherds . . . the wise men who'd come so far since Monday. Her heart swelled with the simple joy on their faces. Who could know fear or doubt or dismay while children sang about the birth of Jesus? If God had so loved the world, wasn't His love the solution to every earthly problem?

And I didn't just imagine it. Mama told Dat to be quiet! And he's going along with it . . . at least for now.

As her father continued to watch her and Seth and Emmanuel, Mary's strength welled up. Seth had slipped his arm around her shoulders, and then they were sitting down together on the hay bales. Lucy scrambled over to climb into Seth's lap and—not to be left out—Sol came over to sit up against Seth, as well. When Teacher Alberta began "Joy to the World," the crowd sang out in full voice. It sounded as though *hundreds* of people had filled Ben's barnyard.

As Mary sang along, thrilling to the way Seth's voice blended with hers, she gazed upward at the shimmering star that swayed so peacefully above them. Yes, she would have to deal with Dat— again. But Mary knew she'd be pondering these other, lovelier things in her heart long, long after their visitors had gone home after this night of wonder . . . this night of love and light.

CHAPTER 10

Seth waited patiently . . . for the crowd to drive away, for the neighbors to go home after celebrating with cookies and cocoa in Ben and Miriam's kitchen, for Mose and Lovinia Miller to depart with Leah and Dan Kanagy. At long last, Emmanuel, Sol, and Lucy were tucked into bed and Ben and Miriam made themselves scarce by going upstairs. In the hush of the late evening, as logs crackled in the fireplace, Mary finally joined him on the love seat.

"What a night!" she murmured as she sank into the cushion beside him.

"Who knew?" Seth asked quietly. "I—I wouldn't have missed this for anything, Mary, and I'm so glad ya talked me into—"

With a gentle finger across his lips, she shushed him. "I've got something for you," she whispered mysteriously. She went over to the wrapped presents arranged beneath a huge, blooming Christmas cactus on a plant stand, and pulled the largest, bulkiest one from behind the others.

Seth's eyes widened. When she offered him the bundle, wrapped in deep green paper, the weight and the plush give of the contents made his thoughts race. "Mary, I wasn't expectin'—ya didn't need to—"

"You have no idea how much I needed to work on this," she

replied in a light yet serious voice. "I made it as my thanks for all your help since we arrived in Willow Ridge, but I . . . well, I just wanted you to have it, Seth. I'm not trying to *commit* you to anything or—well, just open it!"

He held Mary's bright-eyed gaze for a moment as his finger found the taped seam of the paper. When Seth saw the rolled fabric edges of deep green, and then the large squares with a circle of house and diamond shapes around a center star of red and green, he stood up. "Grab the end! I've got to see this!" he said as he unfolded it. "Nobody's ever made a quilt especially for me!"

His heart thumped hard as they held the quilt between them. While he was no expert on sewing, he sensed that Mary truly had a talent for creating wonderful gifts . . . a reflection of the heart and soul she had poured into this quilt. *What if you'd followed your doubts about Sol instead of believing in that dream about the angel? You'd be so alone now, and Mary would be so disappointed in you. . . .*

Seth smiled. It was time to celebrate, rather than to mull over how he'd almost turned Mary away. No other young woman had ever made his heart thrum with such excitement yet such a sense of peace. She was gazing at him with her deep green eyes, her flawless face alight with a future he wanted to share. *Please, Lord, don't let me say or do anything stupid.*

"This is the most beautiful gift anyone has ever given me," he murmured. "*Denki* so much—and I hope, in time, maybe it'll be you sharing it with me. Cuddling underneath it on a cold winter's night."

Her cheeks grew pink but her gaze remained steady. "We could try it out now, maybe."

"Oh, more than maybe," Seth replied. "But first let me fetch what I brought for you."

His heart was thumping wildly. He'd made a play and Mary had responded in the best possible way, as though being with him *mattered* to her. When Seth returned to the love seat with his papers, Mary had arranged the quilt so they could sit on it and then wrap the sides around them as they talked. It was a promising, positive invitation for him to pursue his feelings for her even as she honored her time of mourning her husband.

We all do better believin' we're loved and needed.

Seth let Ben's advice resonate in his mind as he unfolded the sketches he'd drafted earlier in the week. He desperately hoped Mary would like what she saw.

"Seth, it's a house! My new house," she said as she held the paper. Her hands trembled and her eyes filled with tears as she ran her finger over the layout of the simple single-story home. "Oh, but this makes it feel real and—and *possible*, Seth," she whispered.

"With God, all things are possible," he murmured, although quoting the Bible was the farthest thing from his mind as he sat close to Mary.

"*Jah*, they are," she replied with a twinkle in her eye. "After all, He got you through the Nativity tonight without embarrassing yourself. Matter of fact, when you rescued Lucy from the cow poop and quieted the dog and kept our little show going, you were my *hero*, Seth. And when Dat made his scene—"

"How will ya resolve your conflicts with him, Mary?" Seth asked quietly. "When he hears I've designed you a house, he'll only get angrier, ain't so?"

Mary slowly let out her breath. Then she rested her head on his shoulder. "It's like Miriam—and Mama—have told me. Dat will always be Dat. I can struggle and fuss until I'm blue in the face and it won't change him," she said softly. "I told him and Mama the kids and I would spend Christmas Day with them at Leah and Dan's. We'll talk things out, but I'm not changing my mind. I'm staying here in Willow Ridge—because I have family *here*, too. Close family who'll look after us through thick and thin."

Seth badly wanted to kiss her, but this wasn't the time. "*Jah*, you do," he replied. "And you have *me* . . . if you want me."

"I do," Mary whispered. "Or at least I want us to give it a chance while you build this sweet little house. So tell me what we've got here, Seth," she insisted. "Help me see these sketches as rooms where we'll eat our meals and tuck the kids into bed and greet the sun as it comes in through the windows each day."

Tell me what we've got here, Seth. Many romantic, far-reaching ideas sprang to mind, but he decided to keep the images simple for now. Mary had used *we* rather than specifying just herself and the kids, and that was all the confirmation he needed to ride the wave of happiness that welled up inside him. As he pointed out where the stove would go, and how her washing machine would fit into the mudroom off the porch, and the half bath he'd tucked in beside the pantry, Mary settled against him.

"This is a cozy little home, with just three bedrooms," he pointed out. "But someday, should ya want to expand and add another floor, I've designed the house so it'll look like that was your plan all along instead of appearin' that ya tacked on more rooms willy-nilly."

"Seth?"

"*Jah*?" he whispered, hardly daring to breathe.

"This is the best Christmas gift ever." Mary shifted so she could hold his gaze. "My heart's telling me to just go ahead and build the expanded version . . . but my head's warning me to take it slower. What do *you* think?"

Seth could read all sorts of wonderful things between those lines, but he proceeded with caution. "I think you're right on both counts—and you're curbin' that impulsive streak your *dat* keeps harpin' on," he replied with a smile. "I'm glad I'll be in the picture at least long enough to build it for ya, no matter what happens after that."

"That's all I'm asking."

He let out a long, contented sigh. "That said, Miriam and Ben would let ya stay here while we get to know our hearts and minds— and while Sol and Lucy and I get used to each other. It would save me rippin' off the original roof later, to rebuild this house. And it would save you the hassle of havin' all that remodelin' done after you've moved into it, too."

Mary's sweet face lit up and she gazed at him so intently, Seth felt her probing his soul. "You're a wise man, Seth—but without the fake beard and costume," she added with a chuckle. "And you know, when Lucy climbed into your lap this evening, and Sol sat alongside you, I . . . I could already see us and *feel* us as a family. Right there in front of God and everybody!"

Seth slipped his arm around Mary's shoulders. When she tucked the Christmas quilt more snugly around them, he had visions of a different angel from the one who'd come to him in a dream—for Mary was solid and real, the sort of woman who would make his life richly satisfying every day. He, too, had felt a special glow when the kids had joined them on the hay bales, choosing *him* to sit by while their mother cradled the baby. And the whole town of Willow Ridge—and Mary's parents—had witnessed it.

What could possibly be more powerful than God's love come down to earth on Christmas, and the love a family shared on that most sacred of days?

Seth sighed happily. He was pretty sure he had the answer to that.

A CHRISTMAS ON ICE MOUNTAIN

KELLY LONG

PROLOGUE

Christmas Eve, 1975
Ice Mountain, Coudersport, Pennsylvania

Fifteen-year-old John Beider clasped the five dollars he'd earned for a day of helping his community's healer, Grossmuder May, search the snowy mountainside for winter herbs and roots. The money represented the last installment he needed to purchase *auld* Possum Johnson's gun—a twenty-gauge shotgun of legendary renown on Ice Mountain. John had haggled with Smucker Kauffmann for the past two years over the gun and had finally gotten the store owner to agree to sell, and at a fair price. But eighty dollars was no easy thing to come up with, even for someone as hardworking as John, and his greatest fear was that, despite his down payments, Smucker might sell on an impulse for a higher price. Only John and his best friend, Luke Lapp, knew about the deal he'd worked out with Smucker, and tonight was the final payment.

John took the heavily salted front steps of the Kauffmanns' store two at a time and burst into the over-heated, scent-filled air, angling past late-evening shoppers and chatting women, and making his way to the back counter of the store. He glanced nervously up the

88 • *Kelly Long*

wall to the bracket mounts where the gun usually hung. His stomach dropped. . . . It wasn't there.

Without hesitation, John drew himself up to his full height and strode to the counter. *Auld* and grumpy, Amos King was there too, but John could only stare at Smucker, who looked troubled.

"Where is it?"

Smucker sighed. "Now, John . . ."

"Don't ya have any manners, *buwe?*" Amos asked in irritation. "I was here first."

"What did you do with it?" John asked again, trying to keep his voice calm.

In his mind's eye, he tried to focus on the gun as he'd envisioned it a hundred times over . . . fine stock, clean barrel, and the distinctive Buffalo nickel that Possum Johnson had carved a spot for in the forearm of the gun after he'd "brought down a twelve-point buck as big as a buffalo" with the weapon. John had grown up on the legends and had wanted the reality, but now . . .

"Are you going to tell me straight?" he asked Smucker. "How much higher did you sell it for?"

"John, I . . ."

"*Ach*, don't go apologizin' to this whelp, Smucker. Tell him the truth. . . ." Amos spun on John. "It was Luke Lapp, your so-called friend, who bought that gun no more than fifteen minutes ago. So, there." The old man snickered.

John felt his head swim in confusion. Luke—but why? Why would his best friend betray him in such a way? He staggered away from the counter, ignoring Smucker's urging to wait. But John knew what he had to do—a friend who'd betray another was no friend at all. And he would never forget. . . .

CHAPTER 1

Present Day
Ice Mountain, Coudersport

Outside the cabin window, the winter stars flashed like crystal shards against the backdrop of sapphire-blue night sky. Laurel Lapp paused with quiet feet on the bottom wooden stair to study the view for a moment.

"Are you sneaking out again?"

Laurel nearly lost her footing at the plaintive whisper behind her and she turned to glare at her five-year-old sister, Lucy.

"You should be in bed," Laurel whispered back as Lucy cuddled a favorite baby quilt close and took a seat on the second step down.

"So should you."

Laurel sighed, unable to resist her only sibling's sweetness despite the intrusion. She tiptoed back up the steps and sat down next to her little sister, pulling her close for a moment.

"When are you going to tell Dat and Mamm about Matthew?" Lucy asked.

Never . . . or maybe when we've been married for about fifty years. . . . Laurel had to smile to herself at the thought of a lifetime with the impossibly handsome Matthew Beider—if only it weren't for her *dat* and Matthew's *fater* as well. But there was no sense fretting over things now; Matthew was waiting.

Laurel bent and gave Lucy a quick *buss* on the top of her silky blond hair. "Go back to bed, sweetling. And *danki* for keeping our secret."

Lucy nodded with a yawn and rose to pad off with silent feet to their room. Laurel waited until the door closed, then stealthily made her way back downstairs, catching her cloak off its peg, and leaving the warmth of the cabin for the chill of the December air outside. But she smiled as she ran for the line of pines that crossed the back half of her father's land, for she knew how heated she'd become once she reached Matthew's strong arms. . . .

"Dat, I've got to go check on that mare—she might foal tonight." Matthew Beider knew his father didn't like to be interrupted in the middle of a talk, but Laurel would think he'd forgotten her. *As if I could forget to breathe . . .*

He'd been in love with Laurel for as long as he could remember, and now that he was twenty, and she eighteen, he wanted nothing more than to marry her and begin a life together on Ice Mountain.

But their fathers . . . Matthew sighed and resisted the urge to run a hand through his black hair. He glanced out the window at the moon and unwittingly drew the attention of his story-loving *dat.*

"Matthew Beider, as I live and breathe, tell me what I'm known best for on this mountain."

Ach . . . now I've done it. Laurel's going to be cold. . . . And he had to suddenly force his thoughts back to the moment at hand.

"You're known for being able to talk a man to sleep," he answered his father, fighting to keep a smile from his lips as he said it—for it was certainly true. John Beider could talk endlessly, seemingly never running out of a story, tale, or plain, homey gossip.

"Right you are, *sohn.* Now I recall a time that . . ."

"*Dat, sei se gut*—the mare?"

"*Ach*, go on with ya then. You'd think you was going to meet a girl for all your fuss about that horse."

Matthew grimaced faintly as he wound his scarf around his neck and waist. He hated to lie to his family, but there seemed to be no help for it. On all of Ice Mountain, probably in all of the world, for that matter, there was only one man that John Beider would not talk to—and that was Deacon Luke Lapp, Laurel's *fater*—and the feeling was quite mutual.

He wished his *daed* a good night and slipped outside. He walked toward the barn, knowing that the mare would be fine for a bit, then took off at a brisk run through the snow, hurrying to make up time on the quarter-mile distance to the Lapp's tree line.

When he got there, he feared she might have already gone, but then he caught a glimpse of her black cloak moving behind a sapling in the shifting moonlight.

"Laurel?" he called softly, her very name feeling like a caress to his mouth.

He watched her step from the tree and was struck, as always, by the intemperate beauty of her face and form. Her eyes burned liked twin blue jewels against the backdrop of her pale-pink skin, her face a perfect oval in the folds of her cloak's hood. She lifted slender hands to fling back the fabric from her face, then ran with her *kapp* strings streaming to jump into his arms.

He caught her full against him with ease and spun her around until they both grew dizzy. Then he stopped, lowered her to the ground, and bent to press his forehead against hers, steadying himself while drinking in the rosewater scent of the silky red blond curls that had escaped from the front of her *kapp*.

"I've missed you this day," he breathed when she reached up to twine gentle fingers in the hair at the nape of his neck.

"Have you?" Her blue eyes flashed merrily at him.

"You're a fever in my blood, Laurel May Lapp, and you know it well." He lowered his head to steal the first kiss of the evening, the dual sensations of the cold air and her warm lips feeding the fire in his body and brain until he had to break away with a gasp.

He pressed her against his chest, holding her close, letting her feel the rampant beating of his heart, until he'd regained some measure of control. But then she reached to drink from his lips, standing on tiptoe, pressing against him, until he forgot where he was and nothing existed save Laurel.

He heard her voice, calm with soft determination, as if from far away, and he felt himself collide abruptly with the reality of an earthly world beneath his boots.

"We have to tell the bishop about us, Matthew . . . tomorrow."

CHAPTER 2

"Laurel, this is the second batch of sugar cookies you've burned this morning. *Was en der weldt* is the matter with you?" Laurel's *aenti* June stood with her apron stretched about her vast frame and arms akimbo.

Laurel started guiltily, then smiled at her aunt. She could never measure the amount of love and cheer that June had brought to her family when her *mamm* had died four years ago in a sled accident. June had come and taken up the care of the infant Lucy, nurtured a grieving teenage Laurel, and worked to soothe the anger and heartache of their *fater* in the loss of his wife. Now, the older woman was a cherished part of the home and family—one whose empathetic nature kept her attuned to the unspoken thoughts of her charges. She could discern the slightest ripple in the family's usual placid sea of routine life.

Laurel had managed to avoid her *aenti's* gift of discernment lately by sheer force of will, but today, she was distracted. She was to meet Matthew at Bishop Umble's at 1 PM, and she had to make it look like a chance meeting, should anyone from the community be about. Fortunately, there was a quilting frolic at Deborah Esch's *haus* that morning, and Laurel knew she could slip away on some excuse once the women were talking and eating.

"You're moon-eyed, that's what," Aenti June pronounced when Laurel nearly upset the small container of teaberry candies used to sprinkle on the cookies.

Laurel straightened slowly. Denying her *aenti* would only produce more suspicion. "Why would you say that? Who is there for me to be moon-eyed over?"

Lucy rolled her eyes as she sat at the table decorating, and Laurel gave her a warning look.

Aenti June shook her grizzled, *kapped* head. "*Ach*, only a dozen or so willing, single men—eligible too. Any one might make a fine husband, but I think you've got your eyes set and that's the problem."

Laurel bit her lip for a moment, then stopped immediately, knowing her *aenti* knew that it was a nervous habit of hers. *Maybe Aenti June would understand....* The tempting thought drifted through Laurel's mind even as she discarded it. She doubted that even June understood the mysterious reason Luke Lapp and John Beider never spoke to one another—certainly no one else seemed to know. And June would stick by her *bruder*, of that Laurel was sure.

Laurel tried to shrug in a casual manner and plopped two raisin eyes on a gingerbread man. "Well, perhaps you're right—it's making the right choice that's the problem." Lying didn't come easily to Laurel's lips, but she hoped the half-truth would divert her *aenti* into a lecture on choosing a mate.

"Well, not that I've ever been married, but I've thought a bit about the subject and I know that picking the right man can be . . ."

Laurel breathed a silent sigh of relief and avoided the merriment in her little sister's blue eyes. Aenti June was in full lecture mode, and Laurel sat down at the table to ice molasses cookies, letting the older woman's words drift somewhere off into the far distance.

Matthew rolled over wearily when he heard his *fater* call him from below. He hadn't gotten to bed until nearly four because the decoy mare actually did foal, with a nasty presentation, but praise Gott, things had turned round and both mare and filly were doing well.

Matthew gazed at the wind-up clock by his bedside and groaned.

5:30 AM. He inched up in the bed as his fourteen-year-old younger *bruder*, Simon, burst through the door without knocking.

"Matt, what's wrong? Dat's ready to start chores."

"Go away."

Simon adjusted his round glasses and sat down to bounce with vigor on the end of the bed. "Out late with Laurel Lapp?"

Matthew hurled a pillow at his brother's head with alacrity. "Shut up. I've told you to never mention her name anywhere in this house."

Simon shrugged, adjusting his glasses and throwing the pillow back. "Dat's gonna find out. . . . What's the difference? You can't expect to have the engagement announced in church without him or Mamm hearing."

Matthew clutched the pillow over his face and groaned. *Simon is right, of course. And it's not like I haven't imagined the scene already a thousand horrific times. . . . Her* fater *will kill me. . . . My* fater *will kill me. . . .*

He lifted the pillow with a sigh. "Go on down and fend Dat off for a minute, will you, Simon? I'll get dressed."

Simon obeyed with a residual bounce and Matthew lay back in the bed for a brief moment when the door banged closed. He drew his bare arm over his eyes and prayed silently. *Derr Herr, take care of this situation. Be in charge of this, sei se gut, because I don't know how to work it out. . . .*

"Matthew!" His *fater's* voice broke into his thoughts and he hastily jumped up to pull on his pants and shrug into his shirt and suspenders. Hopefully, the meeting with the Bishop that afternoon would go well and the man would offer some wisdom.

It had barely gone eight o'clock in the morning when Laurel packed up the last plate of cookies to take to the quilting. She heard the gay ring of sleigh bells and glanced out the kitchen window to see her *fater* drive the sled and horses out from behind the sawmill.

She watched her *dat*, a tall, bulky man with a graying red beard, as he climbed down from the driver's seat. *Ach, if only Daed would explain what there was or wasn't between him and John Beider, then perhaps I could approach him and talk. . . .* Laurel sighed aloud at the thought. Her father had become even more reserved since his election by lot as a deacon of the church and after her mother's passing.

She pushed aside the unhappy thought as she listened to her father stomp his boots outside the front door. Aenti June was upstairs bundling Lucy for the ride to Deborah Esh's *haus*.

"Ready to go?" Her *dat* poked his head inside the open door and Laurel nodded, catching up the basket filled with cookies.

"*Jah,* Fater."

"*Gut.* Be careful to stay on the cut ruts in the ice. I've got a big order for kitchen cupboards to go down the mountain or I'd drive you myself."

"*Ach, nee.*" Laurel smiled hastily. 'You know I've been driving since I was seven. You needn't worry." She regretted the words as soon as they were out of her mouth. Her *mamm* had known how to drive a sled well enough too, but there was no accounting for sudden snow squalls on the mountain.

She moved impulsively and laid her hand on the dark heavy wool of her *fater's* black coat. "We'll be fine, Dat." She swallowed hard; it was difficult sometimes—how much she missed her *mamm.*

He grunted. "*Jah* . . . as Derr Herr wills."

Laurel nodded as Lucy clambered nosily down the stairs, breaking the quiet moment.

Soon they were piled in the sled with Aenti June balancing the cookie basket on her ample lap and Laurel at the reins. Lucy cuddled between them, waving a dark mitten back to where their father stood watching them go in the crusty snow.

Luke Lapp swallowed hard when the sled carrying the remnant of his family turned the bend in the road and was obscured by pine trees.

It was always like this when he watched a sled slide away— Meg's face would come to mind, her blue eyes bright and sparkling, her fair hair escaping her *kapp* in dear, curling disobedience. . . .

He blew out a harsh breath and turned back to the house, deciding on a quick cup of coffee before finishing his cabinetry order. The house was awful, as usual, in its quietness when no one was about, but he told himself that Derr Herr was with him and that had to count.

He poured a quick mug, then slid down at the wooden table he'd carved for Meg when they'd first married. Absently, he let his callused fingers play over a well-hewn knothole in the wood; it resembled the blackened target of a shot gun and for a *narrisch* minute he was transported back to boyhood. He and John Beider had always gone out together for hunting season, enjoying the talks and long tramps through the tumbled leaves and powdery snow of the woods. It seemed like an eternity ago. . . .

He drew too quick a sip of coffee and burnt his mouth, bringing him painfully back to the present. *Ach*, John had been a rare friend, brooding but faithful, yet like Meg, John too was lost to Luke through time and the heartless beat of an unforgiving past.

CHAPTER 3

"It's a fine filly you brought through last night."

Matthew heard his *fater*'s praise through the tired fog in his brain as he leaned against the barn rail watching the new mother mare clean her baby with diligence.

"*Jah, danki.*"

His *dat* clapped him on the shoulder, and Matthew heard Simon laugh when he jumped. He glared at his younger *bruder* and longed for the warmth of Laurel's arms about him, a fair fantasy to ward off the chill of the icy morning.

"I thought I'd best mend fence with you *buwes* today out in the north pasture. It should keep us busy until suppertime," his *fater* mused. "Your *mamm*'s baking beans and bacon."

Matthew nodded, then recalled his planned clandestine meeting with Laurel and the bishop. He snapped to abrupt alertness. "Uh, Daed, *nee*—I mean, um, it's so cold. Why not let Simon and me have at the fences and you could stay in with Mamm and shave a few more shingles for the front roof? Besides—I, uh—have been wanting some alone time to talk with Simon. . . ." Matthew lowered his voice to a whisper. "The *buwe*'s been asking questions about girls lately."

"Hmm? You don't say . . ."

"What was that?" Simon asked, jumping down from the fence rail.

Matthew caught him by the back of his jacket. "It's all right, Simon. Perfectly normal. Let's get going and give Dat a break."

Simon opened his mouth, and Matthew closed his eyes, waiting for the words to come that would reveal his love for Laurel. But to his cautious surprise, he opened his eyes to see Simon simply give an exaggerated yawn.

Matthew's stomach dropped back into place and he gave his *bruder* a wry grin.

They headed out to harness the horses while their father went back inside the main house. Matthew cuffed Simon lightly on the shoulder when their *dat* was out of sight. *"Danki*, little *bruder."*

Simon scowled. "I'm younger than you be, but I ain't no snitch."

Matthew laughed aloud. *"Gut.* I wouldn't want you any other way."

John Beider entered the warm and fragrant kitchen to find his wife, Ellie, putting the final touches on a cheerful wicker basket with dark green tissue paper. She smiled at him briefly, but he could tell by the way she hummed that her mind was already on ahead to the women's quilting frolic being held that day.

"I could run you over to Deborah Esch's for the doings, if you'd like," he offered, but she brushed him aside with a quick *buss* on his cheek.

"It's a faster walk and I'm running late already. Mind you stir the beans now and then."

She bustled to the door and was off in a flurry of her thick cloak. John sighed aloud at the sudden silence of the *haus. I hate to be alone . . . always have, right, Lord?* The sudden echoing report of a shotgun from a distance outside startled him, and he smiled grimly to himself. Somebody hunting nearby most likely. He used to like to hunt—once upon a time, and long ago. But the thought stirred up a flurry of unpleasant memories within him and he blew out a breath of exasperation; there were some places in his mind that he knew better than to tread upon. . . .

"Time I shaved a few shingles," he muttered aloud, trying to comfort himself with the sound of his own voice. Then a knock at the door gave him welcome diversion. He squinted through Ellie's window curtains and broke into a smile. It was Tab King, a grizzled elder of the community who was always ready for a talk. John began to whistle. The day began to look up a bit.

Laurel relaxed into the comfortable hubbub of Deborah Esch's kitchen. A large, wooden quilting frame had been set up, taking up nearly every inch of the room, but the women of the community jostled about with *gut* cheer as they found seats around the beautiful quilt and took up their needles with the ease of long expertise.

Laurel was glad to recognize the pattern in the fabric as Christmas roses. The quilt was for Grossmuder May, the elder and healer of the community, who had been feeling a bit poorly herself the last few weeks with the onset of truly cold weather. The quilt was sure to bring her warmth and a blessing as it represented a truly communal effort. The centers of the roses were red, but the quilted petals were pieced from the scraps of many sewing baskets, displaying a year's worth of the fabric of the everyday life on the mountain.

Laurel found a seat and was about to draw her needle through a piece of light blue chambray when a pleasant voice made her hand freeze over the fabric.

"May I sit next to you?"

Laurel looked up with a hasty smile at Matthew's *mamm.* "*Jah,* of course."

Naturally, in such a small community, the Beider family was often encountered, but when her *fater* was present, Laurel usually stuck to basic politeness. She'd never had a conversation of any length with Matthew's mother.

Laurel scooted her chair over, accidentally elbowing a rather cranky *auld* woman, Ruth Smucker, on her other side. She muttered a hasty apology and ducked her gaze away from the dark green eyes of Frau Beider—Matthew's eyes. Laurel sought for the whereabouts of her *aenti* as a possible diversion, but Matthew's *mamm* was already speaking.

"I suppose you don't know my secret?" The older woman's voice was low, and Laurel swallowed at the strange words.

"Nee..."

"It's simple really—your mother and I, we were *gut* friends before she passed on."

Laurel stared into the intense green eyes and blinked, trying to recollect ever seeing Frau Beider anywhere around when her *mamm* had been alive.

"Don't look so puzzled, my dear. It was a secret friendship... well, because of our men folk and the silly hindrance of the feud they've kept going all these years." She shook her *kapped* head. "*Ach*, I mean no disrespect to your *fater*—your *mamm* felt the same way I did and you seem very like her with your strawberry-blond hair and blue eyes. You remind me of how dearly I miss her."

Laurel wet her lips as the other woman's kind words reached to warm her to her core. Would Matthew's own *mamm* be a possible ally in a future marriage, or more blessed still, would she be like a second mother to Laurel herself? "I—I didn't know. I miss her too, so very much."

Frau Beider seemed about to speak again when Ruth Smucker gave Laurel a sharp nudge with a bony elbow. "Hiya, quit your mumbling amongst yourselves. I can't even catch a bit of gossip, and I've dropped my needle through. Fetch it for me, girl."

Laurel stifled a sigh. She was far too tall to go crawling beneath the quilt frame to get dropped needles so she caught Lucy's eye as the child ambled past with a handful of cookies.

"Lucy," she called. "Frau Smucker's needle's gone through. Would you get it, *sei se gut?*"

Laurel watched her little sister scamper to obey, crawling happily between chairs and beneath the stretched quilt to bob up triumphantly a few moments later with the missing needle. Frau Smucker took it without a word of thanks, but Laurel patted her sister's hand.

Lucy dawdled beside her for a moment, staring at Frau Beider, and Laurel began to grow anxious at what might come out of the little's girl's mouth.

"Lucy, why don't you..."

"You're Matthew Beider's *mamm*, right?" the little girl chirped.

Laurel clutched her own needle with suddenly damp fingers.

"*Jah,*" Frau Beider smiled. "Matthew and Simon's *mamm*. And you're Lucy."

"My *dat* doesn't get on well with your family, I don't think," Lucy said matter-of-factly, and Laurel longed to sink into the pegged hardwoods beneath her feet. But Matthew's *mamm* simply smiled and nodded.

"*Jah,* that's so, little Lucy."

Frau Smucker leaned over with a snort. "Little girls should be in the front room playing. I still can't hear what you're talking about over that child's squeaky voice."

Laurel frowned in affront, trying to think of a pointed but respectful response on her sister's behalf when Matthew's *mamm* leaned across the quilt.

"Perhaps, Ruth Smucker, you should try listening for the *gut* of what others say, though I would imagine that would be difficult for you to hear as well." Frau Beider's voice carried, and Laurel struggled not to giggle as Ruth Smucker's rather toothless mouth opened and closed like a gasping rainbow trout at the faint rebuke.

Laurel couldn't imagine what the grumpy woman might have retorted had their hostess, Deborah Esch, not sailed past to grasp Ruth's arm. "Fresh gingerbread and tea, Frau Smucker? I've got a little table all set up in the side room—away from the *kinner* and the noise."

Ruth Smucker rose with a sniff and a glare and allowed herself to be led away while Laurel glanced back to Matthew's mother. "*Danki*, for defending Lucy."

Frau Beider laughed. "The Smuckers are meaner than catfish through and through—a little reminder for the good now and then won't ruffle the hairs on her chin much."

Lucy crammed a cookie in her mouth and stroked Laurel's hand. "I thought only men had beards."

Laurel did laugh then, though only a bit, because respect for her elders was so ingrained in her being. Yet she couldn't help but see the shine of a smile in Matthew's *mamm*'s own eyes. She felt as if she'd connected with the older woman somehow. She relaxed into the moment, and the morning seemed to fly by as all of the women worked hard to finish the quilt.

Then Laurel remembered the time. She nearly jumped from her spot when she saw that it was approaching 1 PM.

"Uh, Frau Beider, I'm sorry. I must—um . . ." *Go and make secret plans to marry your* sohn. Laurel frowned in desperation, but Matthew's *mamm* smiled with indulgence.

"Run along, child. I remember what it was to be young and restless at sitting all day. It has been a pleasure."

Laurel nodded and murmured a farewell before carefully circumventing her Aenti June in the large kitchen. She grabbed her cloak from a wall peg and slipped out the back door and into the light snow.

CHAPTER 4

Matthew knew, as all the community did, that the bishop's back door was always unlocked. Bishop Umble didn't hold with not "being open," as he called it in church, and this view extended to the very wood of his *haus.*

"Hiya?" he called, and when no one answered, he slipped off his boots on the rug beside the door and trod quietly across the pristine kitchen to take a seat on one of the comfortable living area chairs. He took off his hat and loosened his coat, glancing around with taut nerves. He hoped the bishop hadn't forgotten, though it didn't line up with the *auld* man's nature.

He listened to the tick of the wind-up clock and the crackle of the woodstove and settled back further, willing himself to relax. Soon, the grueling *nacht* past caught up with him and he closed his eyes against a swimming wave of peaceful drowsiness. *If I fall asleep, I'll surely hear someone* kumme *in.* . . .

Luke Lapp took his role as deacon to the small mountain *Amisch* community seriously. So, when an old widow stopped to ask for a bit of kindling from his scrap pile at the woodworking shop, he gave her his full attention.

"You'll excuse me," he muttered to the *Englisch* customer

who'd made the trek up the mountain to look at some veneer wood for a daughter's vanity.

"Of course." The *Englischer*, Mr. Ray, was jovial. "I'll poke about your shop, if you don't mind?"

Luke smiled with a brisk nod. *Of course I mind—it's a workshop, not Kauffmann's store. . . .* But he'd learned that the *Englisch* had different social boundaries from the *Amisch*, and, after all, the customer meant no harm.

He filled the back of Frau Knepp's sled in a few quick motions, then piled the *auld* woman back in under the blankets. "Don't unload it alone, *sei se gut*," he said politely to the widow. "I'll *kumme* over shortly and do it for you."

He was rewarded with a toothless smile, then watched her pull away. He waited to make sure she navigated the tight turn at the end of his lane and went back in search of Mr. Ray.

He found the *Englischer* admiring the tall gun cabinet that stood along a weather-tight back wall of the shop.

"Cherry, isn't it?"

"Through and through."

"Your scroll work is remarkable. What a gift you have!" Mr. Ray smiled.

Luke shifted on his booted feet, uncomfortable with praise. "As Derr Herr—The Lord—gives."

Mr. Ray toyed with a latch on one of the glass doors. "Nice bunch of guns too—I collect a little. What's the prize in the white sack?"

A small sound, a smothered sigh, escaped Luke's throat as he gazed through the glass at the gun carefully shrouded in white cotton. "It's—nothing. A relic, you might say."

"I'd be interested in . . ."

"I'm sorry, Mr. Ray. We were discussing those veneers? I've got a cabinet shipment to get down the mountain soon."

The *Englischer* cleared his throat, obviously understanding that he was being warned off. "Of course." He smiled. "The veneers . . ."

Luke turned his back on the gun cabinet. *Today need not be a day for ghosts. . . . I have work to do.*

* * *

Laurel knocked hesitantly on the back door of the bishop's *haus*, and when no one answered, she finally gritted her teeth and went inside on tiptoe. Frau Umble was at the quilting of course. . . .

She saw Matthew sprawled on one of the bishop's chairs, his big, lean body deep in repose. His dark brown hair was tousled, his head tilted backward against the simple doily on the chair back.

Laurel smiled to herself as she realized they were alone in the *haus*. It was simply too *gut* an opportunity to miss. So many of their embraces had been stolen ones in the cold outdoors—the idea of kissing Matthew awake in the warmth of a home appealed to her impulsive nature and sent her senses racing.

She bit her lip and made her way to the back of the chair where he lay. Leaning over, she smiled into the perfect bone structure of his upside-down handsome face. A lone freckle, an angel *buss,* as Aenti June called the sun marks, sat parallel to the dimple in his chin and she couldn't resist brushing her nose over the spot. He sighed in his sleep and parted his lips. She leaned farther, feeling the chair back in tight accord with the dizzying place in her stomach, and balanced on tiptoe.

She blew softly on his mouth and he shifted a bit, still visibly deep in sleep. Laurel smiled, then captured his bottom lip with her damp mouth, marveling that such a simple change in position could produce such heady sensations.

She kissed him with artful strokes, tilting her head, until she saw his dark, thick eyelashes flutter against the flush of his skin.

Matthew was dreaming. He had to be. . . . He recognized, in his subconscious, that he'd never burned to such an extent. He felt turned upside down and inside out, as if he were coming apart, and could only think about his next thickened heartbeat and the sensation that his mouth nearly watered with want. . . .

A light hand on his shoulder brought him up from the first depths of sleep and he groaned aloud with reluctance, not wanting the moment to end. He felt like begging for another bit of time and taste in his half-dreaming state and pushed back against the surge of waking. The pressure on his mouth increased subtly and he drew a frantic breath, arching upward in an effort to follow the movement.

"Do you like this?" Laurel's soft voice was a throaty shimmer of sound at the back of his mind.

"*Ach, jah*," he breathed, the words tangled in his consciousness. "Please . . ."

"Please, what, Matthew?"

He smiled, coming half awake when he recognized the light tease in her tone, like a veil wafting through summer air. Then he remembered where he was and reached his hands upward to capture her sweet face, working his mouth hard against her until he heard her own soft sounds of harmonious pleasure.

"Ahem!"

Matthew fell out of the chair at the brisk clearing of the bishop's throat. He staggered to his feet, then bent once more to snatch up his hat, wringing it between his hands. He moved quickly to grasp Laurel's arm from the other side of the chair and then hauled her behind him, shielding her slight body with the bulk of his own.

"Bishop Umble, uh, sir . . ." Matthew resisted the urge to look away from the shorter man's bright blue eyes and craggy raised brows.

"It doesn't appear as though an explanation is necessary as to why you both wanted to see me." The bishop's voice was even but not condemning, and Matthew felt himself relax to a slight degree.

"*Jah*, we wish to marry."

"To say the least," Bishop Umble returned dryly, then indicated the couch with a sweep of his aged hand. "*Sei se gut*, let us sit."

Matthew guided Laurel to the couch, then perched in a tense posture a more than safe distance from her hip. He was ashamed to have put Laurel in such a compromising position in the bishop's own home.

"So," Bishop Umble began without preamble. "By any chance, do either of your *faters* know?"

Laurel struggled to keep her voice level though she could feel her cheeks still heated from the impromptu kissing, but she felt she should speak up as she sensed Matthew's nervousness.

"*Nee*, Bishop Umble. We—we have been courting in secret." Normally, the mountain Amisch kept an impending marriage secret from all until their intentions to marry were announced at the end of a church service at least two weeks prior to the wedding itself. Courting, too, took place at *nacht*, when no other was around but the couple themselves.

The bishop raised a brow. "In more secret than normal, I would imagine."

"*Jah*, sir," Matthew muttered.

Laurel watched the bishop pass a hand over his brow, as if deep in thought. Then he sighed aloud. "I must make it known to you both that I have tried, over the years, to speak to your *faters* in an effort to mend their . . . discord."

"Do you know why they fought?" Laurel asked, unable to contain her curiosity.

The bishop shook his head and spread his hands before him. "*Nee*, it is a secret lost long ago and known only between the two of them. There was a time, when I was a much younger man, that I can remember them as inseparable friends. But, like all fighting of this sort, the reason often becomes lost to time, but the disagreeableness goes on, fueled by pride."

Matthew cleared his throat. "We were hoping that you might . . . prepare them both somehow before the announcement is made next week at church service."

The bishop smiled grimly. "I fear there is no preparation for that moment save an intervention from Derr Herr's own Hand."

Laurel felt her heart sink. A miracle seemed a far-off thing at the moment.

The Bishop seemed to read her thoughts, then laughed with a wise look. "It is the season for miracles, my *kinner*. We will have to see what Derr Herr has in store."

CHAPTER 5

John Beider took a long pull on his coffee and settled back more comfortably in the chair near the woodstove. His legs were crossed at the ankle and his favorite socks showed signs of his wife's *gut* mending around the toes and heels. He glanced at his visibly drowsy companion, old Tab King, and smiled to himself. It was no insult to John when a friend began to drift off after a few of his tales—in fact, he saw it as a compliment to his storytelling prowess.

He was spinning a fair yarn to Tab about the Ice Mine at the base of the mountain, and his guest revived at the mention of silver.

"Now, wait jest a minute here, John." Tab ran a hand through his gray hair, making it stand on end. "I've heard tell of the Cattaguras Indian and the silver, and the farmer what owned the mine lookin' for silver, but I ain't never heard of no silver coins nor government payload bein' lost on Ice Mountain."

"I'm not saying Ice Mountain for sure, but somewhere in these parts anyway. You see, with all the logging and mining going on way back around here, the government set up an outpost with a bank included near Coudersport. But one of the clerks who worked at the bank got upset and quit the day before the payload was supposed to arrive."

"What he get upset over?" Tab asked.

"Hmmm? *Ach*, I don't know for certain, probably no one does, but he quit. He quit and he walked off—with his keys still on him."

Tab looked suitably intrigued and John went on, painting a picture with his words. "That same afternoon, some *Englisch* ladies came into the bank, wanting to set up a jelly display sale for the poor of the area and the lone clerk agreed. Little did he know how much them jelly jars would come to matter in the next few hours."

"Ya don't say?" Tab leaned forward a bit.

"*Jah* . . . the clerk who'd quit earlier that day came back that night. He knew when the payload was to be delivered, and he showed up right after the delivery team of horses had been driven off. The clerk who'd quit was drunk and mad as a rattlesnake. He had a gun and a small leather sack and he demanded that his former coworker hand over the payload."

John deepened his voice to portray the scene. "*I mean it, Sam. Hand over the silver or I shoot.*

"*And raise half the town in the process? I don't think so . . .*

"The former clerk cocked his gun and Sam decided he'd better not risk it, but when he kicked the wooden box—pay in silver coin for seventy-men—toward the robber, he made an interesting point."

"What'd he say?" Tab asked, gratifyingly curious.

"*You'll never fit all that silver in that small satchel and you'll never be able to carry that chest more than a few feet. Give up, why don't you?*"

"*Ach*," Tab murmured in agreement.

"*I'm not giving up and I don't need all the silver anyway.*"

"The robber's eyes swept the dim room and lighted on the stacked jelly jars. He gestured with his gun. *Empty me some of those jelly jars. Glass don't rot when it's buried.*

"*You're crazy. What good is buried silver?* Sam wanted to know, but then he hurried to obey when the gun waved in his direction.

"The jelly spilt out on the floor like a pool of blood and made Sam even more nervous. He opened the chest of silver and filled six sticky jelly jars full of the coins. He carefully filled the robber's satchel and handed it over.

"Then, before Sam could even raise an alarm, the ex-clerk disappeared into the night and the forest. Three days men from the town hunted for him—they even called in U.S. Marshals. When they finally caught up with the ex-clerk, he was collapsed in the woods, lying half-dead with the diphtheria. He was delirious with fever. They got him back to town and tried to make sense of his ramblings. It seemed he was trying to do right in the end and tell them where he'd buried the silver, but all they could make out was 'by a triangular tock where the ground is cold as ice.' To this day, *Englischers* still hunt these mountains for the buried treasure, but none has found it yet because the clerk died without ever truly revealing his secret."

Tab blew out a whistle of appreciation. "Whoo-ee, you know how to tell a story, John Beider. Jest think of it—what that silver'd be worth today."

John was about to speak when the sound of a rifle shot from back on the mountain broke the moment.

"Somebody huntin'." Tab sat up straighter in his chair. "Say, do you remember the story of that *Englisch* hunter who had a camp over on the far side of the graveyard? *Ach*, but you was jest a *buwe* then. . . . They say he dropped a deer as big as a buffalo and . . ."

"Possum Johnson," John said, feeling a tightness around his mouth.

"*Jah, jah*, Possum Johnson it was. *Auld* Smucker Kauffmann bought that rifle from the family when the man passed on, had it hangin' in his store for quite a while. . . . I wonder what happened to that shotgun? Now there'd be a story. . . ."

John rose abruptly. "Tab, I'm sorry, but I've got some shingles to shave. I've been rambling on too long."

Tab laughed and got to his feet. "You? Ramble? That's fun, John Beider. Pure fun."

John knew his smile didn't reach his eyes, and he was only too happy to help Tab off the snowy porch and wave him on his way. Back inside, the silence once again seemed to engulf him and he couldn't resist touching the old wound in his mind, like running a cautious tongue over a canker sore.

He'd gone to Meg Lapp's funeral, of course, but he hadn't been able to bring himself to speak to Luke even then. It didn't feel right. *I had no idea what to say in the face of that kind of loss and with Luke sobbing. . . . Gott, why didn't I speak when I had the chance?*

John swallowed hard in the cozy warmth of the kitchen and decided he'd do a few shingles, then go and check on his *sohns*. Thinking about Luke's wife was a good reminder that anything could happen in the mountains, all kinds of accidents, and his *buwes* were too precious to think about losing. . . .

CHAPTER 6

Laurel slipped back into Deborah Esch's kitchen and was met with loud gales of laughter from the other women that made her freeze in uncertainty. Had someone found out about her and Matthew? Her confusion was compounded when Deborah Esch came forward and bundled the heavy, completed Christmas-roses quilt into Laurel's arms.

"There! *Ach*, stop laughing at the poor girl. She looks as dazed as a rabbit in the lantern light." Deborah hugged Laurel, quilt and all. "You see, my dear, we all decided that the next one to come through the kitchen door would deliver the quilt to Grossmuder May. Naturally, we expected it to be a man, but . . . here you are."

"*Ach*." Laurel smiled weakly, avoiding her *aenti* June's eyes. "*Jah*, here I am. And—and I'd be glad to take it up to Grossmuder May."

"*Wunderbar!*" Deborah clapped. "I'll see your *aenti* and Lucy home safely. Can you manage the quilt up the mountain path?"

"*Jah*, it's only a bit of a ways. I'll be fine."

Laurel caught a tighter hold on the quilt and set back out into the cold.

"You say Matthew went where?" John Beider stared down at his youngest *sohn* as they stood in the cold field. Perhaps the youngster was addled by the frigid air because he seemed to be stumbling over his answer when a look of relief suddenly suffused his small face.

"Here he comes now, Dat," Simon squeaked.

Matthew came jogging across the snowy field.

"Where have you been, *sohn?*" John asked with a frown.

"Well, I started out for supplies, but look what I found on my way back." Matthew opened his coat and revealed a tiny kitten, black with only a white spot on its small head. He closed his coat quickly against the chill.

"A kitten? At this time of year?" John mused aloud in disbelief.

"The mother cat and the other two kittens weren't so lucky. They'd frozen to death, but this little one held on somehow."

"What are we going to do with it, Dat?" Simon asked in clear excitement, and John sighed.

"We're going," Matthew asserted, "to find some girl's lap for it to warm. It would make a nice gift."

Simon scowled. "Sure, it would."

"Well, you know how your *mamm's* nose runs around cats. I don't know that we could manage it in the house," Matthew's father said.

"Don't worry, Dat. I'll take it to . . . some little girl who'll give it a *gut* home. I won't be gone long."

His *fater* nodded. "All right, but hurry. There's a storm brewing up on the mountain, I think. Likely to *kumme* in quick. Me and Simon'll head back home now in case."

Matthew grinned and nodded, cuffing his little *bruder* on the shoulder and gaining a reluctant smile. *Laurel will love the kitten. I wonder if she'll repay the gift with more of her upside-down kissing?* The thought sent him crunching heavily through the snow even as the wind picked up.

Laurel struggled to find her footing along the snow-covered path that led uphill to Grossmuder May's cabin. It had started to snow in icy gusts and more than once, she nearly toppled over from the force of the wind and the weight of the quilt.

Finally, the cheery lights of the *auld* cabin glimmered through the darkening swirl and Laurel fell against the stout wooden door. It was opened so quickly from within that she collapsed against the wizened old woman, then steadied herself with a few gasping breaths.

"Laurel May Lapp, herself, indeed," Grossmuder May said with strangely apparent satisfaction. *"Kumme* to visit in this fine weather, have you, child?"

Laurel shook her head and felt her wet bonnet sag backwards. "It wasn't like this when I started out."

"Nee, nee . . . but you must learn that Ice Mountain is where Gott works His hand at the unexpected—in the weather, and in life."

Laurel shook out the heavy folds of the beautiful quilt, not understanding too much of the old woman's sayings, but it was always that way. Grossmuder May had an attitude about her that was as mysterious as the mountains themselves and left Laurel feeling rather adrift. But she presented the quilt with her best smile.

"The women got together today, Grossmuder. It's Christmas-roses pattern. For you."

"For me, hmmm?" The older woman laughed. "We shall see. Now, *kumme* have some tea by the fire, child." She put her cane under her arm and piled the quilt on the wooden table to the side of the room.

Laurel glanced out the window to the snowy blur. *"Ach*, I'm sorry, but I must go home. My *fater* will worry."

"He will worry more should you become lost in the storm, and Luke Lapp must learn that your mother's fate is not your own. Besides, it is not as bad down below, but *nee*, it is too dangerous for you to go."

Laurel opened her lips to protest, but realized it would do no good and that there was reason in what the old woman said. So, she dropped tiredly into a chair by the open fire and took warm sips of the ginger tea that Grossmuder May had ready. Soon, Laurel began to relax despite the deepening roar of the storm outside.

Matthew saw the sliver of mellow light from inside the Lapps' barn door and knew that Laurel would be at her milking. He would never have risked coming so near the Lapp home but for the storm and the kitten, which had begun to cry piteously inside his coat. He slipped inside the barn and stood stock-still when he spotted the small form of Lucy Lapp, poised with a milk bucket near a calm cow.

"She's not here," Lucy said quickly. "And you'd best hurry. My *dat* is coming out to check on me any minute."

Matthew didn't stop to ponder the coincidence that both he and Laurel had told their siblings they were courting. "Where is Laurel?"

Lucy darted forward even as he opened his coat. She took the kitten in a matter-of-fact grasp and bent to dip her fingers in the steaming milk, offering it to the ravenous baby. "She's up the mountain at Grossmuder May's."

"What?" Matthew exclaimed, feeling his heart began to pound with fear. "In this storm? I've got to get to her. She may not even have made it to the cabin. Why did she go?"

"To take the quilt. Now, hurry! And do be careful!"

Matthew slipped outside into the deepening gloom and realized that Luke Lapp stood on his porch, staring up at the mountaintop. Matthew caught his breath, then pressed hard against the barn, sliding along the far edge and out into the whirling snow

Luke eased quietly into the barn, not wanting to startle Lucy, but to his surprise, she knelt before the doors in the hay, feeding a young kitten milk with her small fingers.

"What are you doing, my child?"

"Feeding this poor kitten. Can we keep it, Daddi?"

Luke felt his gaze trace the corners of the barn and passed a hand over his eyes, wondering if the kitten had simply materialized out of nowhere. *My mind is troubled over Laurel. . . . Dear Gott, let her be safe. Please, let her be safe.*

He dropped to his knees in the hay and pulled Lucy close. "We must get you and the kitten both inside and out of this cold. *Kumme.*"

"*Ach, danki,* Daddi. *Danki!*" Lucy's thin arms were flung around his neck and he breathed in the still baby-fresh scent of her hair. *Ach, Meg, if only you were here . . .*

"I'll name the kitten Friend. What do you think of that?" Lucy chirped as he lifted her, kitten, and milk bucket high in his arms.

"*Gut.* That's *gut.*"

He opened the barn door with his hip and gasped at the dark snow. "Because Derr Herr is our friend, right, Daddi?" Lucy's high voice pierced the howl of the wind, and Luke looked down at his little girl.

"*Jah,*" he whispered, drawing her closer. "*Jah.*"

Matthew knew he wasn't dressed for such weather. It had begun to sleet, turning the snow into icy shards. His hands were nearly frozen in his pliable work gloves and he'd left his scarf hanging over the fence when he'd been working. But the thought of Laurel's safety prodded him onward and upward, even as he slipped and fell many a time. He wasn't even sure that he was going in the right direction and he started to pray when the faint glimmer of a kerosene lamp flashed nearly beside him. He stretched out his arms and ran smack into the side of Grossmuder May's remote cabin. *Another few feet and I would have missed it. . . . Thank Gott. Thank You, Gott. . . .*

He found the door latch somehow and stumbled inward to collapse on the warmth of the hardwood floor.

"Matthew!" Laurel's voice was high with panic. He wanted to comfort her, but he couldn't seem to catch his breath, and the pull of wanting to sleep right there and then seemed to lure him.

"He's frozen through." Grossmuder May's voice swirled somewhere above him. "We've got to get him warm. Help me, child."

Matthew drifted into a pleasant lassitude until the shock of warm water on his hands and feet burned like sudden fire and he could find no refuge from the pain.

CHAPTER 7

Luke Lapp stared out the window at the bleak weather, then slapped his hands down on the kitchen table in sudden decision. "I'm going after Laurel."

"Are you *narrisch*?" his sister demanded, her hands on her hips, as she looked up from where Lucy cuddled the kitten in a box of flannels. "You know she made it to the cabin and is staying the night with Grossmuder May."

But Luke caught the faint waver of uncertainty in June's voice. "I don't know that for sure." He lowered his voice as Lucy gazed at him with a puckered brow. "And neither do you." He cleared his throat. "Lucy, I think I'll take a bit of a jaunt up the mountain and check on your sister. You keep that kitten—I mean Friend—*gut* and warm, all right?"

"Will you be safe, Dat?" the child asked with concern.

"As Derr Herr wills, child."

Lucy's mouth quivered. "But He willed it for Mommli not to be safe, didn't He?"

Luke wet his lips and avoided June's pointed gaze. "What Derr Herr wills is always *gut*, Lucy. It works out for good—someway, somehow."

He drew a breath of relief when the little girl nodded, apparently satisfied, as she looked back down at the kitten. Then he strode past June to make his way to the bedroom to bundle up thick for the hard trek ahead.

John Beider paced the confines of the kitchen despite Ellie's pleas that he sit down and pray instead of worrying. Matthew had not returned and the storm had indeed come on quickly.

"John, most likely he's in town somewhere. Probably at the Kauffmanns' store, sitting around the stove and drinking coffee. Stop fretting."

"I should go and look for him."

His wife threw up her hands. "Go and look? In the middle of a blizzard? *Jah*, that would be wise."

John noticed the quiver in her voice and realized she was worried too, but his going out would only trouble her more. He drew a steadying breath and reached to pat her shoulder.

"All right, Ellie. You've convinced me." He glanced at Simon, who was idly poking at a checkers game. "I'll tell Simon a story while you get supper, and likely Matthew will be home when this all blows over."

Ellie sniffed and nodded, and John silently bent his head to pray for a moment before joining Simon at the table.

The pain had eased somewhat, and Matthew was now conscious to the point of realizing that the torturous warm-water soaks had probably saved his fingers from frostbite. He gazed around the cabin's bedroom, then tried stretching in the big, down-filled bed, only to wince at the attempt. Then Laurel bustled in and even the weight of the heavy quilts piled atop him couldn't distract his mind from the knowledge that he was naked and that he'd had no hand in getting that way himself.

"How are you feeling?" she asked, reaching a cool hand to his brow.

Awkward . . . strange . . . yearning. The words tussled in his brain until he could do nothing but give her a reassuring smile. She smiled back, then bent as if to kiss his mouth, and he tensed automatically.

"Laurel . . . I—I'm not dressed."

The sudden flush on her pretty cheeks told him all he wanted to know about his lack of clothes and he closed his eyes with a groan.

"You were soaked, Matthew. I—I had no choice." Her voice sounded forlorn and he opened his eyes to see the half-shamed expression on her face. He knew immediate regret at his foolish pride and stretched out a swollen hand to awkwardly pull her close.

"Thank you, sweetheart," he whispered.

"Do you think me wanton?"

He smiled. "*Jah* . . . wanton and brazen and perfect. In fact, I'd like to show you how much I appreciate your vices if I . . ."

"There'll be no showing of any kind," Grossmuder May laughed from the doorway.

Matthew jerked even as Laurel jumped and the old woman laughed again. But then she sobered. "Laurel, come lift the bundling board down from the rafters. We haven't much time."

"Bundling board?" Matthew exclaimed. He knew the old custom of his people of bundling among courting couples. It was when a couple would lie abed with each other, fully clothed, with a bundling board bolstered between them while they got to know each other. But, he was not fully clothed and how did Grossmuder May know they were courting anyway?

He opened his mouth to protest, wanting to save Laurel from further discomfiture, when Grossmuder May shushed him. "Enough thinking questions. He'll be here soon, and it must appear as though Laurel sleeps alone in the bed."

"Who'll be here?" Matthew asked, confused by the woman's easy discernment of his thoughts.

Grossmuder May sighed as if annoyed by an obvious answer. "Laurel's *fater*, of course."

Laurel froze in horror as she pulled the thin board down from amongst the dried herbs and onion ropes. "My—*fater*?"

"*Jah*," Grossmuder May answered easily. "Luke Lapp. Hurry on now."

Laurel let the old woman slip the board from her fingertips and followed her back into the bedroom in a frantic daze.

"But what are we going to do? My *fater* will kill Matthew!"

Grossmuder May rolled her eyes. "Don't overdramatize, child.

You and Matthew will bundle in the bed properly. I will tell your *fater* that you are asleep and need not be disturbed. I will sleep in my rocker by the fire and your *dat* will do the same in the opposite chair."

"But . . ."

Grossmuder May held up a wrinkled hand for silence. "In the morning, you and your *fater* will leave first and then Matthew later. It's simple, really." Laurel saw her cast a stern eye in Matthew's direction. "So long as you are quiet, all should be well."

Laurel lifted her hands helplessly. "But how—why—do you know? Why do you help us?"

"I've got eyes, child, haven't I? Any man who'd risk losing his hands to this mountain is worth his salt and a fine match for you, no matter your *faters'* feuding. And moreover, I was young once myself."

A rampant knocking at the cabin door sounded from the next room, and Grossmuder May calmly handed Laurel the bundling board. "Down the center of the bed, child. I'll get the door."

She hobbled out and flung down the thin curtain that separated the bedroom from the front room and kitchen.

Laurel stared at Matthew in dismay as the rumble of her *fater's* voice seemed to fill the cabin with its power.

CHAPTER 8

"*Kumme* in, Luke Lapp. I've been expecting you. *Kumme* and close the door. You're blowing half the mountain in!"

Luke stood tall and uncertain inside the cabin and looked down at Grossmuder May through the layer of snow topping his muffler. "Is she here then?" he asked, his heart beating fast.

"Sleeping like an angel in my bed."

"Praise Gott. I would see her . . ."

"*Nee*, the child is fair worn out and bundled beneath the quilts. Let her sleep while you take your own rest here before the fire. There's no sense trying to get down the mountain until daybreak and the storm passes. Are you hungry?"

Luke realized he was ravenous after his hazardous ascent. "*Jah*, but I don't want to trouble you."

He watched her sweep a bright quilt off the kitchen table and then she brushed away his words with an unladylike snort. "Sit, Luke Lapp. There's venison stew and dumplings. Though I'll put this quilt away first."

His stomach rumbled as he began to undo the layers of his coat and scarves, thanking Derr Herr for Laurel's safety and the coming food.

* * *

Laurel jumped and sat up straighter in the comfortable bed as the curtain was briefly drawn aside and Grossmuder May entered, carrying the Christmas-roses quilt. Laurel had put the bundling board in place and bolstered it with two pillows. But the board provided little true division, rising only a few inches, so that Matthew seemed incredibly close, even though she lay fully dressed atop the quilts.

Grossmuder May came to stand at the foot of the bed. "Your first wedding present," she whispered in her aged voice. And she flung out the Christmas-roses quilt so that it covered Laurel and added another layer atop Matthew.

When Laurel opened her mouth in amazement, Grossmuder May gave a warning frown and Laurel smiled in bewildered, grateful thanks. *If my* dat *finds out that Matthew's in here, there'll never be a wedding....* But such thoughts seemed of little use, especially when the old woman left them alone once more.

Laurel reached to run her fingertips over the quilt top, touching the petals of a single rose in dreamy fascination. It seemed that when Grossmuder May covered them with the quilt, she was blessing them and their lives together. *And how like Derr Herr to give hope for the future...* Laurel relaxed her posture and leaned over in the bed to rest her chin atop the quilt-covered bundling board. She forgot for the moment that her *fater* was only a few feet away when she gazed into Matthew's warm green eyes.

"I love you," he whispered. Laurel felt her cheeks heat with his words, but she knew joy in her spirit that she could shape the words back to him with certain truth.

"I love you too."

John Beider turned his empty coffee mug around, and the light of the kerosene lamp caught on the creases in his aging hands. The storm still howled outside and he sat alone, waiting and praying for Matthew. He looked up when Ellie appeared from their bedroom, her comfortable form wrapped warmly against the chill that permeated the room now that the fire was banked.

"You should come to bed, John." Her voice was tender, mournful. He gave her a rueful smile. "You know, Ellie, it's strange how usually I can't stand to be alone, but sitting here now—waiting—I find myself thinking back over my life and I can't seem to get away from the mistakes I've made."

Ellie turned to lay a hand on his shoulder, and he caught her fingertips in his own. "You're worried, John. That's all."

He shook his head. *"Nee*, I don't think that's it. I can't get it out of my head that maybe if I hadn't—well, stole that dollar when I was eight from Kauffmann's or sassed my *mamm* before she died . . ." His voice lowered. "Or fought with Luke—maybe, maybe Matthew wouldn't be out in this right now."

He felt Ellie draw him close. "John, you know that Derr Herr came into this world to take away our sins, to give us relief from the shame of things we've done or should have done. Matthew's out— or not out—in the storm because he is finding a home for a stray kitten. A kind act—a kind choice, like we raised him. Your past has nothing to do with it."

John nodded. He knew what his wife said was true. *"Danki,* Ellie." He rose and pulled her near for a sweet kiss.

"Now *kumme* to bed. It will be morning before we know it."

John lifted the lamp and followed Ellie out of the kitchen, but not before turning once to see the circle of light reflected against the glass of the window and the driving snow.

Matthew tried to fall asleep, but the sensory overload of Laurel's nearness and the cacophony of loud snoring coming from Gross-muder May and Luke Lapp barely allowed him to close his eyes. And, he was thirsty.

He considered climbing out of bed and getting the tantalizingly close water pitcher on the nearby dresser, where a single lantern burned low. But he couldn't risk Laurel waking and seeing him un-dressed. And, his clothes were nowhere in sight.

"What's wrong?" Laurel whispered, startling him. She gave a hushed giggle and leaned farther over the bundling board near his ear. "Don't worry, Matthew. The way those two are snoring, they'll never hear. What do you need?"

He stared up at her, her innocent question provoking stirrings of desire in his mind. *What do I need? You . . .*

He reached up a tender hand to tease a strand of red-gold hair from beneath her *kapp*, coiling its length around his still reddened fingers. He pulled gently and she stretched even nearer to him, her red lips parted in breathlessness.

"Water," he muttered, trying to get a rein on his thoughts. *Water and your sweet mouth on mine like spring rain . . .*

Laurel frowned in concern and turned to slide with visible caution off her side of the bed. She moved in the shadows like a slim wraith, and he couldn't ignore the swing of her skirts as she stretched to reach a glass tumbler on a shelf above the dresser. He shifted restlessly, painfully aware of his state of undress. Then the gentle trickle of water filling the glass absorbed him and she came back to the bed.

She perched atop his mound of quilts, but he could still feel the press of her hip against his side as he eased himself up a bit to drink. He reached to hold the glass, but she gently pushed his hand away and pressed the rim to his lips.

"Drink," she whispered.

The icy water quenched his hot throat, but the scent and nearness of Laurel sent fresh heat to his bare shoulders and chest. He couldn't stop himself when she pulled the drink away. He caught her mouth in a languorous kiss, slanting his head to deepen the intensity until he lost all sense of reason.

Laurel responded to his kiss with equal desire and only realized that the glass had slipped from her tingling fingers when it shattered on the floor with all the seeming intensity of an unpredicted earthquake.

She froze as the male snoring from the other room came to a sudden, coughing halt and then the unmistakable sound of heavy footsteps pounded across the cabin floor. She felt the slight breeze on her cheek as the curtain was flung aside and longed to lose herself in the intense green eyes staring in mixed determination and desperation up into hers.

"Laurel, are you well?" her *dat* asked, rubbing his eyes as she turned.

She watched her *fater's* eyes adjust to the dim light as he approached the bed and then blaze out with incredulity and fury at the sight before him.

* * *

Luke Lapp could not have been more confused and dazed if someone had struck him broadside with a two by four. But there she was—held protectively against a bare male chest. Luke lurched forward another step, crunching glass beneath his thick socks, then blinked as he recognized John Beider's eldest *sohn*.

Luke struggled to get a word out, any word, but all he heard coming from his throat, as if from a distance, was a low growl of white-hot rage. It surprised him for a second, long enough for him to realize that his hands were clenched in fists and he knew a desire to strike something, break something. . . . He let out a ragged breath. His people were peaceful in nature and he had never struck another human being, and he realized that, by some tenuous thread of control, he was not about to start now.

He lifted a hand and pointed his finger at the young couple, looking past Laurel to meet Matthew Beider's resolute green eyes. "What—is going on?"

"It's my fault, sir," Matthew said quickly. His deep voice was very much like his *fater's* had once been, so that Luke had the eerie feeling that an embodiment of the past had somehow come to meet him in the confines of the small room.

The *buwe* continued to speak, his strong, cleanly muscled arms visibly tightening around Laurel—as if . . . *As if I'd hurt her.* A vein in Luke's forehead pulsed fiercely and a sob caught at the back of his throat as the dissolution of his daughter's honor seemed to stare him in the face. *What would Meg have said?*

"I know how you feel about my *fater*—how you each feel. I sought to court Laurel anyway in deep secret. It is all my doing. I—I came after her here when the storm started because I feared for her. I love her, sir. I want to marry her."

"By your teeth, you surely shall marry her, or I'll . . ." Luke caught a winded breath. *What will I do? The* buwe *will do the right thing or else. . . .* He ground his jaw in mute frustration.

"Fater, please do not be hurt or upset. I love Matthew. I would make him a *gut* wife."

"You're a child," Luke choked.

"I'm eighteen—older than Mamm was when she married you."

"Don't—don't you dare bring up your mother here. If she could see you . . ."

"What is all the fuss about? I was dreaming deep." Grossmuder May hobbled into the room and poked Luke with her cane. "Luke Lapp, so your daughter bundled with a *buwe*. So, what? You know it was common practice not that long ago on this mountain."

"You would have hid this from me," Luke accused the elder with a catch in his voice.

"*Jah*, and for your own *gut*. Because you're acting exactly like I know you would have, had you known from the outset."

Luke shook his head and swung his glare back to the young couple. "Get out of that bed, *buwe*. The sun is beginning to rise and the storm has passed. You and I are going to see the bishop and then your *fater*. You'll marry before this day is out, so help me. Now, get up."

"Fater . . . *sei se gut*, let Matthew have some privacy." Laurel protested weakly.

"What?"

"*Ach*," Grossmuder May snorted. "She's trying to tell you that the *buwe*'s not dressed."

Luke's mind boggled. "Not—dressed . . ." He took an involuntary step nearer the bed.

"Luke Lapp, he was nearly frozen through." Grossmuder May dismissed the issue with a wave of her wrinkled hand. "And the girl intends to be his wife."

"But—virtue—chastity—pureness—only pureness before her eyes before . . ." Luke heard himself rambling but couldn't stop.

"Fater, please," Laurel began to sob.

"There, now you've done it," Grossmuder May snapped. "A cryin' on her first wedding gift. There should be no tears on that quilt at the beginning. Now we will all step out and let the lad get dressed. *Kumme!*"

And Luke found himself obeying with unshed tears in his eyes for his girl. . . .

CHAPTER 9

John Beider was dressing to go out that morning to look for Matthew. The storm had gone, leaving a dazzling display of white against the rising dawn of a blue sky. He looked up from tying his boots when a loud knock sounded at the back kitchen door.

His heart dropped when he thought it might be news of Matthew. Ellie hurried past him to open the door and an odd, bundled trio stepped into the kitchen. Scarves and hats came off and John stood with one boot in his hand to stare at Bishop Umble, Matthew, and finally . . . Luke Lapp.

John cleared his throat, focusing on his *sohn*. "Matthew, we've been worried. . . ." John, usually never at a loss for words, trailed off in uncertainty.

"I'm fine, Daed." But Matthew seemed too serious, almost subdued, and John faced the bishop, ignoring Luke Lapp.

"What's the matter here?" John asked as Ellie slipped past him to gather coffee cups.

"Uh, Frau Beider," the bishop began. "There's no need for coffee. Perhaps if you might give us men a few moments alone."

John saw Ellie nod wordlessly and slip into the bedroom, pulling a reluctant Simon from the breakfast table with her.

"Well?" John asked again when the bedroom door had been closed.

"I found your *buwe* here in—in a bed with my daughter."

In one distant part of his mind, John heard the old cadence of his one-time friend's voice and knew it was something he'd recognize for all his days, but another area of his brain caught the actual words and he bristled at the accusation.

"What's that you say?"

"We were bundling, Daed. That was all." John saw Matthew give Luke a direct gaze, and he recognized the tiredness in his *sohn*'s voice, as if he'd pled the same words many times.

"Of course that was all, Matthew. As you say," John snapped as he dropped his boot and straightened his back.

"The *buwe* was naked. Bundling is no longer practiced and is to be done fully clothed anyway. He has dishonored my girl," Luke bit out.

Bishop Umble raised a placating hand when John took a step forward. "Now, Luke Lapp, show reason. Matthew could not have remained in freezing clothing and Grossmuder May gave her approval to the situation."

"Grossmuder May?" John asked. "Why were you up there?"

"He's been secretly courting Laurel for months. But he'll marry her today, so help me." Luke looked like he wanted to shake Matthew, and John felt his ire rise higher.

"Matthew will marry whom he chooses."

"Daed, I choose Laurel. I love her. I always have." Matthew spoke earnestly.

Luke Lapp snorted as if in disbelief and John clenched his fists. "Look, *Deacon* Lapp, if you have something to say about my *buwe*, then say it out. Right now!"

"He's dishonorable."

"Ha! But he's decent enough to be willing to give his life away to a daughter of yours when he could choose from any of—"

Bishop Umble shook his head and laid his aged hands on the shoulders of the two men, who'd inched fighting close. "Enough. We've heard Matthew. He loves Laurel. The two even came to see me to find a way to make their fathers see reason. But you both choose pride and spite. . . . You both choose poorly."

John swung away, not wanting to listen when his anger was so intense. He grabbed his *sohn's* hand. "You do not have to marry, Matthew."

"He does and he will," Luke growled. "The wedding is set for two o'clock today at my home. I expect all to be put to right when Derr Herr gives his blessing to this unholy union." He turned with a final sweeping glare and stomped out the door.

Bishop Umble paused. "All will be well, *sohn*." He patted Matthew's shoulder and nodded at John. "Think, John Beider. Think . . ."

Then the old man left and closed the door gently behind him.

John wordlessly turned to his *sohn* and caught him close. Matthew didn't resist, and John wished fervently that he could make things right for his *buwe*, the way he had when Matthew had been a *boppli*, but Matt was a man now—it was as simple as that. A man and soon to be wed to his enemy's daughter. And despite the bishop's admonition, it was more than John could stand to think about. . . .

Laurel felt bedraggled by the hike down the mountain, and she clutched the Christmas-roses quilt in front of her like a shield as she entered the kitchen and met Aenti June's searching gaze.

There seemed little point in speaking anything less than the truth, so Laurel dropped down at the kitchen table, put her arm around Lucy, and managed a tired smile. "Well, I'm to marry Matthew Beider this afternoon at two o'clock."

For once, Aenti June appeared nonplussed, and Laurel waited while Lucy gave a happy squeal. "So, you told Dat? And he said *jah*?"

"Something like that, Lucy. Wherever did you get the kitten?" Laurel reached her hand out from under the quilt to pet the small creature.

Lucy gave her a less-than-obvious wink. "From the barn last night. I thought we could maybe . . . share her. I named her Friend."

"That's nice."

Aenti June exploded. "Wait a moment. . . . *What* did you say?"

Laurel looked wearily at her *aenti*. She felt awful about the way her *fater's* face had been set as they'd left the cabin—in despair, anger, sadness—all disappointment in her. It was not the way she wanted to start a life with Matthew.

"I'm marrying Matthew Beider. Dat found us together at Grossmuder May's. . . ."

Aenti June blustered. "Do you want to marry this *buwe?*"

" 'Course she does," Lucy answered stoutly. "She's been seeing him forever and I know he loves her. . . . He's even her *frieeend*," the child finished, emphasizing her last word and looking down at the kitten.

Laurel sighed. "It's true. I love him dearly, but Fater . . ."

Aenti June seemed to rally. "Your *fater* will accept it in time, but right now, it's nearly eight a.m. and you're telling me we're having a wedding in six hours? Why, we've got to get this place cleaned and I need to make a cake at least. And you need a blue dress!"

"I think it will be a very quiet wedding," Laurel pointed out. "No guests but the Beiders and the bishop and his *frau*, maybe."

"Huh! Only the Beiders . . . do you think I'd have those people in this *haus* without it looking just so? Now, you go to your room and get your work dress on. We'll save time for you to bathe and do up your hair afresh. And go through your hope chest to find what you'll be taking."

Aenti June stopped still after she spoke, and Laurel realized the full import of her words. *What I'll be taking . . . away. To live at the Beiders', where my fater is hated. Why have I never thought beyond the wedding to the tradition of the bride going to the groom's home to live until a new home can be made?*

Something of what she was thinking must have shown in her face because Lucy tugged hard on her arm. "Where are you going, Laurel? To Matthew's? But I'll miss you," the little girl whimpered, and Laurel felt like crying herself at the suddenness of everything.

Aenti June dabbed at her eyes with her apron and gave an enormous sniff; then she reached to pat Laurel's hand. "Mind, now, Lucy, don't upset your sister on her wedding day. You'll see her— we'll see her, anytime we like."

Anytime . . . Laurel repeated in her mind, praying that all might go well.

* * *

Matthew winced as he tightened his boot strings, and Simon must have caught his expression.

"What's wrong with your feet?"

"Nearly frostbitten—they're still sore a bit."

Simon huffed. "Is a girl really worth all this trouble?"

Matthew grinned despite his tiredness. "You'll see one day, little *bruder*. Now bundle up. We're going to the Kauffmanns' store."

"What for?"

"Wedding coats. I expect you to stand up with me."

"Me? Really?" Simon pushed his glasses farther up on the bridge of his nose and smiled from ear to ear.

"*Jah*, you. Who else would I have but my *bruder*?"

"Whoo-ee!"

"Simon Beider," his mother admonished from the doorway. "Stop screaming and step out for a minute, will you? I want to talk with Matthew alone."

Simon bounced off the bed. "All right. I'll go get my scarf and stuff."

Matthew studied his mother's face when his *bruder* had gone. "I'm sorry, Mamm," he said finally. "I didn't expect things to turn out like this."

"How did you expect them to turn out?" Her voice was curious. "Were you simply going to allow the deacon to announce the impending marriage after a service and surprise us? Shame us because you didn't trust us enough to let us know the girl you love?"

Matthew hung his head and his mother came and sat down next to him on the bed. "Matthew, I don't want to hurt you, but it is to be a mother's joy to help with the planning and preparations for a *sohn*'s marriage."

His head began to ache and he ran his hands through his dark hair. "Mamm, it was never you. . . . It's Dat. I thought—with the feuding—well, that I'd never gain his blessing. I didn't know what to do."

His mother was silent for a few very long, uncomfortable moments. Then she slapped her hands down on her knees. "Well, we'd best get moving. Since you normally sleep with Simon, I'll air out the guest room for you and Laurel. I know you'll be anxious to have a home of your own *kumme* spring, but we'll get along all right with Derr Herr's help."

"*Danki,* Mamm. I love you so much." He leaned over and gave her a quick *buss* on the cheek. She reached to pat his face, then slipped her hand down to lay some money in his palm.

"I want you to take this, Matthew. I know you have your own savings, but I'd like to help with the coats and the fast tailoring Ben Kauffmann's going to have to do."

"Mamm, I can't . . . really."

She rose to her feet. "You can and you will. Now get a move on. You've only a few hours."

Matthew smiled and nodded, then watched her bustle from the room. He closed his eyes and prayed silently. *Maybe things will go better than I expect. . . .*

CHAPTER 10

Luke plunged through the snow at the Amish cemetery, discovering that the simple white headstones were nearly covered by the past storm. He counted stone tops as he walked, four over from the large pine tree that gave such pretty shade in the summer, and two rows back. He dropped to his knees in front of the stone, and dug with his dark gloved hands to clear the small space. There was snow, then wet leaves, then grass in wilted disarray. He eased his hat off, careless of the cold, and stared at his wife's name, carved in plain letters. He knew the *Englisch* put flowers on their loved ones' graves, even plastic things in the winter, but it was not his community's way. Yet he wished it was today. . . . He wanted to bring something to Meg besides his troubles, not that he was really sure if she heard him. He knew he should talk to Derr Herr alone, but simply voicing his thoughts out loud at Meg's grave gave him comfort that he did not believe *Gott* would withhold from him.

He swiped his arm across his eyes, feeling at ease to cry here, as he had many times in the past. "Well, Meg, our girl's getting married today—to John Beider's *buwe*. . . . I never would listen to you when you tried to reason with me about John. I'm sorry for that. It seems so much easier to keep on with the anger—and the hurt. And Laurel . . ." His voice broke as he recalled the scene in the bedroom cabin. "Laurel—will do the right thing, but I—I'll miss her about the place. Like you, sweetheart . . . like I miss you." He lurched to his feet and fished out a red handkerchief and blew his nose and dried his face, then turned with resolve toward home.

Laurel knelt beside the large carved cedar chest and eased open the lid. Lucy was next to her and the little girl clapped her hands as though a great masterpiece were being unveiled. In truth, Laurel had always kept her hope chest as a private thing, and she found the rich, aromatic scent of the wood to be calming as she prepared to share her hopes with Lucy.

On top were several intricately crocheted white doilies in tissue paper. An *Amisch haus* was plain in decoration, but doilies were acceptable on chair backs and end tables.

"Oooh, they look like snowflakes," Lucy cooed. "However did you learn the patterns?"

Laurel smiled as she remembered. "I found one in a newspaper from Kauffmann's store and Aenti June taught me another. I suppose I'll have to teach you sometime soon."

Lucy wriggled in excitement, clutching the flannel-filled box and the kitten closer.

Next, there was a beautiful nine-patch quilt that Laurel had worked the year she was fourteen. Although the pattern was a simple one, the intricate piecing of colors and fabrics was a cheerful sight in the bright morning light. "Mommli helped me with some of this," Laurel said softly, remembering her mother's industrious, care-worn hands and feeling a wave of loneliness. She laid the quilt aside and drew out two tablecloths, both snowy-white linen and edged with pale blue embroidery. Then came fine linen napkins, tied in bundles of four with light blue satin ribbon.

"*Ach*, what happened here?" Lucy's little fingers touched the brown mark of a very obvious iron burn on one of the napkins.

Laurel laughed. "I was twelve and noticed a starling outside the kitchen window while I ironed. Its song was so beautifully clear through the open window, and Mamm said I should keep the napkin, not to recall my poor ironing but to remember the starling. And I still do."

"Mommli was smart," Lucy said wistfully. "I wish I knew her better."

Laurel felt her eyes swim with tears. "Oh, Lucy, I know. I want her to be here now today, too. But I'm glad that we have each other."

"And Friend." Lucy stroked the kitten with tenderness, and Laurel had to smile through her tears.

"*Jah*, and Friend."

"What's next?" Lucy asked, quicksilver in her curiosity.

"A box of recipe cards." Laurel opened the brown box with the faint outline of two strawberries on it and flipped through the cards, each done with the careful penmanship of a different hand.

"But you can cook *gut*," Lucy protested.

Laurel shook her head. "It's not so much the recipe as it is remembering each woman's handwriting and what she loved to make and share. I expect it'll make me feel less alone when we have our own *haus* and I'm cooking for Matthew."

Lucy smiled with broad innocence. "You mean before the *kinner kumme*.... Then I'll be Aenti Lucy."

Laurel couldn't help the blush that stained her cheeks and hurriedly lifted the pillowcases embroidered with Bible verses out of the chest. The white cases were large enough to fit the giant feather pillows common on the mountain and were also a keen reminder to trust Derr Herr even during sleep.

Next came a tightly woven berry basket. "This was from Alice King. She passed on before you were born. But when I was little, I was permitted to go and watch Alice weave her baskets. She said I sat as still as a baby rabbit and gave me this as a gift. It's one of the first things I put in my chest."

"*Ach*, will Daed make me a hope chest?" Lucy asked, gently fingering the intricate weaving on the shaved wood basket.

Laurel felt her heart rise with sudden impulsive inspiration. "He won't have to, sweetling. I'm giving you this one. It was Mamm's and should rightfully go to you."

Lucy's cherubic mouth froze in a perfect O and Laurel laughed in delight. "*Kumme* on, we'll slide it onto your side of the bedroom."

Lucy set the kitten box carefully aside and pushed with all her might as Laurel slid the bulk of the weight. It was something *gut* to do that kept her mind from thinking that her new bedroom would be at the Beiders' this *nacht*.

Matthew groaned silently when he saw Bishop Umble talking as men from the mountain gathered around the stove in Ben Kauffmann's store.

"Right on the stroke of two, today . . ." Matthew heard the bishop gently gossip and knew he was talking about the rushed wedding. *Men gossip more than the women on this mountain*, Matthew considered, plastering a smile on his face and squaring his shoulders. Although it was the way of things that everyone knew everybody else's business, he wasn't about to be caught looking sheepish about the whole situation. *After all, I'm marrying the girl of my dreams. . . .*

Bolstered by his thoughts, he stepped nearer to the warm stove and let his gaze swing around the faces of those gathered. He recognized Professor Jude Lyons, the *Englischer* who'd recently married a mountain girl and announced his desire to join the *Amisch* community. Matthew thought that Jude could probably understand things a bit from his perspective as the professor had himself been pushed into marriage by an angry father.

Matthew was grateful for the professor's welcoming smile while many others merely hushed up and looked uncomfortable for a minute.

The bishop cleared his throat when Matthew arched an eyebrow at him. "*Ach*, Matthew and Simon . . . I was explaining your situation and I, um, imagine you're here to see Ben about some wedding clothing?"

"*Jah*," Matthew returned drily. "And, since it's no surprise that the wedding's today, we'll need to make do with what the store's got." He looked to Ben Kauffmann and found the tall *Amischer*'s eyes to be bright and kind.

"*Kumme*, Matthew and Simon, let's see what I've got ready made in the back." Ben shouldered a path through the small crowd, and Matthew followed in relief, ignoring the teasing whispers behind him.

"Ignore everyone, Matt," Ben advised when they'd reached a

small section of premade clothing. "You'd get teased whether you had two months or two hours to prepare—you know that."

"I know." Matthew smiled, feeling himself relax. He glanced at Simon, who grinned back, and soon they were attired in black wedding coats with long tails that covered the seats of their black pants. Simple white shirts completed the outfits.

Ben walked around them both, making small pulling adjustments here and there. "Hmm . . . some hemming on Simon's sleeves and I think we'll be *gut*. It'll only take me half an hour or so. Why not go in through to the *haus* and visit Grossdaddi? He's been down with a bad cold. But remember that he forgets sometimes—talks like he's in the past and all that."

Matthew entered the small side door that led to the main *haus*, grateful that Ben hadn't suggested they go back and wait around the stove.

Matthew and Simon sat down near the frail *auld* man bundled on the couch near a bright window. The gentle hum of the Kauffmann women's voices could be heard from somewhere deeper in the house.

Matthew leaned towards the couch. "Hiya, sir."

Smucker Kauffmann turned his gray head. "*Ach*, who's there?"

"John Beider's *sohns*—Matthew and Simon."

"John Beider—John Beider. Angry young man."

Matthew looked at Simon and shrugged, unsure of what to say.

Smucker Kauffmann stared at them without appearing to see them. "Always that gun. Hounding me day and *nacht* . . . let me be."

Matthew leaned back in his chair, puzzling over the elder's words about his *fater*. *Could Smucker know something about the feud between my* daed *and Laurel's* fater*? And what gun? As far as I know, Daed hasn't hunted since before I was born. . . .*

Smucker drew a sighing breath. "John Beider and Luke Lapp, I've sold you *buwes* more licorice today than a body could know what to do with . . . going to rot your teeth, both of you! *Ach*, no laughing at your elders!"

The *auld* man's voice rose and Ben's wife bustled into the room, stopping short when she saw Matthew and Simon. "Hiya, *buwes*. Is Grossdaddi having one of his remembering spells? Please don't let him disturb you."

"Uh—" Matthew got to his feet. "*Nee,* Frau Kauffmann—we are the ones who do not wish to disturb him. We'll head back out into the shop."

She nodded with a pleasant smile, and Matthew nearly tripped over Simon in his haste to leave the room.

"Did you hear that?" Matthew hissed. "Daed and Luke Lapp were friends. The bishop told me that, but I couldn't picture it."

Simon shrugged. "It's a mystery, for sure."

"*Jah,* a mystery that might be solved and make my married life with in-laws a whole lot easier. . . ."

CHAPTER 11

John soberly helped Ellie into the cutter sled. Matthew and Simon were seated in a second sled behind. It was quarter to two in the afternoon and an eight-minute ride to Luke Lapp's. John bit the inside of his mouth against the cold and thoughts of Luke Lapp as his soon-to-be kin. He hadn't set foot in the Lapp cabin for nearly forty years—even when Meg had died, he'd only gone to the service at the cemetery.

"Are you going to pick up the reins?" Ellie asked, interrupting his thoughts.

"What? *Ach, jah* . . ." He released the brake and called to get the horse moving.

He listened to the comforting sliding sound as the sled cut through the snow and tried to calm the nervousness he felt inside. *How will it be to have Luke's daughter in the haus? To invite the Lapps to every picnic and frolic . . .*

"For our *sohn's* sake, I hope you will give up this feud with Luke Lapp." Ellie's voice was quiet.

John looked at his *frau's* set profile and some imp of pride made him tighten his jaw. "I am accepting Luke's daughter as my own— that will have to be enough. More than enough."

"Huh," Ellie snorted in obvious disdain, then did not speak again until they pulled up to the Lapp cabin.

"The bishop is here already. We'd best hurry. Forgive me, John, for telling you how to manage your life." Ellie patted his hand and he squeezed her fingers in return. It felt good to walk in unity up the steps as Matthew and Simon followed behind.

Luke knew he should be downstairs already to greet the *buwe* who would be his son-in-law, but Lucy had caught his hand and pulled him back inside of his room.

He glanced rather shyly at her little blue dress, wondering how Laurel would look in the traditional marrying color. *Surely I've seen her in blue before....*

"Daddi," Lucy spoke up, her small voice demanding his attention.

"What is it?"

"I think you should give Laurel something of Mamm's to go with her wedding dress."

"What?" *The child is right; I should have thought of it myself. Instead, I've avoided my daughter, likely shamed her....*

"Something of Mommli's, like one of her handkerchiefs." Lucy ran to the dresser drawer where he kept some of her *mamm's* things.

"This one," Lucy cried, pulling out a dainty scrap of fabric, carefully edged with a single strand of blue.

I can remember Meg using that.... He cleared his throat as Lucy laid it in his hand. "Perhaps you are right, little Lucy. I'll take it to Laurel and you go down and greet our guests."

"All right. But only for a minute. Then I get to walk downstairs with Laurel." The child snatched the kitten box from the bed and hurried away, leaving Luke to stare at the handkerchief. He brought it instinctively to his nose and caught Meg's scent—faint, but like lilacs in May. Then he steeled himself and walked down the hall to Laurel's room.

Laurel started at the knock on her door and glanced at the wind-up clock on the dresser. She'd thought she still had a few minutes. She drew a deep breath and stepped away from the small mirror to open the door. When she saw her *fater*, she bowed her head. They hadn't spoken since coming down the mountain from Grossmuder May's, and Laurel still felt embarrassed by the situation her *dat* had found her in with Matthew.

"Laurel, I know our time is short. I wanted . . . to apologize for my temper this morning, and I wanted to give you this to keep to remember your wedding day."

She looked up and saw the dainty handkerchief in his hand, recognizing it as her *mamm's*. Suddenly she felt as if she were a little girl again, sobbing when she skinned her knee or found a wounded bird. Her *fater* had been there to bind up every wound. She stepped into his arms and was engulfed in his embrace.

"*Kumme*," he said after a moment, clearing his throat. "You'll muss your hair and dress. It's beautiful that you are, and I'll not guard against vanity in saying it. Matthew Beider is a blessed man."

"*Danki,* Daed," she whispered. She wanted to say more as a kaleidoscope of images of the strong man before her seemed to swirl in her mind. She had his red hair; she knew she had his strength and would be a *gut* wife, even in a strange household.

Lucy's urgent chirp broke the moment. "Daed, you must go down. It's time for Laurel and me."

Laurel watched her *daed* nod and turn away, his broad shoulders down bent for a moment before he straightened and she heard his heavy footsteps descend the wooden stairs.

Laurel smiled down at Lucy, and the little girl caught her hand, swinging it in excitement. "You look pretty, Laurel."

"So do you, sweetling."

"*Gut*. Let's go."

Laurel drew a deep breath, standing in the doorway of her old bedroom, poised on the precipice of a new world, then slowly stepped forward into her future.

Matthew wanted to scratch his right shoulder badly but decided it wouldn't do to fidget while the bishop was in the middle of the wedding sermon's admonitions and exhortations. Matthew felt that the whole thing had been going on forever, but Laurel's beautiful

face and her downcast eyes, as she sat in a hard-backed chair opposite him, were enough to make any man anxious. He'd spent so
much time fantasizing about her, but now that the wedding was at
hand, his head throbbed at the idea of the wedding *nacht* itself.
And he still couldn't banish the image of his *daed* and Laurel's po-
tentially brawling across the wedding cake once the bishop was
through. He was pondering how pink icing would look against
black wool when the bishop's stern voice broke into his thoughts.

"Uh—*jah*—what, sir?"

There was a general murmur of laughter from the limited number of guests behind him, and he threw Laurel a look of apology.

"I said," Bishop Umble continued, "that my expectations for
your marriage involve you keeping 'the love of your espousals' over
the years. Do you not agree?"

"I agree," Matthew answered, ignoring the bishop's hazardous
grammar.

"And how will you do that, young Matthew Beider?"

Matthew resisted the urge to run a finger under his seemingly
too tight collar and thought hard. The bishop was known for
putting people on the spot, no matter the occasion. *Please, Derr
Herr . . . give me the answer, an answer. . . .* And then a calm filled
him, soothing, like the breeze of a summer's day, and he looked at
Laurel and smiled.

"Well, it's not looks that keep a relationship strong, though my
wife will have plenty of those." A titter ran through the small gathering and Matthew felt a growing confidence. "And it's not *kinner*,
because I know firsthand how much trouble a *buwe* can bring to
his parents. *Nee*, perhaps the answer lies in the smallest of things—
being friends as well as lovers, telling the truth no matter the cost,
remembering to laugh together as well as to cry. Listening to the
rain with each other, praying, dreaming, working, and believing in
what Derr Herr can do with the future." He trailed off and realized
that the room had grown silent. He glanced around, feeling as if
he'd rambled on, when the bishop took out a large handkerchief
and spoke with a loud sniff.

"Anything else you can teach us, young man?"

Matthew realized it was a serious question and thought hard.

"No grudges." The words were out of his mouth before he considered their implication. *Was en der weldt* was wrong with him? *No grudges . . . and both of our* faters *sitting right here . . .*

But the bishop latched with preaching verve on to the simple phrase like a wolf with a bison bone, and Matthew literally bit his tongue, though he knew it was too late. Still, when he looked at Laurel, her eyes held him and he felt cherished inside. At least she was pleased with him . . . and maybe that was all that mattered.

CHAPTER 12

Laurel snuggled closer to Matthew in the sleigh. The wedding and rather stilted eating of Aenti June's delicious cake afterwards all seemed to have passed in a blurred dream. And now, she clutched her brown satchel, which held most of her possessions, and was headed for a new home. She swallowed back tears at Lucy's emotional farewell, then blinked, not wanting Matthew to see her cry on their wedding day.

"At least they didn't fight," he said, navigating the horse around a bend in the road.

"Jah," she agreed. "Though I think they stayed as far apart as possible, even with the bishop's admonitions." She glanced at him shyly. "I loved how you answered when Bishop Umble questioned you."

Matthew caught her hand and pulled it to his lips. "Derr Herr gave me that answer, sweetheart, but I meant it and I'll try to live by it."

She nodded. *"Danki.* Me too."

She watched the snow being thrown up by the horse's hooves and wet her lips in the cold air. "What will it be like, living with your folks, I mean?"

He sighed, which didn't do much to reassure her. "I expect it'll take some getting used to, but don't worry, they'll be kind to you—

no matter how Daed might feel about your *fater*. And, *kumme* spring, we'll have a cabin raising and you'll be mistress of your own *haus*. It's only for a short while."

"I know. I don't mean to sound nervous, but I am I guess. Still, it's Christmas in a few weeks. My favorite time of year . . ."

"My *mamm*'s too and this year, I will not have to go hunting for a tree with Simon alone. You'll come, sweetheart, and save me from my little *bruder*, who thinks he's an expert on all holiday traditions."

Laurel laughed out loud, the sound carefree and full even to her own ears, and suddenly, all things seemed new and possible.

John bowed his head for silent grace, thinking how strange it was to have a girl sitting next to Matthew. His *frau* . . . John had always wondered what it would be like to have a daughter. His *buwes* were *wunderbar* of course, but girls seemed different in their gentleness and manner. And now, Gott had blessed his table with Laurel Lapp—*nee*, Beider. It made him feel both anxious and responsible at the same time.

He asked Ellie for more bread after grace was finished, then noticed the cloud of silent tension that seemed to fill the room. It bothered him. He glanced at Laurel in her wedding dress, her head bent, taking small bites of food, and realized it would be difficult for anyone to leave home and come to a strange *haus* to live.

He sought for something to say, but Simon beat him to it. "It's weird that you're here." The *buwe* gestured to Laurel with his chin while he chewed.

John saw Laurel flush and Matthew give his *bruder* an icy glare.

"Uh—" John interrupted. "What Simon means, Laurel, is that we are happy to have you here, truly. You must move about and *kumme* and go as you please. Think of this as your home . . ." he finished lamely as he realized how he must sound as her *fater*'s enemy.

"*Danki*," she whispered, her slender shoulders still bent toward her plate.

John was relieved when Ellie reached across the table to pat the girl's hand. "It will be well, Laurel. You will see."

John nodded in quick agreement. He'd have to talk to Simon

later about his speech, though he knew the *buwe* meant no harm. But for now, he would enjoy his wife's cooking and the pork chop and apples 'n' onions she had prepared. Things would grow easier in time; Ellie was right, as usual.

"I miss Laurel!"

Luke Lapp sighed as Lucy gave an uncharacteristic wail. It made his heart hurt and he glanced in mute appeal to June, but his sister, too, seemed absorbed in the strangeness of the *haus*, bereft without Laurel.

"Lucy, darling, she's but right down the road," he tried to reason.

"But I want her here."

So do I. . . .

Friend, the kitten, meowed, and he latched on to the sound. "There, Lucy, you must not upset your kitten with all of this crying. Friend probably misses Laurel too. You can help her."

"How?" the child sniffed.

"Why—why—hold her close, speak softly, and—perhaps Aenti June will sleep in Laurel's place in your room this *nacht*."

Lucy picked up the kitten in gentle consideration, and John saw her glance with appeal in June's direction.

"*Jah*, Lucy—for tonight, to make us both less lonely. I'll sleep in Laurel's bed." June sniffed. "But tomorrow, you must think of it as your own bedroom and be a *gut* girl."

"*Jah*," the little girl agreed, then seemed to think of something. She stared straight at Luke. "Where is Laurel going to sleep at the Beiders'?"

Luke suppressed a groan and tried not to think of a response.

Alone in what would be her and Matthew's bedroom, Laurel sat tentatively on the side of the bed and tested its softness. The bed springs squeaked alarmingly and she stilled, biting her lip. She understood well enough what went on between a man and woman on their wedding *nacht*—Aenti June had felt it her duty to educate Laurel in a straightforward, no-nonsense manner.

But now that the moment was at hand, Laurel felt uncertain, though her desire for Matthew tempered the emotion. But how *en der weldt* were they going to have their first *nacht* together on a bed that sounded like an *Englisch* untuned trumpet, with his parents right next door? She sat pondering until she jumped when the door creaked open. Matthew came in, carrying a lantern.

"What's wrong?" he asked with concern.

She gave a half plop on the bed and the springs echoed.

"*Ach*." He smiled his white smile. "I see."

He set the lantern on a dresser top and paused to run his hand in obvious appreciation down one of her work dresses, which she'd hung on a peg next to his shirt. She shivered because she felt as if he were actually touching her.

"I have an idea—get up, *sei se gut*." He reached for her hand and pulled her to her feet. Then he surprised her by sweeping all of the bedding and the mattress tick off the bed and onto the floor. "There."

She giggled and felt more relaxed. This was the Matthew she knew and loved and whom she had risked so much to sneak out and see on chill evenings. She went into his arms easily, standing on tiptoe, and kissing him with an abandon she'd never known before.

He made an appreciative sound deep in his throat, then pulled her down with him to land on the pile of bedding. She bit his lip and noticed him wince; she drew away in embarrassment. "I'm sorry," she murmured.

He laughed, biting her back. "Don't be silly, Frau Beider, it's my boots that are feeling a bit tight."

"*Ach*, Matthew, I forgot about your feet—and your dear hands." She bent her head and lapped gently at the skin on the knuckles of his right hand.

"Laurel," he choked, after a moment. "Help me undress."

Matthew caught a handful of her red-gold hair. He'd always dreamed of what it would look like unbound, and now it spread in glorious, cascading waves around them both, spilling across his chest and hip, and framing them in a secret curtain of intimacy.

By the shimmering light of the lantern, he watched the rise and fall of her snow-white breast and tried to fathom once more that she was now his wife in every sense of the word.

"Are you sleeping?" he asked, nuzzling the length of her neck and watching the lift of her thick lashes as she smiled.

"*Nee*—dreaming, of you." Her voice was a languorous whisper that sent chills racing down his spine.

"No need to dream, my love. I'm right here."

She looked up at him, her blue eyes like twin jewels in the lamp light. Then she wriggled from beneath his hand and knelt upward. "I almost forgot," she whispered in excitement.

"What?" He shivered with the absence of her warmth.

She rose, a slender thing of beauty, and slipped to the wardrobe against the far wall. She withdrew a white bundle and came back to shake it out over his head. He laughed as the cotton settled about his head and shoulders; then he lowered the quilt to peer up at her.

"Grossmuder May's quilt?" he asked in amusement.

She hurried to join him beneath the comfortable fabric. "*Jah.*" Her teeth chattered. "And our first wedding gift."

"You are a gift," he said, pulling her slight form close, then moving to kiss her.

She ran artful fingertips down his bare chest and then lower, and he forgot all else but the blessed night before them.

CHAPTER 13

John sat at the kitchen table the next morning, sipping a cup of coffee. He and the *buwes* had already been out at the chores, and Ellie was unfortunately in bed with a head cold. Matthew and Simon had gone out to exercise some of the horses in the bright morning. He was about to make some toast for Ellie when the guest bedroom door creaked open and Laurel appeared. She made as if to retreat when she saw him alone in the kitchen, but he put his cup down and motioned her forward.

"*Kumme,* Laurel. Will you have breakfast with me? Ellie's not feeling too well and Matthew's out and about with the horses already."

"*Ach*, I'm sorry for rising so late." She flushed prettily. "I don't usually do so."

He waved away her words and started toward the woodstove.

"Let me, *sei se gut*," Laurel intercepted him. "I'm a *gut* cook and you can finish your coffee."

John heard the faint anxiousness in her voice and knew she longed to have purpose in this new home, so he sat back down.

For someone who was known as being able to talk a man to sleep, he felt oddly unsure of what to say to his new daughter-in-law. But he found that she was a spritely conversationalist herself, once her hands were busy, and he knew a certain pride in Matthew's choice of a wife.

"Would Ellie like toast and eggs, do you think? Or only the toast? I can also make some fresh orange juice—I know my *daed* always likes . . ." She dwindled off, and John bent his head in frustration that she should feel uncomfortable mentioning her *fater*.

"I'm sorry," she recovered quickly. "I don't mean to cause any trouble or bad feelings."

John sighed. "You should feel comfortable in your new home. *Sei se gut*, speak of your *fater* as you will. You do not offend me."

He was pleased with her quiet smile and soon was enjoying the breakfast she'd made for him. She'd shredded some cheese in the scrambled eggs, giving them a rich and different flavor, and his toast was laden with sugar and cinnamon.

He watched her prepare a small tray for Ellie, taking the time to take a flower from the Christmas cactus in the windowsill to put in a cup of water, to brighten the food. In all, he again knew thankfulness to Gott, for his new daughter and the future she represented.

Laurel knocked softly on the master-bedroom door and entered to the sound of a deep cough from Ellie.

"You're newly married, child," Ellie wheezed. "Don't wait on me."

"It's my pleasure." Laurel smiled. She put the tray on a tabletop, then helped Ellie sit up against the pillows, bringing her a washcloth from the bowl and pitcher. Laurel was relieved that Ellie's forehead did not feel too warm, and she soon settled the tray on the older woman's lap.

"*Ach*, fresh orange juice—what a treat. John wouldn't know how to squeeze an orange if you paid him."

Laurel giggled. "He was very kind to me this morning."

Ellie blew her nose in a white handkerchief and nodded. "John's a *gut* man, same as your *fater* is. They're both simply too stubborn."

Laurel sat down in a small ladder-back chair near the bedside. "Can you tell me what I can do to help get ready for Christmas? I've told Matthew that it's my favorite holiday."

Ellie smiled though her eyes watered from congestion. "I usually put the tree up about now. Why don't you and Matthew go out and find one today when he's done with the chores?"

Laurel clapped like a little girl. "*Ach*, I'd love to, but may we take Simon—and possibly my baby sister?"

Ellie arched a graying brow. "The day after your wedding, you want to be saddled with *kinner*? I think you need time alone with Matthew."

"*Nee*, truly. Matthew and I are—fine...." Laurel blushed, remembering the previous night. She was grateful, though, that her new mother-in-law seemed not to notice and was concentrating on her toast.

"Well, suit yourself, child. And if you take some gloves and shears, you might get some pine boughs and holly for the windowsills."

"*Wunderbar*," Laurel exclaimed. She loved the scents and sights of Christmas, and she was expert at stringing holly on fishing line without getting pinched overmuch.

"I appreciate your help," Ellie sniffed. "And I would hug you, my dear, if I didn't worry you'll catch my cold."

Laurel leaned forward from her chair and caught the *aulder* woman in a tight embrace. "*Danki* for letting me help and for giving me a warm welcome."

"You're more than welcome, child."

And Laurel rejoiced at the gentle hand that brushed at the back of her *kapp*.

"Here *kummes* Laurel.... Whooee, I didn't know a girl could ride a horse like that." Simon whistled in appreciation and Matthew turned in the saddle to see the vision of his wife coming across the snow-laden field, riding a black gelding sidesaddle. Her dark wool cloak flowed in the wind and her *kapp* strings blew out behind her like twin miniature banners. She was truly a sight for any man to behold.

She slowed to a neat stop next to them. "Hiya." She smiled, nodding at Simon.

Matthew wanted to kiss her right there, but saw no practical way of doing so without startling the horses, so he let his eyes touch her face with tender intimacy instead and was pleased to see her blush.

"You know your *mamm's* not feeling well, so she asked if we might go and find a tree and some greenery for the *haus*. I thought you might *kumme*, Simon, and maybe we can stop for Lucy."

Matthew wanted to be alone with her but couldn't deny the look of pleasure on his *bruder's* face. "Surely, we can head back now."

"Let's race," Laurel called, turning her horse with an expert hand and galloping away. Matthew grinned and followed, Simon's second whistle of appreciation that morning ringing in his ears.

Luke Lapp returned to the bright morning kitchen to find Lucy talking excitedly to June, but she turned to him instead even before he could get his boots off.

"*Ach,* Daddi, I had a dream!" The little girl hopped up and down like a bubbling brook.

"A dream, hmm? What about?"

"*Nee*, listen, *sei se gut*—this dream was special. I believe it was from Derr Herr."

Luke grew serious and looked at June over his daughter's small head. June shrugged.

Luke sat down on the couch and drew Lucy onto his knee. "All right, little one, tell me of your dream."

Lucy's brow furrowed in thought as she visibly concentrated on how to begin. "It was about my kitten, Friend, and John Beider."

Luke blinked, not expecting such a combination. "*Jah?*" he questioned.

Lucy let out a gusty sigh. "I think John Beider is a lonely man, and Gott told me in my dream to give Friend to him so that he wouldn't feel so alone."

Luke frowned in thought. As a deacon, he took very seriously what the Bible says about Gott sometimes speaking to people in dreams, but surely not to such a little child. . . . Then he felt a certain ire rise in his throat. *I've already had one daughter pay a high price to John Beider. Why should my other have to give to the stubborn man as well?*

"Lucy, child, sometimes we think of something in the back of our minds, but it doesn't mean that Gott actually wants us to . . ."

Lucy jumped down from his lap. "You don't believe me, just like Aenti June—and only because you fight with John Beider because of why? Nobody knows!" Her voice became shrill and she stamped a small foot.

Luke gave her a stern look. "Lucy. You will hold your tongue and temper as a child should in this *haus*."

She bit her lip, struggling with tears, then nodded, grabbed Friend's box, and ran upstairs.

Luke exhaled slowly. "What do you think this is about?" he asked his sister.

"Nothing, most likely," June said. "The child is missing Laurel—that's all."

And I *am too*, Luke thought silently, weary before the day had hardly begun.

CHAPTER 14

Laurel found it strange somehow to come home, even as Matthew pulled the double sleigh up in front of the cabin where she'd been raised. It was almost as if there'd been some subtle shift in her spirit that acknowledged that she belonged with Matthew, wherever that might be. And she knew she was no longer a little girl, but a woman, full grown, with a life and dreams of her own to be met and fulfilled.

"Come in, both of you," she urged as Matthew and Simon seemed to hesitate. "Please," she added and they both hopped down from the sled.

She opened the cabin door to find her *daed* sitting alone at the kitchen table, his back to them. But he turned upon hearing the door and there was no mistaking the look of joy in his eyes as he rose to greet her with a hug. Then he shook hands with Matthew and Simon.

"Sit down. Have some coffee. June is doing laundry and Lucy's upstairs."

"*Ach,* Daed, we can't stay but a minute. I wondered if Lucy might go with us to look for a Christmas tree?"

Her father appeared to consider. "*Jah*, she may," he said finally. He turned and walked to the staircase, calling for her little sister.

But there was no sudden patter of footsteps in response, and Laurel saw her dad frown.

"I'm sorry. She was upset earlier, and I had to speak firmly to her. Perhaps she is still troubled." He called again, and then Laurel spoke up.

"I'll go and fetch her, Daed."

But when Laurel went upstairs, she passed through each room and found no sign of Lucy or her kitten.

She went back downstairs feeling oddly worried. It was not like Lucy to avoid coming when called.

"Well?" Her father looked up with a faint frown.

"She's not up there."

"What? Maybe she's with June."

Laurel saw the worry on his face as he went to the back room and spoke rapidly to Aenti June. Soon, she appeared with him, and they both were visibly troubled.

"Would she run away?" Matthew asked in the silence.

"*Nee.*" Laurel shook her head. "At least, she's never done so before."

Her father sighed. "I know where the child is—at your *daed's haus*, Matthew."

Laurel listened to the explanation about the dream and then quickly went with Matthew and Simon out to the sled.

"I'll follow," her *daed* called, and Laurel felt sorry for the worry he must be feeling.

She slipped into the sled next to Matthew and was glad when he urged the horse to hurry.

Ellie was sleeping and John had finished drying the last of the dishes when he heard the soft knock at the door.

He went to open it and had to peer down at the little girl standing on his front porch with a small box. "Lucy Lapp?" he asked finally, perplexed.

"*Jah.*" The child nodded. He saw that she wore only a light cloak and hurried her inside out of the cold.

"Does your *fater* know you're here?" John asked after a moment while the child stared up at him with big blue eyes.

She shook her head. "But Gott knows."

John put his hands on his hips in thought. "That's true." He smiled to himself. *Bright little thing she was. . . .*

"I had a dream last *nacht*—about you," she announced.

"About me?" He was truly surprised. "What about?"

"I know you and Daddi don't like each other." There was no accusation in the child's voice, but John ducked his head all the same.

"I don't—I don't 'not like' your *fater*. It's more . . ."

"You don't like him or else you wouldn't be mad at him all the time."

Oddly frustrated by this simple logic, John had the urge to call for Ellie to help deal with the youngster. Then he noticed the box again.

"What's in the box?"

She held it up to him. "She is part of my dream. Gott told me how lonely you are, and He said I was supposed to give her to you." Her little voice wavered, but she went on with visible bravery. "Now you won't mind being alone so much."

John took the box carefully, feeling as if he were moving in a dream. *How can this little one know so much about me?* He put his hand in the box and lifted the scraps of flannel to reveal the kitten that Matthew had found.

"So," John murmured. "This is where he got her to. I'd say Matthew found her a *gut mamm* in you."

Lucy nodded, biting her bottom lip. "But now she's yours."

John looked into the little girl's face, struggling so clearly to do what she thought was right, no matter the cost to herself. He knelt down next to her, cuddling the kitten under one palm.

"Lucy Lapp, I don't think I've ever had so selfless a gift in all my days. And I would love to have the kitten. . . ."

"Friend," she interrupted. "Her name is Friend."

John smiled. "I'd love to have Friend, but the truth is that we can't have cats about because Ellie has allergies from them—her nose runs too much."

The child looked at him, puzzled. "I don't understand. Then why did Gott tell me to bring her here?"

He shook his head, thinking hard, knowing the answer mattered. "Well, simply because Ellie's nose runs doesn't mean that you and Friend can't *kumme* here and visit as often as you'd like. In fact, I'd enjoy that." And he realized it was true. Somehow, through Derr Herr's Light, Lucy had found a way into his heart, and he felt the years of enmity between himself and her *fater* begin to melt away.

Matthew, Laurel, and Simon all tumbled over themselves to get into the Beiders' back door. Luke Lapp hurried behind.

Matthew drew a deep sigh of relief when he saw Lucy, seated on the floor with his *daed* and playing with the kitten and a small ball of yellow yarn.

"Praise Gott," Laurel cried, flinging herself down next to her sister and catching her close in a tight embrace.

Matthew moved to kneel behind his wife, rubbing her back.

"What's all this?" his *fater* asked.

"Lucy ran away. Her dad thought she'd be here, but we weren't certain." Matthew glanced over to where Luke Lapp stood stiffly on the edge of the circular rug.

"*Ach . . .*" his *daed* murmured.

Matthew watched his *fater* put down the yarn and rise to go and greet Luke Lapp. Amazingly, his *daed's* hand was extended and somehow then engulfed by Laurel's *fater's* hand. It was a brief moment, but it took Matthew's breath away as he watched the seeming dissolution of an old enmity. *And all because of a kitten, and a dream . . . and Gott.*

"I will take Lucy home," Matthew heard Luke announce finally. "But after the tree is chosen, perhaps you—John Beider—and yours would *kumme* to my *haus* for supper."

"Uh, Luke—*danki.*" Matthew's *daed's* voice was shaky with emotion. "We'd love to, but Ellie is feeling under the weather."

"Ellie wouldn't miss this for the world," Mathew heard his *mamm's* voice carry from the bedroom archway, where she'd obviously been watching the whole thing.

Matthew looked into Laurel's blue eyes, which were awash in amazement and luminous with unshed tears, and he knew the Christmas season had truly begun for their two families.

CHAPTER 15

"Well, Lucy, your dream was indeed from Derr Herr." Luke looked down at his little daughter as she held the kitten box close in the confines of the sled.

"So you're not mad at me for running away?"

Luke had to laugh, a free sound that gave him refreshment inside. *John Beider held out his hand to me in goodwill. . . .* "*Nee*, little one. I'm not mad, but please don't make a habit of running. My heart could not take it."

Lucy snuggled close to him. "I promise to be *gut*, Daddi."

Luke smiled down at her. "And I promise to listen more closely when you tell me that you have a message from Gott."

He turned his focus back to the snowy road and remembered that he'd have to tell June she'd be having five unexpected guests for supper. The thought made him laugh again and he felt like a much younger man inside.

Laurel laughed aloud in the clear mountain air as she darted behind a pine tree only to be caught in Matthew's strong arms as he swung her off the ground for a lingering kiss.

"Matthew," she protested when he let her catch her breath. "Simon will see."

"Simon saw," the younger boy called from beside a nearby tree, and Laurel smiled at his dry tone.

She nuzzled closer to Matthew's chest, still filled with disbelief at her *fater's* show of goodwill that morning.

"I know what you're thinking," Matthew said, resting his chin atop her bonnet. "I can't fathom it either. But I wish..." He stopped, and she tilted her head backwards to stare up at him.

"What?"

He shrugged his broad shoulders. "Well, I wish that you might have been able to have a big wedding. I know a girl must dream of those things."

"I dreamed only of you, my love," she whispered. "And I wouldn't trade our wedding for all the guests and gifts in the world."

He rewarded her answer with another deep kiss, and she heard Simon snort nearby.

"Look, can we stop the mush and pick a tree? I'm freezing."

"*Ach*," Laurel exclaimed. "Let's get two trees—one for each home. The Beiders' and the Lapps'."

"Great idea," Matthew said, grinning.

"Oh, boy." Simon shook his head. "*Jah*, it's a great idea, but you'd think that, Matt, even if she asked to go round up ostriches with orange plumes."

Laurel lifted her nose and suppressed a giggle. "I'll have you know, Simon Beider, dearest *bruder*-in-law, that I'd only ask to look for purple-plumed ostriches and never during a Christmas tree outing."

She was secretly pleased to see Simon smile. She so wanted her new family to accept her. Then she caught Matthew's hand and pulled him into a clearing of long-needled pines.

"Here we are. Any of these would be perfect. And the long needles will hold the bread-dough decorations nicely." She ran a gloved hand caressingly down a fragrant tree branch.

In the end, they chose two trees that barely fit in the back of the sleigh, and Laurel knew they'd have to wrestle the pines into the doors of the cabin homes. But she believed in big trees to match the ebullient spirit she felt inside at this time of year and in especial thanksgiving for the healing going on in their fathers' hearts.

* * *

John watched in fascination as his new daughter-in-law twisted the ornament bread dough with deft and artistic hands. In the past, Ellie had normally used cookie cutters and food coloring to paint the ornaments, leaving the *buwes* not all that much interested in decorating. But Laurel had an infectious smile and encouraged everyone to try their hand at making more individualized ornaments.

"At home," the girl chattered happily, "we paint them after with a coat of lacquer and some of the ornaments have lasted for years."

"What a *gut* idea!" Ellie exclaimed, still hoarse, but up and joining in the fun.

Soon, an odd but creative assortment of decorations was spread out on cookie sheets. John watched Laurel take Matthew's hand and guide it to leave a thumbprint next to hers in the dough. Then she carefully etched in the date of their wedding. A small straw was used to leave a hole in the top of each piece, where ribbon would be tied later.

John was surprised to see how deeply Simon concentrated on his piece of dough and his penknife. He soon bashfully revealed a full wreath, with leaves neatly displayed, as well as holly berries and a bow. Then the ornaments went into the oven and were properly painted with food coloring to finish.

While the decorations baked, Ellie served a quick lunch of chicken salad, dumpling soup, and fresh lemonade. Then, Laurel gathered them all near as she, with simple garden gloves on, threaded holly leaves onto fishing line to create a full, beautiful garland to place atop the mantle of the fireplace.

John was happy to see that Ellie showed genuine joy in Laurel's work. He imagined it did not always go so well when a new woman was about in the kitchen or adding to family traditions. But he was blessed in his home, his table, and now his new relationship with Luke. John still had no true idea how he'd gotten up the nerve to extend his hand to Luke. It truly had to be Gott's work, but now that it was done, and Luke had responded in kind, John thought of all the time they must catch up on. And he also realized how foolish he'd been to sacrifice a friend over a shotgun so many long Christmases ago.

* * *

Once the decorating and the afternoon chores were done, Matthew discreetly sought out Laurel in their room.

"What are you doing?" he asked quietly, closing the door behind him.

"*Ach*, mending my *gut* apron for tonight." She bent forward in the small rocker near the window to get closer to the fading light.

She glanced up at him briefly. "What are you doing?"

He pretended to consider. "I did my chores, made my ornaments, had my lunch, listened to my wife's instructions ... and now, I think, we should do something together."

"What is that?" Her pretty brow wrinkled in thought as if trying to remember something she might have forgotten, and he took a step backwards to the bed. He caught the top quilt of Christmas roses in his hand and flung it out onto the pristine hardwoods with a gentle flair and an arched brow.

"Matthew," she protested in hushed shock. "It's broad daylight."

"It is not," he contradicted, raising a hand to the fading afternoon outside the window.

He was pleased to see her blush and he moved to take the apron and needle from her carefully, laying them aside on a small worktable. "*Kumme*, lie with me, my *frau*."

"But what will your parents think, and Simon?"

He grinned. "Simon's currying the sled horse, Mamm is rebraiding her hair, and Daed is dozing in front of the fire. Any other protests?"

She rose to her full, slight height and straightened her spine, which pushed her breasts out delightfully. "I am not protesting. I know my duty as a wife."

"Duty?" he scoffed. "Duty on the second day of our marriage?" He made himself take on a discouraged expression. "And to think that I believed you enjoyed our, um—time on the floor."

She laughed then, moving toward him. "I suppose I do sound a bit prudish. I expect it's only the second year of marriage before a wife may mention duty."

He enjoyed her teasing and gave her a wolfish smile. "My love, so long as I have will in my body, what we do together will never be duty to you, and never be less than all the pleasure I can give."

"Is that a promise?" she breathed as he caught her close.

He kissed her until she felt like melting beeswax inside and would have lain with him anywhere.

"That, Laurel Beider, is my word of honor."

CHAPTER 16

"I tell you, Luke, it feels like Christmas Eve already," June called from the kitchen.

Luke walked away from the tree where Lucy was hanging paper chains. "I know what you mean." He smiled at his sister. "What are you making for the dinner I sprang on you?"

June sniffed. "I fancy I'm about ready for anything that comes my way in the kitchen—Pork chops, mashed potatoes, gravy, corn off the cob, pickled beets, raisin pie, and hot cider."

Luke grinned. "Sounds *gut*."

"It smells *gut* too, Aenti June," Lucy called. "Me and Friend are hungry."

"Well, you won't have to wait long, Lucy. Here they come." Luke hurried to the front door as the sound of sleigh bells rang out in the dark air. *I still cannot believe I'm going to greet John—John Beider, after all these years. It seems too gut to be true . . . but that is how Derr Herr works—what we least expect and when we least expect it.*

Luke went out on the porch to take Ellie's arm as she balanced a huge casserole of baked beans and molasses. Laurel and Matthew followed arm in arm, and then Simon and John. Luke once again took great pleasure in the hand John extended to him, and he returned the handshake with gladness. *Ach, how happy Meg would be to see this . . . but perhaps she did.*

Lucy immediately caught hold of John and declared Friend's intention of sitting next to him at the table. Luke was happy to see the gentle way his old friend treated his younger daughter, and he knew that the Beider *haus* would easily become home for Laurel if John had anything to do with it.

The rooms were filled with merriment as wraps were taken off and boots unlaced, and the tree was admired with fervor.

Then an impulse came over Luke and he caught John's arm as he bent over his bootlaces. "John, *sei se gut*, would you *kumme* out to the wood workshop with me for a quick moment before we eat?"

"Surely." John smiled, bending to pat Lucy's head and promising to return quickly.

Luke led the way outdoors and over to the shop. He turned up several lanterns, then showed John through the shop.

"It's beautiful work you do with wood," John murmured, pausing to finger a carving. "I knew when we were young that you had talent, but didn't imagine this."

"*Danki*," Luke returned soberly. "I know that is not idle praise."

"*Nee*, it's not. I mean it, and I mean to take the time as days go by to speak a lot more things to you, old friend. Things I should have said long ago."

Luke nodded and set the lantern he carried down on a workbench. "Do you remember the last time we spoke?"

"You mean screamed, on my part, don't you?" John recalled with sad remembrance. "I wouldn't hear you out, no matter what you said, and all over a silly shotgun."

Luke turned to a large cabinet nearby and brought out a long, white cloth bag. He laid it on the table in front of John and cleared his throat. "I know we don't usually give gifts until Second Christmas, but this one has been waiting a bit too long for the giving. Merry Christmas, John."

John stared down at the cloth, his heart starting to beat fast. He undid the drawstring slowly and slid the material down to reveal the shotgun inside. For once, he found himself speechless as Luke moved the lantern closer.

"Turn it over," Luke suggested.

John did and saw the legendary Buffalo nickel that old Possum Johnson had carved a space for on the stock, but then John looked closer. He rubbed his eyes and stared again at the fine-grained wood.

Beneath the nickel, carved in perfect penmanship, was his own name and *Christmas—1975*.

"I—I don't understand . . ." John whispered, feeling his eyes well with tears.

"You wouldn't let me explain or I would have told you that I bought the gun to carve it for you as a special surprise for Christmas." Luke's voice was gentle, full of hope.

John put the gun down on the table and caught his old friend in a hearty embrace. "Blamed fool, I was. Forgive me. Forgive me, Luke."

Luke hugged him back. "I already have. And forgive me for not picking a time to tell you the truth over all these years."

John shook his head, his voice catching heavily. "They say it's never too late to do the right thing."

The sudden opening of the workshop door caused the lantern light to dance. Lucy darted inside. "Aenti June says it's suppertime, but wait—*ach*, you two look like . . . friends."

John reached out and caught her within the circle of his arms, drawing her close to her father. "Friends and family—that we are, little one. This Christmas, and for all those Gott allows to *kumme*, that we are."

A PERFECT AMISH CHRISTMAS

JENNIFER BECKSTRAND

CHAPTER 1

"Our grandson Gideon is going to Mexico, and we've got to stop him," Anna Helmuth said as she tied a bright red ribbon around a jar of huckleberry jelly.

Felty, her husband of sixty-three years, shoved a log into the cookstove. "Why would we want to stop him? Mexico sounds mighty nice this time of year."

"Not as nice as spending Christmas in Bonduel with Dorothy Schrock."

"I might agree if I knew who Dorothy Schrock was," Felty said, squinting at his wife as if trying to make sense of what she was hinting at.

"Now, Felty. Dorothy lives not ten miles down the road."

"These days I don't get much farther than down my own lane."

Anna picked up another jelly jar. "She's that nice young lady who is cousins with Ada Stutzman, who is a cousin to Gideon."

Felty stood up straight and scratched his head. "Wouldn't that make her our granddaughter?"

"Of course not, Felty dear. Gideon's *mamm* Abigail is our daughter, so Gideon is our grandson."

"*Jah*, I know that."

"Gideon is on Ada's *dat's* side and Dorothy is on Ada's *mamm's* side. Gideon and Ada are cousins, and Ada and Dorothy are cousins, but we're not related to Ada, and Gid isn't related to Dorothy."

"*Gute.* For a minute I thought I'd forgotten one of our grand-children," Felty said.

A column of wrinkles appeared between Anna's eyebrows. "I'm starting to wonder about your memory, Felty. I'm helping Dorothy make a Christmas quilt for her *mamm.* She came to our house twice last week. You sat in your recliner and shot the breeze with her for twenty minutes."

Felty scratched his head again. "Are you talking about Dottie?"

"Oh, thank goodness. I thought for a minute you were getting demented."

"You can't blame me for being confused. I've never heard you call her Dorothy before. She's a nice girl. As busy as a beaver yet."

Anna nodded vigorously. "So you see why we must convince Gideon to come to Bonduel instead of Mexico for Christmas."

"*Why* do we want to convince our grandson to come to Bonduel?"

Anna smiled as if she was sharing a delightful secret. "He's got to marry Dottie Schrock, that's why."

Felty finished loading his wood and closed the door to the fire-box in the cookstove. "Annie-girl, you're not thinking of making another match, are you? You're already working on Tyler Yoder and Beth. One match at a time is enough, don't you think?"

Anna pinched the ribbon between the scissors blade and her thumb, sliding the dull blade the length of the ribbon and turning the ribbon into a bouncy curlicue. The jelly jars were to be sold at the Christmas bazaar next week. She held it out for Felty to see. "Isn't that charming?"

"Anna, you are the charmingest girl I know. But what about Dottie and Gid?"

"Oh, Felty. I'm so pleased that you're worried about them. What should we do about Dottie and Gid?"

"We don't have to do anything. Let Gideon go to Mexico in peace," Felty said.

Anna scolded her husband with her eyes. "We most certainly will not. He and Dottie are perfect for each other."

"I'm sure Gideon would be glad to know you're so concerned about his love life."

"Just because our daughter and son-in-law are going to Mexico doesn't mean Abigail and Dan have to take Gid with them. Gideon wants to be here in Bonduel celebrating Christmas with his cousins," Anna said.

"Are you sure about that?"

"Of course. He'd much rather be falling in love with Dottie than sitting on some muggy Mexico beach wishing for a white Christmas."

Felty gave in. "I'm sure he would. But I don't know how you'll convince him of that."

Anna tapped her finger to her lips, deep in thought before her face lit up like a jumbo-size propane lantern. "Felty, how would you like a new pair of snowshoes for Christmas?"

"I thought you were going to get me that manure spreader from the Sears catalog."

"I've changed my mind."

Felty stroked his horseshoe beard. "I ain't never been snow-shoeing before."

"Perfect. Gid won't be able to resist."

"Resist what?" Felty said.

"You'll see. I'll write Abigail a letter immediately. They're leaving for Mexico in less than two weeks." Anna's eyes twinkled with the delights of a thousand Christmases. "It's going to be a wonderful-*gute* holiday."

Felty wrapped his arm around Anna's waist. "As long as I'm with you, Annie, it couldn't be anything but."

CHAPTER 2

Mamm gasped and clapped her hand over her mouth.

"Bad news?" asked Gid, looking up from his breakfast and flinching in alarm at the expression on Mamm's face as she read her letter.

"*Ach, du lieva*, Gid! Your *mammi* is going to worry me into a heart condition yet."

Dat didn't seem quite so concerned as he scooped another helping of hash browns onto his plate. "What's the matter, Abigail? Did your *mamm* accidentally give everyone in the district food poisoning again?"

Mamm arched an eyebrow and glared at Dat. "Oh, Daniel, of course not."

"*Gute.* I don't think anyone at *gmay* will ever eat tripe stew again—as if they ever wanted to eat it in the first place."

"So what happened with Mammi?" Gid asked. He had a soft spot for his lovable grandmother, who sent him mittens every winter and cooked bad-tasting food seasoned with plenty of affection.

"Of all the crazy things, she's buying your *dawdi* a pair of snowshoes for Christmas."

"That doesn't sound like such a bad gift," Dat said.

"It is if he actually tries to use them," Mamm insisted. "Listen to this." Her eyes found the troubling part of Mammi's letter. "*Felty will want to go exploring the minute he tries on his new snowshoes. I'm hoping he won't get lost in the woods or fall into a lake or some other such nonsense. I know I worry too much, but I'd feel so much better if Felty had someone like Gid watching out for him on his first snowshoeing trip. Gid camps and fishes and snowshoes all the time. He practically lives in the woods. What a wonderful-gute grandson he is. Tell him I'm sending a hug with this note.*" Mamm held out the letter and waved it toward Gid. "A lot of good a hug will do us if Dat breaks his neck."

"Dawdi shouldn't take up snowshoeing," Gid said. "He's eighty-five years old."

Mamm smirked. "Oh, he thinks he can do anything."

"Write to your *mamm* and tell her to get your dat a pair of slippers instead," Dat said.

Mamm massaged that spot just above her right eyebrow where a headache was surely starting. "She wouldn't pay me any heed. She and Dat refuse to behave like old people."

Gid took the letter and read the important parts. Mammi had sent him a hug, for goodness sake. A hug. Her affection tugged at his heart. He couldn't leave Dawdi at the mercy of a pair of snowshoes. "Maybe I should go to Bonduel for Christmas."

Mamm sighed, and the tension seemed to slide off her shoulders. "Oh, *denki*, Gid. I'd feel so much better."

"And forget about Mexico?" Dat said.

"Keeping Dawdi out of the hospital is more important than Mexico." Gid glanced at Dat. "Unless you want me to be with you."

Dat shoveled some scrambled eggs into this mouth. "It's just nasal surgery so I can breath better at night. The doctor says it should cure my sleep apnea. The surgery's routine and quick. Besides, your *mamm* will be there. I planned on you being at the beach most of the time anyway. Won't you feel bad missing the beach?"

Gid grunted dismissively. "Ice fishing is better than the beach."

Mamm finally relaxed enough to take a sip of coffee. "You'll have to stay with Endie Elsie and Onkel Joe. Beth and little Toby are at Mammi and Dawdi's house."

Gid smiled. "Even better. Junior and I can go snow caving."

Mamm reached over and patted Gid on the cheek. "You're such a *gute* boy to give up your Christmas in Mexico."

Gid shrugged off her praise. "It'll feel more like Christmas with the snow. I'll have a wonderful-*gute* time snowshoeing with Dawdi and caroling with Uncle Joe and Aunt Elsie. It may turn out to be the best Christmas ever."

CHAPTER 3

Did anyone truly appreciate how hard it was to fashion poinsettias out of frosting?

Dottie Schrock kept her hands steady as she put the finishing touches on the homemade cream puffs for her Christmas party. She took shallow breaths so not even the slight rise and fall of her chest would nudge her arms a fraction of an inch and possibly ruin her delectable creations. With a pastry bag of cherry-red frosting, she carefully piped five tiny petals in between each pair of green frosting leaves, creating a charming miniature poinsettia on the top of each cream puff.

Holding her breath, she squeezed out the last petal and stepped back to admire her work. She could already imagine the compliments and squeals of delight from her friends and her *mamm* when they saw her Christmas cream puffs.

Look at those snacks. You are so talented!

They look too beautiful to eat.

Dottie, you shouldn't have gone to so much work.

Aunt Elsie came into the kitchen and slipped her arm around Dottie's shoulder. "The cream puffs look wonderful-*gute*. Everybody will want to look at them instead of eat them." Gray streaked Aunt Elsie's chestnut hair, and the lines around her mouth indicated she'd spent much of her life smiling. Dottie wanted to be just like her someday.

Dottie did her best to think humble thoughts. The cream puffs did look delectable, but she shouldn't be proud. She had spent all this time on them because Mamm deserved the best Christmas ever. And Dottie was determined to see that everything down to the last leaf on the last poinsettia was perfect.

That's why she had carefully planned her Christmas party, hand-picking twenty people to attend. Eight boys and eight girls, plus Mamm and Dat and Aunt Elsie and Uncle Joe. In her head, she'd already formed *die youngie* into couples. Not that anyone would necessarily couple up, but she had the perfect number of boys and girls in case they wanted to.

And there would be an even number of people to play Mamm's favorite Christmas game. The game would only work with an even number, and Dottie was determined to make it perfect for Mamm.

The party was only the beginning of what she had planned for Mamm's special Christmas holiday. Dottie had a few more stitches to put into the Christmas quilt she was making, and her siblings had been drilled on their parts for the family's Christmas Day program. Tomorrow she would bake stollen, a special holiday bread, and *lebkuchen*, and decorate the house with pine boughs and red ribbon—all the things Mamm used to do before she got sick. It would be the best Christmas the family had ever celebrated.

Dottie's cousin and best friend, Ada, came skipping into the kitchen like a seven-year-old and threw her arms around Aunt Elsie. "Mamm, did you see the veggie tray Dottie made? It looks like a wreath."

"Does it now?"

"She trimmed the broccoli and formed the little trees in the shape of a circle and decorated the top with cherry tomatoes and jicama slices shaped like stars. It looks so festive."

"Our Dottie never does anything halfway."

Dottie squeezed the leftover frosting into a plastic dish and put it in the fridge. "I just want it to be nice for my *mamm*."

Aunt Elsie gave her a squeeze. "Bless you for wanting to give her a happy Christmas. You're a wonderful-*gute* daughter."

Ada reached out and dusted some flour from Dottie's cheek.

"Your *mamm* will be so happy. How could anybody have a bad time with poinsettia cream puffs and bell-shaped Rice Krispies treats? She'll love all of it."

"I hope so." Dottie laid five cream puffs on a paper plate and set it aside. Tomorrow morning, she'd take them to her shut-in neighbor across the street.

"I'm glad you decided to have the party at our house," Aunt Elsie said. "We have more room, and your mamm won't be tired out by a passel of guests at your house."

"But you get all the mess," Dottie said, giving her aunt a peck on the cheek. "*Denki* for hosting."

"Anything for you, Dottie."

"What else can I do to help?" Ada asked Dottie. "We've got one hour yet."

"Will you check on the napkins? Junior folded them, but he's not always so careful."

Dottie shut her mouth right quick as Junior strolled into the room. Junior was Ada's brother, younger by a year, and too big for his britches.

"I'm not always careful about what?"

"Everything," Ada said.

When Dottie had informed him that he wouldn't be able to fold napkins properly, Junior had insisted on taking the task, rejecting help from anyone. If a girl could do it, then, he assured her, he could do it with his eyes closed. Three times Dottie had showed him how to pleat the middle of the napkin so it looked like a bowtie. He'd gotten all indignant about it, insisting he was capable of folding a few measly napkins. Then he had told her to go away and leave him alone while he folded. Sometimes that stubborn streak of his tried her patience something terrible.

"Did you do the napkins?" Dottie asked, trying to act as if she had all the confidence in the world that Junior had actually finished the task.

"*Jah*," Junior said, his mouth twitching into a self-congratulatory smirk. "But the bow thing looked stupid, so I just folded them in half."

Ada gasped and her mouth fell open. "Junior, that's not how Dottie wanted them done. You've ruined everything."

Junior grunted at his sister as if she didn't even deserve a response.

Dottie took a deep breath and told herself to be patient. With few exceptions, nobody did things quite to her standards, and Junior's efforts were always well below her standards. She would hold her tongue. Hopefully, she could fix the napkins before the party started, but she must leave herself enough time to arrange the cookies into a charming star pattern on the plate. If she didn't, the cookies would look awfully plain sitting next to her tower of Rice Krispies treats.

Dottie did a quick intake of breath as Junior reached out to snatch one of her cream puffs. Ada slapped his hand away. "Not until the party, Junior. Can't you see how pretty the plate looks? You're going to ruin it. You're going to ruin everything."

Junior held his hands out innocently. "Somebody needs to sample them. What if they taste bad? You don't want all the guests gagging at the party, do you?"

"They taste just fine," Aunt Elsie said, taking Junior by the shoulders and steering him in the direction of the hallway. "Go make sure the sidewalk is shoveled. It's started to snow again."

Junior grabbed a piece of chocolate from the bowl on the table as his mamm pushed him out of the kitchen. "The sidewalks are clear, and someone is at the door for Dottie."

Ada threw up her hands. "And *when* were you going to tell us that? Three hours from now?"

"I just told you."

"You've been shooting the breeze with us for five minutes," Ada said. "Whoever is at the door is probably frozen to death."

Aunt Elsie propped her hands on her hips. "Oy anyhow, Junior, sometimes I don't know where your head is."

Junior popped the chocolate into his mouth and shrugged his shoulders, grinning unashamedly. "Right on top of my neck, where it's always been."

Dottie took another deep breath. Junior loved to raise the hackles of the female members of his family. "It wonders me if I should go see to the door."

"*Jah*, go," Aunt Elsie said, waving her hands to hurry her along, "and apologize to our guest for Junior's rudeness."

"Who is it, Junior?" Ada asked.

Junior pressed his lips together and his eyes flashed as if he were keeping a great secret. "You'll see."

Dottie walked down the hallway to the front entryway and stopped in her tracks. Her stomach fell to her toes and shot back up again as if she were riding an unpleasant roller coaster.

Hat in hand, Gid Stutzman leaned against the doorjamb, his brow cocked and his mouth twisted into a wry grin. His loose brown curls fell across his forehead and his dark eyes flashed with a mixture of amusement and annoyance.

He wasn't supposed to be here. He should have received Ada's letter a week ago.

Dottie's stomach did a double back flip and three somersaults. It had been two years since she had seen Gideon Stutzman and he'd definitely grown up. His shoulders and arms had filled out nicely, and that square jaw and tan face made her heart flutter even as her stomach kept bouncing. But his appearance didn't matter. She'd always think of him as Junior's annoying teenage cousin who never stopped teasing her and made a point to make a pest of himself.

He'd sure enough received Ada's letter, because it dangled casually in his fingers like a used tissue. She swallowed hard. Oh, he was annoyed all right. And it was a good guess the letter had something to do with it.

"Dottie Schrock, I would have a word with you about this letter."

Her stomach stopped its roller coaster ride and lodged in her throat. "I'm wonderful busy right now," she managed to squeeze out.

He nodded. "Oh, I'm sure you are." His other brow rose to meet the first one. "Getting ready for the party I'm not invited to."

Dottie feigned innocence. Either that or die of embarrassment. She'd rather not pass away at the young age of twenty. How had Gid found out about the party? "What do you mean?"

"Hmm," he said, studying her as if he were a cat ready to pounce on an unsuspecting mouse. He looked as if he wasn't about to let her get away with anything. "Let's see here." He unfolded Ada's letter. "*Dear Gid, We are so happy you will be spending Christmas with us while your parents are in Mexico. Junior wants to go camping with you so you can show him how to make an ice cave.* And so on and so on," he said, his gaze scrolling to the bottom of the page. "Ah, here it is. *It wonders me if you could postpone your arrival until Christmas Eve.*" He glanced at Dottie.

Her face felt hot, as if she'd been standing next to the roaring wood stove all afternoon. She resisted the urge to squirm and tried to look mildly interested even though she knew what came next. She'd helped Ada write the letter.

Gid kept reading. "*Dottie is sure we're going to be extra busy up until Christmas, and we don't want you to feel ignored. I hope you understand how busy we will be. We really think it's better if you don't come until Christmas Eve. Or maybe even Christmas Day. Love, Ada.*"

"It wondered me why Ada was so concerned about my arrival date."

"You read that part. She was afraid you'd feel ignored. Everyone is too busy to entertain you."

Gid's eyes flashed, and he looked as if he wanted to laugh. "*Jah,* I'm sure that was the first thought that came into my cousin's head when I told her I was coming."

Gid was a cousin on the other side of Ada's family. Dottie was very glad that she and cocky Gid Stutzman were of no relation whatsoever.

He held the letter up like a stop sign. "When I saw your name in her letter, I got suspicious."

Gid *would* get suspicious. He probably couldn't fathom why anyone wouldn't be eager to have him at her party. Any party. No doubt, he thought he was everybody's favorite. Dottie pursed her lips. Well, he was not her favorite.

"Ada and I are best friends. Are you saying she's never mentioned me in a letter before?"

Gid smirked. "When I got Ada's letter, I wrote to Junior. He told me that you were throwing a party on the very day I had planned on coming into town."

Dottie resisted the urge to growl. Junior couldn't fold napkins, and he couldn't keep his big mouth shut. At the moment, he was not on her good list. Truth was, he never had been.

Gid narrowed his eyes and stared her down. "You don't want me at your party," he said. The very idea seemed amusing to him.

Dottie thought she might suffocate with embarrassment. Though she hadn't seen him for two years, she remembered how blunt Gid could be, and his wide grin only made it worse.

Boys! Tilting her head back, she clamped her eyes shut and clenched her teeth. "Okay. You're right. I asked Ada to write and tell you to come a day later than planned."

He seemed on the verge of laughing. "You wrote the letter for her, didn't you?"

"Maybe," she grudgingly admitted, wondering if her face was as red as the poinsettia frosting.

Her admission pushed him over the edge. He threw back his head and laughed. "I thought so, Dottie Schrock."

"Thank you so much for laughing at my humiliation." He'd done it before. She didn't know why it irritated her now.

That brought him up short. For the first time since he'd arrived, he lost the aggravating smile. If she didn't know better, she'd think he almost looked contrite. "I'm not laughing at you. Honest." His lips curved upward again as if he found it impossible to keep from grinning. "I'm laughing at how clever I was to figure it out."

Dottie ground her teeth together until she thought they might crack. Gid was nothing if not arrogant. But the lack of an invitation to her party must have taken his confidence down a peg or two. She didn't want to feel smug about that, but she couldn't help herself.

She pasted a look of sympathy on her face. "You're upset that I didn't invite you to the party. I'm sorry that I hurt your feelings."

He ran his fingers through his curly hair. "I'm not upset about your party. I'm irritated that you tried to meddle in my life. You might be pretty to look at, but you are a fussy busybody."

In vain, Dottie tried to pretend Gid hadn't just called her pretty. What did he mean by saying such a thing to his cousin's cousin when he hadn't seen her in two years? He was angry with her, for goodness sake. She willed herself to calm down before her cheeks burst into flame. They felt hot enough. "I am not a busybody. You should appreciate that I wanted to spare your feelings."

His grin drooped a little at the corners. "I'm perfectly capable of governing my own feelings. And making my own choices, thank you."

Dottie slumped her shoulders. "I just . . . I didn't know, and I couldn't have been sure you wouldn't be offended."

"I am offended." A grin tempered his rebuke. "No harm done as long as you promise not to poke your cute nose where you shouldn't."

He thought she had a cute nose? Dottie gave a little cough and remembered why she was standing in the entry arguing with Gid Stutzman. "My *mamm* got sick last Christmas."

"*Jah*, I'm sorry," he said with sincere compassion.

"Well, she's feeling better all the time. I wanted this Christmas to be perfect since Mamm and the *kinner* missed out on one last year."

"And your Christmas will only be perfect if I don't come to your party?" His lips twitched playfully, and he pretended to think about it. "Makes perfect sense to me."

Dottie grabbed the offensive letter from his hand and swatted him lightly on the shoulder with it.

He stepped back and raised his hands to parry another attack. "Hey, no violence."

"Ada and I planned the party before she knew you were coming. We had already invited certain people because they are close to my *mamm*. And it has to be an even number because games are only fun with an even number playing."

He grabbed Ada's letter back and waved it in front of her face. "I suspect that's not the only reason you don't want me at your party."

She felt as if he'd backed her into a corner with that gaze of his. "Okay," she said, as her throat dried out like an old piece of toast. She'd already insulted him. Might as well be perfectly honest about her feelings. "If you must know, you're annoying and immature. I was afraid you'd ruin my party."

The playful quirk of his lips was not the reaction she expected. "You think *I'm* annoying, and yet you're letting Junior in."

"He lives here."

"This is about those pies, isn't it?"

Dottie bit her bottom lip. Several Christmases ago, Gid, showing off as usual, had picked up two of Dottie's Christmas pies and tried to balance them on his index fingers. The pies had ended up on the floor, Dottie had ended up in tears, and Gid had ended up mopping floors on Christmas morning. "Those were the first pies I ever made," she said.

"Dottie, that was six years ago. I was a *deerich* sixteen-year-old."

She lifted her chin, frustrated that she felt the need to defend herself to Gid Stutzman. "And I was a tender fourteen-year-old."

He held out his hands in surrender as a doubtful yet cocky grin spread across his face. "I'm really sorry."

"You enjoyed embarrassing me."

"I used to be a teenage boy, Dottie. I liked to tease every girl who came within ten feet. Can you show me a little mercy for that?"

"I suppose," Dottie said, folding her arms across her waist. She cleared her throat. "But I still don't want you at my party."

He huffed out a breath, seemingly unimpressed. "Why didn't you explain all this in your letter? I am a reasonable person. No need to try to trick me into things." Gid reached for his extra large suitcase sitting on the porch. "I'm really fun in a crowd."

"This party is really important to me."

He smiled mischievously, as if he had no intention of letting her meddle with his choices.

She let out a dejected sigh. If Gid wanted to come to the party, he was going to come, no matter what she said. She couldn't very well grab his arm and force him out of the house. He was arrogant enough to believe that his mere presence would make the party fun. Her heart sank. "What does it matter? The napkins are ruined anyway," she said. So were her dreams of the best Christmas party her *mamm* had ever had.

Aunt Elsie appeared in the entryway and spread her arms wide for a hug. "Gideon! We didn't expect you until tomorrow. What a nice surprise."

Gid crumpled Ada's letter into a tight ball, stuffed it into his coat pocket, and hugged his aunt. "I got the last seat in the van," he said.

"*Cum reu.* Come in and shut the door. You're letting all the cold air in." She patted his wide shoulders then pinched his upper arm. "Look at you. More like your *dat* all the time. And what have you been doing to work yourself into all those muscles?"

"Nothing really. I cut and heft logs all day."

"That'll do it." Elsie put her arm around Dottie. "You remember my nephew on the other side, don't you?"

"*Jah*," Dottie murmured, wishing she'd never laid eyes on him.

Aunt Elsie clapped her hands. "Well, this is a wonderful-*gute* happening. Now Gid can come to our party." She smiled at Gid. "Dottie's been planning it for weeks."

Gid shook his head. "I wasn't invited."

Elsie put her arm around him and looked at Dottie, not guessing how unwelcome Gid was to her. "You don't mind, do you, Dottie?"

Dottie shrugged. She feared she'd burst into tears if she spoke.

Aunt Elsie beamed. "You always make gatherings so fun, Gid. We couldn't have a party without you."

Gid glanced at Dottie with a hint of a tease shining in his eyes. "I think I'm going to have to miss the party tonight."

Dottie's hopes fluttered back to life. Was he really giving up on the party or just poking fun at her? She held her breath and kept a straight face.

"I hurt my big toe ice fishing yesterday, and I can barely stand."

"Stuff and nonsense, Gid," Aunt Elsie said, brushing away such a ridiculous notion. "You can sit the whole time. We've plenty of chairs."

How did someone hurt his toe ice fishing?

"*Nae*, but *denki* anyway. I think I'll soak my toe and then hit the hay early."

"Of course you won't," said Aunt Elsie. "Dottie, help me talk him into it."

Gid held up his hand, laughter alight in his blue eyes. "No use, Aunt Elsie. I'm not coming." He turned his face away from Aunt Elsie and winked at Dottie. She thought she might melt like a snowman in May. Or probably more like a snowman in July. She took back every unkind feeling she'd harbored for Gid Stutzman.

"All right, Gid. If you don't feel up to it," Aunt Elsie said. "*Cum*. I'll show you where you're sleeping."

As Elsie led him away, he craned his neck to glance at Dottie. "Sorry to disappoint you," he said, a charming smile stealing across his face.

She involuntarily grinned back and stifled a giggle as he adopted an exaggerated limp. Had he fibbed to his aunt?

Now she kind of wished he were coming to the party. He might be irritatingly cocky, but he had a reputation for being extra fun at a gathering.

If only she could uninvite Junior.

CHAPTER 4

The grandfather clock in the front room chimed six o'clock just as Dottie poured ice into the punch bowl. Her little dust-up with Gid Stutzman had cost her fifteen minutes, and after mixing the punch and helping Ada with the hot wassail and warm cocoa, she'd run out of time to fix the napkins. She hoped Mamm wouldn't notice.

The front door opened, and Mamm and Dat ambled into the house. Mamm wore her customary black coat with a fire-engine-red scarf and her black bonnet. Dat looked equally festive with a forest green scarf and a nose bright red from the cold.

Mamm smiled. She still had a gray cast to her face and walked with a cane, but the doctors said that the cancer was gone. Dottie was overjoyed that she was walking again.

"Here is my long-lost daughter," Mamm said. "You left before I awoke this morning. I didn't even get to say good morning."

Dottie motioned to the eats table spread with all the desserts she had made today. All things considered, it had turned out nearly perfect. "What do you think?"

"Wonderful-*gute*," Mamm said. "Look at the cream puffs. They must have taken you hours."

Dottie's heart swelled. She'd known Mamm would like the cream puffs. "Worth all the trouble for that look on your face."

Mamm gave Dottie a firm hug. "I'm just eager to spend time with you tonight."

"Me too. It's going to be *gute* fun."

Dottie frowned as she glanced at the place where the napkins were supposed to go. Junior hadn't even had the sense to bring them in from the kitchen. Probably a *gute* thing. They'd only mess up the beauty of her table. If she could manage a perfect party without napkins, she would leave the ugly things in the kitchen.

But cream puffs were too messy to do without napkins.

Ada marched into the front room with the napkin basket in her hand. Thank goodness for Ada. At least one of her cousins paid attention to the important things. "Aunt Saloma," she said, revealing the deep dimple on her cheek. "It is so *gute* to see you. How are you feeling?"

Mamm patted Ada's cheek. "Happy to be getting out after being cooped up so long. Oh, look at those darling napkins. Dottie, you thought of everything."

Darling napkins? Not by any stretch of the imagination. Dottie looked down. In the basket sat a stack of perfectly pleated bowtie napkins secured with red ribbons. She looked at her cousin and beamed. "Ada, thank you."

"Don't thank me," Ada said. "Gid dragged Junior up to his room, and they folded together, although Gid did most of the folding and Junior did all the complaining."

Dottie opened her mouth and closed it again. Gid Stutzman, the boy who hadn't been invited to her party and was too cocky for his own good, had folded her napkins? The guilt wrapped itself around her chest, and she felt her face get warm. Was it too late to kick Junior out of the party and find a quick replacement?

A knock at the door. She couldn't spare time to nurse her conscience. It would take all her energy to host her grand party. Fannie Kiem and her sister Frieda arrived first, almost giddy with excitement.

"Oh, Dottie," Fannie said, unwrapping the scarf from around her neck. "I'm so excited for your party."

"Adam Burkholder is coming," Dottie said.

Fannie squeaked and grabbed Dottie's arm. "I know. That's why I'm so excited."

Dottie took Frieda's coat. "Perry Newswenger is coming too."

Frieda sighed loudly. "*Denki* for trying, but Perry likes his cell phone and nothing else."

Perry had not yet been baptized, and he seemed glued his new phone. He had over a hundred games on it. "He's not bringing his phone tonight," Dottie said.

"He's not?"

She nodded. "I wrote a personal note on the bottom of his invitation."

Frieda raised her eyebrows. "Maybe I'll get a little attention after all."

Hopefully all Frieda's dreams would come true tonight. It was going to be that kind of party.

Dottie made a point to greet all the guests as they arrived. It may have been Aunt Elsie's house, but Dottie was the hostess, and she was the one who had to make sure that everyone had a wonderful-*gute* time.

By a quarter after the hour, nearly everyone had arrived. Adam Burkholder and Mark Hoover. Sarah Nelson and Marvin Eicher. By Dottie's count, only four people unaccounted for.

Just as she thought about them, someone else knocked on the door.

She opened it eagerly. Her last four invitees stood on the porch. Suzy and Emily Miller, Roy Kanagy, and Mahlon Graber looked like a charming group of carolers.

Then Dottie nearly fell backwards. Erla Schmucker poked her head from behind Roy. "Hi, Dottie. I hope you don't mind."

Grinning like tabby cat, Suzy brushed the snow from her bonnet, stepped into the house, and unbuttoned her coat. The rest followed her. "I told Erla she'd could come along with us tonight. She's heard all about your famous cream puffs."

Dottie stretched a smile across her face and felt as empty as an abandoned well. All her careful plans had just blown out the window because Suzy had the nerve to bring an uninvited guest. She couldn't very well ask Erla to leave.

Could she?

No. No. Mustn't even consider such a thing. Erla's feelings couldn't come at the expense of her perfect party.

Right?

Right.

She couldn't do it, even though she was sorely tempted.

Dottie deflated like a balloon with a slow leak. They had to play Mamm's favorite game, and that favorite game required an even number of people.

She knew what she had to do.

"Ada," she said dully. "Will you get the door if other people come?" Other uninvited guests.

"Of course, silly. It's my house."

Dottie paused at the eats table long enough to pull a candy cane from the little tin can she'd decorated with sparkles. A peace offering. She hoped Gid would accept it.

She trudged up the stairs. He'd gloat, of course, but what other choice did she have? There simply must be even numbers at Mamm's party.

She steeled herself against his reaction and prepared to eat a little crow. She'd eat a whole flock if he'd just agree to come down to the party he wasn't invited to. He'd folded the napkins. Maybe he would be eager to see how people admired them.

She knocked lightly a couple of times, almost afraid he'd answer it. Then she threw all caution to the wind and gave the door five good, strong raps.

He opened the door, and with a curiously amused look, propped his hand against the doorjamb two feet above his head. Dressed in his coat, snow pants, winter beanie, and heavy gloves, he looked as if he was ready for a snowball fight.

"Is your room cold?"

"*Nae*," he said. "I'm going snowshoeing."

"It's dark outside," she said, stating the obvious. Wouldn't he rather attend her really fun party than go snowshoeing?

"The moon reflects off the snow. I can see well enough."

"It's cloudy. There is no moon."

"I'll take a flashlight," he said, with a casual shrug of his shoulders. "I'm not fond of being cooped up in this room all night."

Feeling worse by the minute, she swallowed the dust in her throat and held out the candy cane. "I . . . I brought you this."

One corner of his mouth quirked upward as he took her offering and slipped it into the pocket of his snow pants. "Isn't there a party going on downstairs?"

"Thank you for folding my napkins."

He bowed his head in an uncharacteristic show of modesty and burst into a wide grin. "No thanks necessary. It's a talent I share freely with others."

That teased a smile out of her despite how sheepish she felt. "I didn't mean to meddle in your life."

"*Jah*, you did." He tempered his words with a smile.

"And I'm sorry for disliking you so much."

He shrugged. "I destroyed your pies. You have good reason."

They stood staring at each other, Gid eyeing her curiously, Dottie trying to work up the courage to ask him.

He pointed down the stairs and broke the silence. "Don't you have a party?"

"That's the thing," she stammered. "Erla Schmucker showed up."

"Does she smell bad?"

"What?"

He chuckled softly. "Is that why you've left your own party?"

Dottie tried to join in his merriment but couldn't muster anything better than deep mortification. "Erla wasn't exactly invited."

He raised his eyebrows. "Oh."

Jah. Oh.

"I know you planned on snowshoeing." She nibbled on her fingernail and studied his face. "And after all that's happened, I shouldn't even have the nerve to ask, but please will you come to my party?"

She waited for him burst into laughter or at least fix that cocky, self-assured grin on his face and say something clever that would make her feel about three inches tall. She'd certainly brought it upon herself.

Instead, the empathy in his voice knocked her completely off-kilter. "I'd be happy to. We want it to be extra *gute* for your *mamm*."

"Oh, okay. Yes. For my *mamm*." Had he noticed how she had to scrape her jaw off the floor?

He peeled off his gloves and pulled the beanie from his head, then slipped out of his coat and snow pants and threw everything on the bed in the small guest room. "I have to warn you," he said, as he stepped into the hall and shut the door, "I usually win all the games. So if you don't like to lose, you better not play."

"I usually win all the games," Dottie countered. "So maybe you better watch out."

"We'll just see about that."

They sauntered down the stairs together, Dottie feeling almost overwhelmed with Gid's uncommon kindness. "What about your sore toe?"

A teasing glint flashed in his eyes. "I can play through the pain."

"It might give me an unfair advantage in the games," Dottie said.

"With me as your opponent, you'll need all the advantage you can get."

CHAPTER 5

Gid pulled to a stop in front of Dottie Schrock's white brick house. Last night's snow clouds had disappeared, and the sky looked as if someone had taken a paintbrush to it with cerulean blue paint. The winter air was crisp, like a Granny Smith apple, and he loved how it sliced against his face when he spurred the horse into a trot.

He hadn't warned Dottie he was coming this morning. She seemed like the kind of girl who wasn't fond of surprises, and that's why he'd decided to surprise her. He couldn't resist the way she wrinkled her cute nose when something flustered her.

As soon as he'd gotten Junior's letter last week, he'd been annoyed enough to come to Bonduel a day early and make sure Dottie knew he didn't appreciate her meddling in his life. But he hadn't counted on the difference two years had made. The last time he'd seen Dottie, she had been a skinny eighteen-year-old—one he only briefly interacted with at Onkel Joe's Christmas parties and one who was too young to be interesting to a grown man of twenty years. At least that how he had seen himself.

But the minute he'd laid eyes on her yesterday, he'd felt as unsteady as a leaky canoe on the lake during a thunderstorm. Before she had come to the door, he had been annoyed with her. He hadn't expected her to throw him entirely off balance with that nose thing she did.

It was very kind of Onkel Joe to let him borrow the sleigh. After last night, he wanted to see Dottie again in the worst way. He couldn't seem to keep from smiling when she was close. Plus, he wanted to find out if he had the power to befuddle her the way she had befuddled him.

He squinted in the bright sun as he jumped out of the sleigh and bounded up the porch steps to Dottie's front door.

Dottie's sister, probably twelve years old by now, answered the door. "Hey," Gid said, taking off his hat and giving her one of his best smiles. "Diana? Is your name Diana?"

She smiled to reveal a mouth full of braces. "Hi, Gid. Dottie said you came to her party last night."

"You remember me?"

"I remember. You're Junior and Ada's cousin." She tilted her head to one side as she gazed at him. "You took Junior hunting for Bigfoot two years ago."

The Bigfoot hunt. He'd never live that down. "*I* was snowshoeing. Junior was looking for Bigfoot."

"He still goes out every weekend to search."

Gid winced. "I know. I regret ever planting that seed in Junior's head." Bigfoot and snipes. He'd never been able to convince his cousin they didn't exist.

"Dottie says Junior isn't the sharpest tool in the shed," Diana said before clapping her hand over her mouth. "Don't tell anybody I said that. Dottie swore me to secrecy. She doesn't usually talk bad about Junior, even when he deserves it."

Gid chuckled. Mostly, Junior was a teenage boy, and boys grew out of that eventually. Gid had. "Is Dottie home?"

"She says you lost every game at the party last night."

Gid dropped his jaw in mock indignation. "I did not. Dottie wasn't keeping score correctly. In golf, the low score is the winner. By that standard, I won every game."

"Ha ha," Diana said as she walked away. "I'll get Dottie."

"Thanks, Diana."

"It's Eva."

"What? I asked you—"

"I didn't want to hurt your feelings."

He shook his head as she walked out of the room. Not making a good impression so far.

Diana, er, Eva came back with Dottie in tow. Her smile was like the sun peeking over the horizon, and Gid forgot to breathe for a second. Her hair was tied up in a blue bandanna, and a smudge of flour dusted that crinkly nose.

"Gid. What are you doing here?"

"I stole Onkel Joe's sleigh."

Her eyebrows lifted half an inch, and a grin twitched at her lips. "Are you running from the police?"

"Okay, I didn't really steal it. I got his full permission. It's a wonderful-*gute* day for a sleigh ride yet."

An attractive blush tinted her cheeks. "You want me to go on a ride with you?"

"The snow is perfect."

She glanced at Eva, and her smile faded. "I'm sorry, Gid. It's Christmas Eve."

"A perfect day for sledding."

"I haven't stuffed the turkey, and I'm the only one who knows how to make stollen and *lebkuchen*."

"I can make *lebkuchen*," Eva said.

Dottie laid a hand on her sister's shoulder. "*Nae*, Eva. It has to be just right, remember? You don't know how to arrange the almonds the way Mamm likes them."

Eva seemed to deflate before Gid's very eyes, but she didn't argue. He suspected it was a conversation they'd had many times.

Gid fingered the brim of his hat. "You *do* owe me a favor for saving your party last night. Erla Schmucker had a very *gute* time, and I let you win every game. And I did it all with a swollen toe."

"You did not let me win, Gid Stutzman. You are simply a very bad hummer."

"But I did put up with the humiliation of having to hum in front of everyone."

Dottie thought about it for a moment, and her lips twitched at the memory. "*Jah*, you did."

"Half an hour?" Gid said.

"I could boil the almonds while you're gone," Eva offered. "I know how to boil almonds."

"I can spare ten minutes," Dottie said.

Gid raised an eyebrow. "Twenty-five."

"Fifteen at the most."

"I feel like an auctioneer," Gid said. "I've got fifteen, who'll give me twenty?"

Dottie folded her arms. "Fifteen is my final offer."

He slumped his shoulders in mock defeat. "That will get us to the end of your lane and back. You drive a hard bargain, Dottie Schrock, but I accept."

She exploded into an irresistible smile that made Gid's heart thud wildly. Their gazes locked, and he couldn't look away from those stunning hazel eyes. He sure was glad Uncle Joe owned a sleigh.

Clearing her throat, Dottie broke eye contact and turned to Eva. "You can skin the almonds."

"Yeah!" Eva said, doing a little jig.

"Pour boiling water over them and let them sit for two minutes. Only two."

"I can do it, Dottie," said Eva. "I will chop them so you won't have to do that when you get home."

Dottie retrieved her coat from the hall closet. "*Nae.* I will chop. You skin."

Eva's countenance fell slightly, but she obviously wasn't the type of girl to wallow in disappointment and was clearly excited to be allowed to help at all. "I'll do a really *gute* job."

Dottie sprouted a doubtful smile. "I know you will. We want the *lebkuchen* to be just the way Mamm likes it. And"—she paused for a fraction of a second—"why don't you look at the recipe and get all the ingredients out of the cupboard and ready so that it will save me time when I return?" She must have noticed her sister's eagerness.

Eva's grin couldn't possible be any wider. "*Jah, jah.* I will do that. Do you want two bags of apricots or one?"

Gid took Dottie's coat and helped her into it. "I just want to be clear that all this talk of *lebkuchen* does not count against my fifteen minutes."

Dottie's eyes sparkled. "Okay then. The timer starts now."

CHAPTER 6

Dottie gripped the side of the sleigh until her knuckles turned white. She'd forgotten that Gid liked to go fast. Two years ago, the last time Gid's family had come to Bonduel for Christmas, they'd all gone sledding at Beechy Hill, where Gid and Junior had built a four-foot-high snow jump. The two boys had taken that jump over and over again, and after a while, Dottie hadn't been able to watch. Their sleds had flown through the air for several feet and most often ended in a spectacular crash at the edge of the trees. Gid was fearless. That's why Junior tagged after him like a puppy whenever Gid came to town.

"Do you think you could slow down?" she squeaked over the sound of the runners cutting through the snow and the muted clip-clop of horse hooves on the frozen road.

Gid widened his eyes in feigned shock. "Slow down? It's only fun if you go fast. Just sit back, close your eyes, and feel the breeze on your face. Tourists pay good money for stuff like this."

"I'm not a tourist."

He glanced at her and smiled. "Will you still give me a tip?"

"Nae. You give very poor service."

Shaking his head in amusement, he pulled up on the reins and slowed the horse to a walk. "Is that better?"

"Much."

"You said I could only have fifteen minutes. I want to make the most of the time."

"I'm sorry. It's just that my *mamm's mamm* made *lebkuchen* every Christmas. I think it will make Mamm really happy if we have *lebkuchen* tomorrow."

He studied her face. "You're really anxious to make it special for her."

"Last year, three days before Christmas, she had surgery. She was so sick, and Dat was busy taking care of her. We children took care of each other. Except for some cookies a neighbor delivered, we didn't celebrate Christmas at all. It's going to be different this year. I'm making stollen and *lebkuchen*, and I have a very special surprise waiting at Anna Helmuth's house. I'm going to pick it up this afternoon."

"Anna, my *mammi*?"

"*Jah*, she and your cousin Beth are very *gute* at sewing."

"My favorite thing about Christmas is being together with family and remembering the Christ child."

She lowered her eyes. "Your parents are in Mexico, and I didn't even want you to come to my party. I'm sorry."

He brushed aside her apology. "Dat needed nasal surgery and this was the only week available. I'll have more fun in Bonduel than I would in a hospital in Mexico over Christmas. Aunt Elsie and Uncle Joe take *gute* care of me, and Uncle Joe was kind enough to let me borrow his sleigh so I could be with a pretty girl on Christmas Eve morning."

"Oh," she teased. "Are you going to give her a sleigh ride too?"

"I only plan on taking one pretty girl for a ride today." He winked at her and laughed. His bold gesture made her feel giddy. If she weren't on such a strict time schedule, his wink would have made her want to leap out of the sleigh and make a snow angel, just for the pure joy of it.

The way he looked at her made her blush all the way to the top of her head. It would be much safer to change the subject. She nudged a brown paper grocery bag at her feet. "What's in the bag?"

"I need to make a delivery to an old friend."

"What kind of delivery?"

He smiled as if it were a great adventure. "He's only a few minutes from here. I wanted to take him a few groceries to tide him over for the holidays. Would you like to come?"

Dottie took a deep breath. She really, really should be getting back. She needed time to put those finishing touches on Mamm's Christmas quilt.

But the brisk wind felt so lovely against her cheeks, and the snow sparkled in the sun like a field of diamonds, and Gid Stutzman smiled at her as if she were the only girl in the whole world.

Gid waited patiently, his hands wrapped casually around the reins, his face turned halfway toward her.

"Okay," she finally said.

He nodded and his lips quirked upward slightly as if he'd anticipated that if he were too happy about it, she'd change her mind.

"But it won't take very long, will it?"

"Only as long as you say." Mischief glinted in his eyes, and he snapped the reins. "But since we're in a hurry, we'll have to go faster."

She caught her breath as the horse sped to a quick trot, pulling them over the snow as if they were flying on a meadow of fluffy clouds. She gripped the side of the sleigh and sat up straight so her face could catch the wind. Exhilaration rendered her breathless. Maybe Gid's preference for speed wasn't so bad after all.

It seemed like they had just started moving fast, when Gid slowed his horse and turned down a snow-packed road. The horse trotted in the direction of an old farmhouse surrounded by a half-dozen bare and snarled oak trees. The exterior of the two-story house was half made of light brown bricks and half of peeling white siding. Icicles hung from the eaves over the porch, indicating several leaks in the rain gutters.

Gid tied the reins, grabbed the grocery bag from the floor, and smiled as if they were about to embark on a marvelous adventure. Dottie tried to push her uneasiness away. She wasn't altogether comfortable with the condition of the house or the property. What had Gid gotten her into?

Gid knocked on the screen door, which tilted slightly to the left, and they waited. When there was no answer, he knocked again, louder this time, and kept that smile in place.

The inside door creaked as if its hinges were two hundred years old. Dottie couldn't see well into the dark house, especially in the brightness of the snow outside, but she could make out an old man with sparse wisps of gray hair and a thin, weathered face behind the screen door.

"Go away," he said, as if just voicing the words made him tired.

Gid nodded to Dottie reassuringly. "Lou, it's me, Gid Stutzman. Remember? I dropped by last summer a couple of times."

"You're just like the rest of 'em. Leave me alone," Lou said, squinting to see through the screen.

"This is my friend Dottie Schrock. We came by to wish you a merry Christmas."

Lou paused briefly and slapped his hand against the screen door handle. The door popped open. "Well, come in then, if you have to," he said, complaining about it.

Dottie decided she'd rather not, but Gid held the door open for her and she had no choice. It wouldn't look very neighborly to turn around and slink off the porch.

A wall of oppressive warmth and the smell of stale laundry accosted her as she walked into the room. Lou eyed her suspiciously before ambling across his living room and easing himself onto a threadbare brown sofa.

Gid nudged her forward, followed her into the house, and shut the door.

The scuffed wood floor was bare except for a small rug that sat directly underneath Lou's feet. Vertical blinds covered the bay window that faced the front of the house, but at least a third of them were either missing or broken. A brown upholstered chair with faded blue flowers matching the old sofa stood under the big window, and a massive upright piano seemed to lean against the wall opposite the bay window. Dust and grit covered every surface, especially the floor, which looked like it hadn't been swept in years.

"You might as well sit down," Lou said, motioning to the chair. Gid plopped next to Lou on the sofa, and Dottie, grateful for the distance between them, sat in the chair.

Lou sat back and rubbed his hand down the side of his gaunt face. "What did you say your name was?"

"Gid Stutzman. And this is Dottie Schrock."

Still frowning persistently, Lou concentrated on Gid's face. "I remember you. You're the Amish boy who brought me the apples."

"Did you like them?"

Lou turned to Dottie and studied her carefully. "You brought a pretty girl with you this time."

Gid's gaze flashed playfully in Dottie's direction. "We came to give you some Christmas groceries."

This news seemed to make Lou very unhappy. He propped his elbows on his knees and laced his shaky fingers together. "Christmas," he said, a lump of bitterness in his voice. "Nobody cares about that. They don't bother coming. They don't even call." His voice cracked, and he looked as if he was about to lose his composure. His pain was so palpable, Dottie could almost hold it in her hands. "It doesn't matter anyway. They'd rather go to Florida."

A deep line of worry appeared between Gid's brows. "Your son?"

The moment of vulnerability passed. Lou cleared his throat and squared his shoulders. "Can't blame 'em. I'd rather go to Florida too."

"So you're not going to see your family for Christmas?" Dottie asked, hiding her disbelief. How could anybody let his father spend his holidays all alone?

"Joanne's in New Mexico and Brent's in Chicago. His kids wanted to do Disney World."

Dottie's heart sank as she looked around the dirty, unloved room and imagined sitting here all alone night after night. She couldn't stand the thought.

She shot from the chair and snatched the grocery bag from Gid's arms. "That's why we came to make you Christmas dinner."

Gid gaped at her as if she'd just folded all her napkins wrong on purpose.

Lou simply looked puzzled. "Christmas dinner?"

Gid had told her there were groceries in the bag. Hopefully she could turn the contents into an adequate meal. She probably couldn't make it fancy enough to be considered a Christmas dinner, but at least Lou might get something hot to eat and a little company. He was obviously starving for both.

Without waiting for Gid to respond, she marched into the small kitchen and found a place to deposit her grocery bag. After taking off her coat, she piled the dirty dishes from the counter into an already crowded sink and started pulling things out of the bag.

Gid joined her in the kitchen. She relished that look of uncertainty on his face. He was always so confident he knew everything. "You're going to cook him dinner?"

She nodded.

"I don't really want to remind you of this, but you don't have time."

She pulled a package of chicken breasts out of the bag. "It doesn't matter if I don't have time. Nobody should be alone at Christmastime, not if I have anything to say about it."

A smile formed around the edges of his eyes. "Okay."

Pulling a jar out of the bag, she tried to ignore the way his piercing gaze made her heart soar like a sled going over a ten-foot snow jump. "Really, Gid? Green olives?"

Lou hobbled into the kitchen. "We had green olives for breakfast, lunch, and dinner when I was stationed in Germany. They're candy to me."

She rolled her eyes when Gid smugly folded his arms across his chest and winked at her. "I know my condiments."

She took a bag of potato chips and a jar of peanut butter from the bag, plus a loaf of bread, four cans of soup, a bag of apples, and a bar of cheddar cheese.

Gid watched her reaction as she pulled food out of the bag. "I wish you would have consulted me first," she said, earning an indignant smirk from Gid, "but I think I can work with this. Lou, can I peek in your fridge?"

"And the cupboards too, if you want." His tone still sounded as if her cooking in his kitchen was a huge imposition in his life, but Dottie could tell by the softening of the lines around his mouth and the way he tucked his hands into his pockets, that he found their visit an immense comfort.

Gute. Hopefully she could bring a little Christmas cheer where cheer was in short supply.

"First," she said, rummaging through his cupboards for a clean bowl—a clean anything, "let's have an appetizer." She found a coffee mug in one of the bottom cupboards, popped open the bottle of olives, and poured the olives into the mug. "Sit at the table, and we can visit while I make a casserole."

Gid pulled out a chair for Lou and sat next to him. There was barely room on the table for the mug, as it was covered with an eight-inch pile of bills and letters and other papers that spread out over the entire surface of the table. Did all these need to be paid? And would Lou be offended if she asked him to move the stack so they'd have a place to eat?

Gid saved her the trouble. "Can we put these the living room?" he asked, laying his hand on the stack.

"I save 'em for shredding," Lou said, popping an olive into his mouth. "Brent says I'll get my identity stolen."

"Do you have a shredder?"

"That's the trouble. It's down in the basement. I haven't done stairs for months."

Gid smiled. "If you want me to get it, I'll help you shred everything. We can clear off the table one sheet of paper at a time."

Lou wrinkled his brow. "Well now. You don't want to do that," he said, as if he really wanted someone to clear the pile away for him, but didn't want to impose.

"Why not?"

"It's Christmas Eve."

Gid stood up. "It sounds like a fun Christmas Eve activity to me. I'm Amish. I never get to play with a shredder."

Lou's expression could have passed for a smile. "Well then. Go and get it. I haven't eaten at this table for months."

"It will be my Christmas present," Gid said.

While Gid and Lou sat at the table shredding documents, Dottie searched through the cupboards until she'd salvaged enough supplies to throw together a fairly decent chicken casserole. She cut up three breasts of chicken and laid them in the bottom of the pan, then mixed some cream of mushroom soup and rice she'd found in the cupboard and poured them over the top. She layered grated cheese over that and finished with a handful of crushed potato chips.

Once she'd slid that into the oven, she went to work on the cake and the peanut butter cookies. Lou didn't have any brown sugar, but he did have white sugar and a small amount of molasses. It would be just enough for the apple pudding cake. Lou had a small bowl on the counter filled with Hershey's Kisses. She'd make peanut blossom cookies and press a Hershey's Kiss into the middle of each one.

She glanced at Gid out of the corner of her eye. He acted as if shredding bills were the most fun thing in the world while he listened in rapt attention to Lou, who was telling him about being in the Army and falling in love with his wife.

Warmth spread through her veins. Not even creating the perfect frosting poinsettia had made her feel this good. She thanked the Lord that Gid had brought her and that they were here together. How could she have ever believed that she didn't want him at her party? He was completely indispensable.

Once the cookies were finished and the cake was in the oven, Dottie started on the dishes. It really could be a nice little kitchen if it were clean. Filling the sink with soap and dirty dishes, she stifled a shudder at the sight of mold growing on some of the bowls and cups. Hot, soapy water would do the trick.

While the dishes dried, she sponged out the cupboards so the dishes would have a clean place to perch and wiped down the counters, spraying them with a solution of water and white vinegar. At least Lou had vinegar. Mamm always said it was the most important ingredient in the kitchen.

Would Lou be offended if she worked her way into the living room? Biting her lip, she glanced at him as he and Gid made their way through the pile of bills. She simply couldn't stop now. He'd be so much more comfortable in a clean house.

She took a deep breath and forged ahead. "Lou, can I do your floors?"

Gid gazed at her as if she were a Christmas angel. She held her breath as a ribbon of warmth slid down her spine. He was certainly good looking. A girl could get too *ferhoodled* to think straight looking into those eyes of his.

Lou lifted his head and gazed at Dottie without really seeing her. "Kumi used to do the floors. She's my wife. We were married forty-nine years and eleven months. Cancer took her." A sigh came from deep in his throat. "That's the only day I ever cried."

"My . . . my *mamm* had cancer," Dottie said. "She's in remission."

Lou studied Dottie's face and then pointed a finger at her. "She'll be all right," he said firmly. "Don't you lose your faith. She'll be all right."

Dottie was surprised by the tears that filled her eyes. Lou didn't even know her *mamm*, but it was oddly comforting to hear his adamant reassurance, as if it would be okay simply because he was so certain.

"Thank you," she whispered. "She will."

"And you can mop my floors if you want. Kumi loved clean floors, and my back's too stiff to do 'em anymore."

Dottie found a broom and a ratty mop and quickly dispatched them on the wooden floors in the kitchen and the living room. While she wiped down the dust on the piano, Gid took four garbage bags full of shredded paper out to the trash bin.

Once she was satisfied with the floors, she wiped off the table and set it with three mismatched plates and cups.

"Just a minute," Lou said. He disappeared into the back and came out with a pot of plastic poinsettias and placed it in the middle of the table.

Dottie ignored the dust that caked each petal and the cobweb hanging from one of the leaves. The table would be more festive, and even if it wasn't perfect, Lou liked it.

Gid hadn't seen the need to buy vegetables, canned or fresh, so Dottie opened a jar of peaches from Lou's pantry. The label on the peaches, written in a dainty woman's hand, indicated that the peaches had been canned nine years ago. But the bottle was still sealed and the fruit looked okay inside. She decided to chance it.

Dottie brought the casserole to the table with the peaches and three pieces of toast. The chips on top of the casserole had baked golden brown, and it smelled delicious. Lou's Christmas dinner was a little bit of a letdown after the beautiful eats she'd made yesterday, but it was the best she could do. She'd feel horrible if he was disappointed.

"I didn't think you could do it," he said, as they sat around the table. "Dottie, you are like Julia Child the way you conjure up a meal out of nothing."

She didn't know who Julia Child was, but the way Lou said it, bursting with gratitude like that, made Dottie believe it was a deep compliment. He reached across the table and laid his hand over hers. He scowled like the grumpy old man he was. "You didn't need to come over, you know. I would have been fine either way." He let his frown sink deeper into his face. "But Kumi would have been happy that you came. She worried about leaving me alone when she died. I told her I'd be okay either way, but she still worried. You know how women worry too much."

Dottie stood and made a great show of looking for the salt and pepper so Lou wouldn't see her tears. She didn't want him to think there was any pity behind her emotion.

She couldn't find the pepper. Once she retrieved the salt, she sat and scooted her chair closer to the table.

"Shall we join hands in prayer?" Lou said.

Dottie clasped hands with her companions and tried to ignore the pleasant sensation of her hand in Gid's. She loved the feel of his calluses against her palm and the way his long fingers wrapped all the way around hers.

"Lord," said Lou, "bless this food that it will taste as good as it looks. Amen."

The chicken casserole turned out better than Dottie had expected. Among the three of them, they finished the entire pan. Gid and Lou raved about the moist apple pudding cake, especially with creamy sauce drizzled on top. Dottie smiled. Butter made everything taste better. After the cake, Dottie set out the cookies.

"This is a feast," Lou said. "I haven't eaten this much since Kumi passed away."

Gid insisted on helping with the dishes, and he acted like getting his hands all soapy and wrinkly was the most fun thing in the world. "I'm the dishwasher at home," he said. "It's my favorite job."

While the two of them cleaned up the dishes, Lou went into the front room and played Christmas carols on the piano.

Gid handed Dottie a plate to dry. "Lou used to play for his church," he said. "Now he can't see the music so well."

"It's beautiful."

"He knows the Christmas ones by heart."

Dottie watched Gid out of the corner of her eye as he drained the water from the sink and swabbed the counters. In her few encounters with him at Ada's house, she'd never seen this side of him. Gid was Ada's annoying and adventurous cousin who loved to hunt and fish and camp. He'd once spent four nights in a snow cave. Dottie had no idea he did dishes and looked after elderly people and had a smile that made her think of springtime. "How do you know Lou?" she asked.

"I'm not sure."

She gave him one of her best quirky smiles. "Okay."

Gid chuckled. "He and my *dawdi* Stutzman were friends. Since my *dawdi* passed away, I've tried to watch out for him. His children are pretty busy."

"But you haven't been to Bonduel for two years yet."

"Sure I have. I just haven't been to Ada's house at Christmas for two years. I come to Bonduel five or six times a year to visit Mammi and Dawdi Helmuth. Greenwood's only a couple of hours away by car."

Dottie felt quite disappointed that she'd missed out on all those other times he'd been in town.

"Gid," Lou called. "Get in here and sing the tenor part."

Gid handed Dottie his towel and flashed an overconfident smile. "I might be a bad hummer, but I am a very good singer."

They went into the front room, and Dottie sat on the threadbare chair while Gid took his place next to Lou at the piano. Gid wrinkled his forehead and widened his eyes at Dottie as if to say, "Get ready for something wonderful-*gute*."

She stifled a giggle. It was best not to encourage his arrogance.

Lou played the introduction, and they began to sing, Gid on the melody and Lou booming a lower harmony. "*Oh come, all ye faithful, joyful and triumphant.*"

Dottie couldn't hide how impressed she was. Gid, so eager to brag about what a good game player he was, hadn't exaggerated his singing skills. His beautiful tenor voice seemed to spiral in the air and envelop her like a mantle of silk.

"*Oh come ye, oh come ye to Bethlehem.*"

Lou's playing became more energetic until they finished the song together in full voice. Lou turned to look at Dottie and pointed at Gid. "He should have been in a band, don't you think?"

"A band?"

"But then, he wouldn't be Amish," Lou said, "so I guess it's just as well."

Gid winked at Dottie, too sure of himself by half. "And all this with a sore toe."

Dottie gave him a teasing grin. "You are a very *gute* singer, Gid. It wonders me why you can't hum to save your life."

"I wanted to let you win," he said.

Oh, *sis yuscht!* His smile could have charmed the beard off a bishop.

"What's this about humming?" Lou said.

"It's a game my mamm made up," Dottie said. "Everybody writes down the names of Christmas songs on small strips of paper and puts them in a bowl, and then you have one minute to get your team to guess as many songs as they can. But instead of talking, you have to give your team clues by humming the songs." She looked at Gid sideways. "Gid is pretty bad at it."

"I am not," Gid protested.

"I wouldn't mind playing that," Lou said. "Gid and I will hum, and you can guess."

"Okay," said Gid. "But I warn you, I have been known to make grown men cry when they lose."

They spent the next half hour playing the humming game. Gid was indeed the worst hummer in the world. It seemed that humming made it impossible for Gid to put tune and rhythm together. He failed miserably. The three of them got to laughing so hard, neither Gid nor Lou was understandable after a while.

Gid lost the humming game, twenty-seven to six.

When the game ended, Lou looked at his watch. "If you stay another couple of hours, it will be time for supper."

Dottie's heart skipped a beat. She'd completely lost track of time. The *lebkuchen* and stollen weren't going to make themselves. And the baking was the least of her worries. She had to get to Anna's house and fetch the quilt, the present she had spent three months working on. If this was going to be the best Christmas ever, she must get home immediately.

Gid seemed to read her thoughts. "Lou, much as we'd like to stay, our families will be needing us at home."

Lou nodded in resignation and averted his eyes. "Everybody should have family at Christmas."

Dottie's heart just about broke at the look on his face, but he squared his shoulders, took a deep breath, and shook his finger at her. "I'll be just fine, young lady. I don't need anybody's pity. You should be with your own folks. My son gave me a thirty-two-inch LED TV for my birthday last year, and Bing Crosby's on tonight."

She nodded and tried to smile as if she felt better about it.

He shook his finger at Gid next. "You owe me an ice-fishing trip."

"How about a few days after Christmas? I'll be here for another week."

"I'll hold you to that," Lou said.

"Do you mind if I bring my cousin Junior?"

"Nope, just as long as he don't scare the fish away."

Dottie walked out the door with a lump in her throat. There were just too many people who needed her.

Gid drove home, not quite as fast as he had gotten them there, but fast enough that Dottie knew he was concerned at how late they were getting back. "I'm sorry that took so long," he said as they pulled off the road and onto her lane.

"I'm not," she said. "I had a *gute* time."

He stopped the sleigh in front of her house, and she almost jumped out of her skin when he took her hand. "*Denki* for cooking and cleaning and playing that aggravating game."

She couldn't concentrate on what he was saying when his surprisingly warm hand enveloped hers. "I like it when . . . when you . . . hum," she stammered.

She liked it when he did a lot of things, not the least of which was taking her hand and smiling at her as if she were a whole batch of gooey cinnamon rolls fresh from the oven.

She *felt* like a gooey batch of cinnamon rolls fresh from the oven. With cream-cheese frosting on top.

"I'll never forget your kindness," he said. "Especially after I sort of kidnapped you."

She giggled like a giddy teenager. "You asked nicely, and I should still have time to get the baking done for Mamm."

"I'm sure your *mamm* counts you as a great blessing."

"I just want her to be well."

He grew serious. "Are you scared?"

"About my *mamm*?"

He nodded. "But maybe I shouldn't ask. Am I being nosy?"

Doubt blurred the edges of her vision. "I am scared. We came so close to losing her last year. This Christmas is a celebration of her recovery as much as it is a celebration of the Christ Child. I'm baking all her favorite Christmas foods, and I've stitched a quilt. I worked on it at your *mammi's* house so Mamm would be completely surprised."

"I don't wonder but you'll make her very happy."

She could have stared at him until New Year's, but she really had to get the stollen into the oven. She stepped down from the sleigh.

"Will I see you tomorrow?" he asked.

Her heart was like to jump for joy. He wanted to see her again? "If we visit the cousins."

"Then I will pray that your *dat* gets it in his head to visit the cousins. If you don't come, I might borrow Onkel Joe's sleigh again."

"Only if you promise to go slow."

He grinned. "I like to go fast."

"I know."

Eva came tripping out of the house with a plate in her hand. "Dottie, look! You were so late in coming that Mamm said why don't I go ahead and make the *lebkuchen*." She held up her plate of slightly blackened cookies for Dottie to see.

Dottie sucked in her breath. "Eva, I told you not to do them yourself."

Eva lifted her chin and forged ahead, trying to convince Dottie she'd done a good thing. "Mamm wanted me to do them."

"You left them too long in the oven, and they're all different shapes. And look at the almonds. They're crooked. We only had enough almonds to do one batch."

Eva's voice trembled. "Mamm says they look delicious."

"They're all wrong, Eva. I told you to wait."

With red eyes, Eva pressed her lips together and marched back into the house. How could she have tried to do the *lebkuchen* herself when Dottie had given her express instructions not to?

She turned to Gid, expecting a little sympathy, but instead encountered a deep frown. He didn't frown often. She didn't like it.

"I think she was only trying to help."

Irritation sliced through her. "But you heard me. You heard me say for her to wait."

"Your *mamm* won't mind burned *lebkuchen*. She'll probably like them better because Eva tried so hard."

Dottie was so frustrated as she saw her time slipping away that she turned on Gid, even though she didn't mean to. "How do you know what my *mamm* would like? Have you ever had cancer? Were you ever afraid that the next Christmas might be your last?"

Small lines gathered around his eyes. "*Nae,* but I can't imagine that a plate of burned *lebkuchen* will ruin your *mamm's* Christmas."

"You just don't understand. All this, all these little things I do show Mamm how much I care. It's got to be perfect."

"It doesn't have to be perfect. It just needs to be from your heart." He smiled as if he were teasing her, like he had at Ada's front door yesterday. Did he think this was a joke?

The bitterness rose inside her. She deserved to be taken seriously, especially by someone as arrogant and shallow as Gid Stutzman. "Well, you might not care enough to make it special, but I do. You don't know anything."

The look he gave her was almost resentful. "No plate of cookies is worth hurting someone's feelings."

She felt as if he'd thrown a large rock at her, and she was dizzy from his rebuke. He spoke forcefully, as if he didn't care how his words stung.

"Don't for one minute think you know better than I do, because you don't," she snapped. "You came to town yesterday with all your boasting and bragging. Just because you're so cocky doesn't mean you know everything."

He raised his hands in surrender. "Okay, Dottie. I'm sorry. What can I do to help?"

"I don't need your sarcasm."

"Sarcasm? I want to help."

"No, you don't. You just want to make me feel guilty."

"Look, Dottie. I think you're wrong with the way you treated Eva, but that doesn't mean I don't want your Christmas to be nice."

"It will be very nice without you." She turned on her heels and marched to the house. "I'm wasting time."

"Until tomorrow then?" he said with a tinge of doubt in his voice.

She didn't answer him as she stormed to the door and slammed it behind her. Tomorrow, she'd be too busy celebrating her perfect Christmas to entertain guests or visit cousins.

And that's the way she wanted it.

CHAPTER 7

Anna Helmuth slipped into the kitchen chair next to Dottie as if trying to sneak up on her. "How are things coming along with Gid?" she asked.

Gid? What did Anna care about Gid—well, besides the fact that he was her grandson? The better question was, what did Anna care what Dottie thought of Gid?

Dottie glued the last glittering star onto her very special Christmas card for Mamm. She'd attached little rounds of foam onto the card and glued the stars to the foam so they stood out in relief against the midnight-blue paper. At the bottom of the card was the silhouette of a little stable she'd fashioned out of crinkly brown paper. It had taken her an hour to create, but she knew Mamm would be thrilled when she opened it.

Anna's great-granddaughter Beth sat on the other end of the table feeding her toddler. Toby bounced in his highchair, but there was little chance that he would get baby food on her beautiful card.

"Your mamm is going to love it," Beth said. She smiled as if she couldn't stop if she tried. Dottie had heard that Beth and Tyler Yoder were coming along very well. Like as not, that explained why Beth seemed to float on air.

Dottie glanced at Anna's bird clock. The time was much later than she anticipated. Once she had stuffed the turkey, baked the stollen, and remade the *lebkuchen*, she'd ridden as fast as she could to Anna's to put some finishing touches on the quilt. Even with Beth's help, the little embroidered holly leaves at each corner had taken more time than she'd expected. The hour was late, but Mamm would be delighted, no matter what Gid Stutzman thought.

As far as Dottie was concerned, Gid could find some other girl to scold. What did he know about making Christmas special? She didn't wonder but his idea of "special" was cutting an extra big hole in the ice for fishing and picking the dirt out of his hot dog before he ate it.

He could just take those icy-blue eyes of his and use them to *ferhoodle* some other girl who didn't mind being teased and didn't care that he had a serious humming disability.

Who needed that whooshing roller coaster feeling every time he looked at her, anyway?

"Do you want to eat supper with us before you leave?" Anna said.

Felty sat in his recliner and perused his paper. "*Jah*," he said, without looking up. "Zucchini lentil soup will warm you up for the ride home. You don't want to miss it."

Dottie gave them a tired smile. "They'd worry about me. I didn't tell anyone where I was going." No one but Gid, and he didn't count because he obviously thought surprises were folly.

Anna went to the stove and stirred the thick sludge that must have been her zucchini lentil soup. "I made enough for all of us."

Dottie smiled to herself, glad she had an excuse to miss Anna's zucchini soup. Anna was famous for her cooking, but not in a good way.

She ran her hands along the quilt. It was magnificent, if she did say so herself. She'd paired a country-red and a forest-green fabric with two different shades of cream in a log-cabin pattern that seemed to zigzag the entire length of the quilt. Log cabin was Mamm's favorite quilt pattern.

After neatly folding the quilt, Dottie placed it in a plastic garbage bag and stuffed it into her canvas bag with Mamm's Christmas card. "It won't take me half an hour to get home, and if I leave now, I'll only be a few minutes late for dinner. Mamm wants the whole family together tonight. I'm sure she'll hold dinner for me. Six-thirty isn't all that late to eat."

Anna went to her hall closet and pulled out eight colorful potholders. "Give these to your brothers and sister from me, and tell them merry Christmas."

Dottie stuffed them into her already-full bag. "*Denki*, Anna. Everybody loves your potholders." Unlike her cooking.

Felty practically leaped from his recliner, went to the fridge, and took out two apples. "And give these to your pony as a Christmas present."

"I will," Dottie said, glad she'd brought a big bag. "Brownie loves apples."

She put on her coat and bonnet and donned the red mittens Anna had knit for her several weeks ago. She wore sweatpants under her dress to keep her legs toasty. Hopefully, she'd be warm enough for the short ride home.

Anna opened the door. Outside, snow was beginning to fall, but the flakes weren't thick. Dottie wasn't worried about the gathering darkness. She had a flashlight and could navigate the roads between here and her house with her eyes closed.

A wall of frigid, moist air accosted Dottie as she stepped outside and retrieved Brownie and her little one-person sleigh from the barn. Eva and Barty used the sleigh on school days, and Dottie took it when she just needed to make a quick trip to the country store. Brownie, their little Shetland pony, pulled the sleigh in winter or a little cart when the snow melted.

As she headed down the hill, the breeze made her shiver, and Dottie tossed her scarf around her face with a sweep of her hand. By the time she reached the road at the bottom of Huckleberry Hill, the snow swirled like feathers in a pillow fight. Dottie could still see the road by the light of the flashlight, but landmarks and trails were slowly starting to lose their shape under a blanket of snow.

Dottie jiggled the reins and prodded Brownie into a trot. They must get home before the storm got worse.

Brownie slowed down as the drifts deepened and he could no longer trot easily through the snow. She could still see the road, but her flashlight wasn't bright and the coming darkness threatened to leave her driving blind. She might be forced to test that theory about getting home with her eyes closed.

The snow pelted her face, and the icy wind slashed at her cheeks. It had grown a hundred times worse than when she'd left Huckleberry Hill. Why, oh why had she waited so long? Was Mamm's special card really worth the extra hour it had taken her to make it?

Fearing she had missed the turnoff she needed, Dottie slowed Brownie even further. Raising her flashlight, she shielded her eyes from the snow and stared into the void of swirling ice and gathering darkness.

Was that the lane just ahead? It didn't look quite right, but nothing seemed familiar covered with a new layer of snow. She twitched the reins, and Brownie obediently turned off the road.

Dottie could see nearly nothing. Her flashlight reflected off the falling snow and visibility was almost better without it. She occasionally caught a glimpse of the shadow of an aspen and, once or twice, a sumac bush. Although she thought she was going the right way, the trees suddenly became thicker, towering above her for as high as she would see.

Her hands gripped the reins in panic as Brownie kept moving, now plowing his way through the snow. Soon he wouldn't be able to find purchase in the deep drifts. Dottie pulled on the reins, tied them to the bar, and got out of the sleigh. Her shoes crunched in the snow and the wind howled against her ears as she tromped to Brownie and nuzzled her face against his.

"Where do you think we are?" she asked.

Brownie nodded his head and shook the snow off his mane. The wind blew the snow sideways, swirling it around Dottie and Brownie like an arctic tornado. Dottie shivered. Her feet and hands stung with the cold, and her jaw ached from clenching it hard enough to keep her teeth from chattering.

She didn't think she could find her way out of the woods, and if the storm got worse, they would need to find shelter. She tromped back to the sleigh, retrieved her bag, and slung it over her shoulder. She could hardly bear to do it, but going back to Brownie, she pulled off her mittens and unhitched him from the sleigh. Then she grabbed his lead and walked him back the way they had come. Or *was* it the way they had come? The path that seemed so plain just minutes earlier had disappeared as if someone had taken a broom to it.

Using the flashlight to illuminate her path, Dottie strained to see past the snow and darkness for something, anything that might provide a little shelter for her and her pony. It was no use. In this blizzard, she might as well be blind.

Tears oozed from her eyes and seemed to freeze before they made it down her cheeks. She sniffed and pressed her mitten against her face. Tears would do no good. She had to find a way out of this.

Wrapping her arms around Brownie's neck, she bowed her head. "Heavenly Father, Mamm deserves a *gute* Christmas, and no one else can organize it like I can. Please, will You help me get home? I'd rather not freeze to death tonight. Amen."

She took up Brownie's bridle, but they only went about twenty feet before she realized *that* particular prayer wasn't going to get her very far.

Pursing her lips, she bowed her head again. "Heavenly Father, I'd settle for shelter if You don't lead me home." Then the most important words. "In all things, Thy will be done."

She never liked saying that, but tonight she knew she needed to stretch her faith.

The trees seemed to crowd around her, as if there had never been a lane or a road or even so much as a path. Soon, she and Brownie were dodging trees and bushes in an attempt to find the easiest way through the suddenly thick forest.

She stubbed her toe on something hard beneath the snow, probably a rock, and tripped over her frozen feet. She grunted at the pain of the cold that sliced through her sweatpants as she fell into the snow. Her knee throbbed, and she didn't know if she would even be able to stand up again. There was no stopping the tears now. She was going to freeze to death in the middle of nowhere. A sob escaped her lips and was carried away from her on the howling wind.

Something caught her eye as, moaning in pain, she pushed herself up to her hands and knees. A dark mass loomed off to her left. She shined her light in that direction. By what she could make out, it looked big enough to be some sort of shelter. Her heart fluttered as she rose to her feet. If she hadn't fallen, her head wouldn't have been turned in that direction, and she would have missed it.

Thank you, Lord, that I fell.

"*Cum*, Brownie. Let's hope I'm not just seeing things."

Brownie, as steady as ever, let her lead him along until they reached the structure, which appeared to be some sort of hut.

Looking for a way in, she trudged around the corner and found a door with a knob that turned only after she put some muscle into it. The door protested loudly when Dottie pushed on it, scraping against the dirt floor as she shoved it open and coaxed Brownie inside. Then she forced it shut with a bang, leaving her ears ringing.

Before venturing any farther, she shined her flashlight into the profound darkness. She stood in a barren room, probably ten feet wide by ten feet long, with rough-hewn log walls and a small window with no glass. The snow blew into the window, leaving a drift across the floor.

A doorway in front of her revealed another small room with a light dusting of frost on the floor.

A hunter's cabin.

More like a hunter's shack. But it was shelter. She wouldn't look a gift horse in the mouth.

Even though snow blew in the window, it felt warmer just being out of the wind. She let go of Brownie's bridle and stepped into the second room. It also contained a window, but this one was boarded up so the snow couldn't get in. A small brick fireplace with a metal grate sat in one wall with an ample stack of wood next to it.

A smile tugged at her mouth. She couldn't feel her toes, her sweatpants were soaking wet, and she shook violently, but she had a flashlight, a roof over her head, and a fireplace. God was watching out for her after all.

If she wanted to keep from freezing, she must find a way to

build a fire. There was wood but no kindling or matches. And the chimney might be plugged. She had no idea how long it had been since this cabin had been used.

Maybe someone had dropped a match somewhere inside the cabin. Saying a silent prayer, she took off her mittens and felt around the cracks in the fireplace and under the logs. She shook like a dry leaf in the wind, searching the floor and around the windowsills in both rooms.

She found a dented tin cup with no handle, a galvanized metal bucket, and, surprisingly, a worn leather jacket and a flannel shirt hanging on a hook in the room with the fireplace.

Checking the pockets of the jacket, she found three dollars and some sort of energy bar. She opened the bar, smelled it to make sure it was still good, and then fed it to Brownie. He seemed to like it. Something told her the owner of the jacket wouldn't mind if his snack got fed to the pony.

She laid the shirt and coat over Brownie's back. It wasn't much, but it would be warmer than not having anything.

But still no matches.

Even if she had flint and steel, she couldn't begin to know how to make a spark with them, and rubbing two sticks together would be equally futile. Nobody could actually start a fire by rubbing two sticks together—except maybe Gid Stutzman, the person who camped as often as some boys took a shower.

Thinking of Gid took her breath away. Would she ever see him again? Would she ever see Mamm and Dat? No matter how badly she wanted to deny it or how adamantly she had tried to justify herself to Gid, she'd hurt Eva's feelings today. Would she ever have a chance to apologize, not only to Eva but to Gid for being so stubborn?

How long before they realized she was missing? Certainly by now they would be looking for her. But she didn't even know where she was. How would anybody find her?

Jiggling the flashlight in her hands, she wondered how long the battery would last. She sat it on the windowsill in the first room with the light pointing out into the storm. Maybe someone would see it. Panic clawed at her throat and nearly choked her.

Probably they wouldn't.

Despair threatened to smother her. She was cold, so cold, and without a way to make a fire, she had little chance of survival, even inside the sheltering walls of the cabin. With no other plan, she sat in a corner, clasped her arms around her knees, and cried until she was too exhausted to care.

CHAPTER 8

Gid picked at the food on his plate. Aunt Elsie had probably spent all day baking bread and chopping onions and roasting chickens. He'd seem ungrateful if he didn't have at least three helpings of everything. But his heart and his appetite just weren't in it.

His head was still swimming with Dottie Schrock and her stormy hazel eyes. Oh, she was pretty all right, but her beauty was not what had stolen his appetite. He was enchanted with the way she crinkled her nose when she was angry and how her graceful hands sprinkled cheese on top of a casserole and how his gut clenched when she twisted her lips into that cute, reluctant grin.

And how he'd ruined his chance with her.

He'd never been one to pussyfoot around the truth, even to spare someone's feelings, but he hadn't been prepared for Dottie's reaction. He'd hurt her feelings something wonderful, and she probably didn't want to lay eyes on him ever again.

The heaviness pressing on his chest made it hard to breath. In twenty-four short hours, Dottie had taken over his reason, his senses, and his life. She'd been worried to the point of anxiety about finishing everything for Christmas Eve, and yet she'd spent hours at Lou's house making him feel a little less lonely and a little more loved.

The way she'd marched into that kitchen as if she'd owned it and made dinner with chicken and a few potato chips was nothing short of amazing. He could have sat at that table for hours just watching her move around the room while she worked her art with those graceful hands. Even the sight of her sweeping the floor, caring for Lou's basic needs, made his throat dry up until he thought he'd never be able to swallow again. She filled every space in his chest and made his heart sing a joyful carol.

Could he really have grown this attached to someone in such a short time? Whether it made sense or not, the emotion was as real and tangible as his own heart beating forcefully in his chest.

Junior and Ada sat on his right with Onkel Joe and Aunt Elsie. His cousin Katie with her husband and two small children sat on Gid's left. Onkel Joe and Elsie's three other children would be here tomorrow morning with their families to open presents and eat Christmas dinner. There would be plenty of company to help him take his mind off Dottie, to help him forget the memory of her face when she'd stormed into her house this afternoon without so much as saying good-bye.

"Don't you like it, Gid?" Aunt Elsie asked.

He lifted his head and smiled halfheartedly. "*Jah*. I love it. Chestnut stuffing is one of my favorites." He shoved a big bite into his mouth.

"I hope so. We're having chestnut stuffing again tomorrow. But this time inside the turkey."

"And cheesy potatoes," Junior said, with his mouth full of green Jell-O salad. "Lena is bringing the cheesy potatoes. They're the best part of Christmas."

"Junior," Onkel Joe scolded, "the Christ child is the most important part of Christmas."

"Yes, Dat," Junior said, lowering his head in a brief show of humility before taking a monstrous bite of his roll. "I meant the best thing to eat at Christmas."

"Junior, don't talk with your mouth full."

Maybe Gid should stroll over to Dottie's place. Just for a visit. Maybe to deliver an apology. It was only a ten-minute walk from Aunt Elsie's.

Nae. He would end up ruining Dottie's perfect Christmas Eve with her family, just like he'd almost ruined her party last night. He wouldn't care for a repeat of that scene at the door. He'd go tomorrow, after all the celebrating, and see if she'd agree to talk to him. Gid glanced out the window. The sky was blacker than a coal bin, and wispy flakes of snow fell lightly to the ground. It looked to be a bad storm. He'd go tomorrow. Hopefully more than the storm would have blown over by then.

A knock at the back door sent Gid to his feet. Maybe Dottie had decided she couldn't wait. Maybe she had come to see him.

He shook his head, a little annoyed with himself that he would even imagine such a thing. Dottie was not coming tonight, not in his fondest dreams.

Gid was a little surprised to see Dottie's *dat*, Melvin, standing on the back porch. Shouldn't he be home with Dottie for the perfect Christmas Eve celebration?

"Is Dottie here?" Melvin said, stepping inside and brushing the snow off his coat.

"No . . . no," Gid stammered, giddy with the thought that she might be coming. "Is she supposed to be?"

"She's not here," said Onkel Joe, rising to offer Melvin a seat.

Melvin shook his head at the empty chair. "She left home more than three hours ago and hasn't returned. She was very firm that we start supper at six. That was almost half an hour ago."

Aunt Elsie knitted her brow. "That doesn't sound like Dottie."

Melvin took off his hat and curled his fingers around the rim. "Do you know where she might be? She left the house at three and told Eva she had one more Christmas surprise to fetch, but she didn't tell Eva where she was going. She loves secrets at Christmastime."

"I know where she went," Gid said. Dottie would probably be irritated that he spilled her secret, but her family was worried. He'd let her give him a stern talking-to tomorrow. "She's been making a gift for your wife, and she's been keeping it at my grandparents' house so you wouldn't find out. She told me she was going to pick it up this afternoon before supper."

Melvin's shoulders sagged with relief. "She probably got held up at Anna Helmuth's. Sometimes she loses track of time when she's doing one of her projects."

Onkel Joe nudged the curtains aside. "It doesn't look too good out there. I hope she makes it home soon. Buggies have a rough time in the snow."

"She took the little sleigh Eva and Barty use for school. Do you think she'll be okay?"

Aunt Elsie joined Onkel Joe at the window. "I don't wonder but it will be mighty cold if she gets stuck in the snow on the way home."

"If I need to fetch her," said her *dat*, "I don't want to wait. We could be in for quite a blizzard."

Gid's chest tightened. If Dottie saw a storm blowing in, she'd have enough sense to stay at Mammi and Dawdi's overnight, wouldn't she? He ran his fingers through his hair. Not when she wanted so badly to give her *mamm* the perfect Christmas. She'd trudge through a mountain of snow before she'd ever miss Christmas Eve.

The possibility of Dottie being in danger made him feel ill.

"I'll ride to Huckleberry Hill," Gid said.

Melvin gave Gid an anxious smile. "No, I can go."

"I don't mind. It will give me a chance to say hello to my grandparents."

"It's making down hard," Melvin said doubtfully. "Are you sure? It's almost a thirty-minute ride."

Gid was already plucking his coat from the hook. "Onkel Joe, can I take your horse? Like as not, he'll make it better through the snow without being hitched to the sleigh. I've done a lot of winter camping on a horse. I can take him through the snow yet."

"I'll have Junior saddle Pete."

Junior groaned at the prospect of going out into the cold to ready the horse.

"No whining, son," said Aunt Elsie.

"She's probably on her way home by now," said her *dat*, "but I would be grateful if you'd make sure she gets in safely. Lord willing, you'll meet her coming here on your way there."

"Can I take a lantern?" Gid asked.

"*Jah, jah*, anything you need," Aunt Elsie said. "Do you want me to pack some food?"

Gid shook his head. "We won't be gone that long, and it will only weigh down the horse. If she's still at my *mammi's* when I get there, I think we should stay the night at their place and not risk riding home in the storm."

"I think that's best," said her *dat*.

"If Junior will let me borrow his cell phone, I can call Onkel Joe's phone when I find her." Onkel Joe had a phone in his wood shop for out-of-state orders.

Aunt Elsie's eyes widened to the size of two shiny Christmas plates. "What cell phone?"

Gid glanced at Junior and winced. "Sorry, but I need a phone."

Junior turned a bright shade of pink and averted his eyes as if he were playing that game where if he couldn't see his *mamm*, she couldn't see him.

It didn't work. Aunt Elsie wasn't about to let him get away with anything. "Joe Junior, what do you have to say for yourself?"

Junior shrugged his shoulders and grimaced sheepishly at his *mamm*. "It's all charged up and ready to go?"

"Not good enough, young man. Get your phone for Gid and then go out there and saddle Pete and think hard on your sins."

"But Mamm, I'm in *rumschpringe*."

"*Rumschpringe* or no *rumschpringe*, you know better than to keep such a secret from your *mamm*. *Ach, du lieva*, Junior, it wonders me how you were raised."

As sorry as Gid was about spilling the beans, he'd do the same thing again in a heartbeat. Dottie's safety was more important that Junior's secret cell phone.

Gid took the stairs two at a time. After putting on a pair snow pants and his warm wool socks, he laced up his snow boots, put on his coat, and pulled a beanie over his hair. Should he take his snowshoes? Maybe, just in case.

The anxiety rose like water in a flood. Dottie had to be all right.

Gid took a deep breath. Not one to lose his head in an emergency, he reined in his galloping thoughts. Dottie was probably walking into her house at this very minute, and they'd have a laugh about how everyone had worried.

He stomped into Junior's room and pulled the cell phone from its hiding place at the bottom of Junior's drawer. He wouldn't turn it on until he needed to. Lord willing, Junior hadn't been mistaken and the phone was charged. His heart bounced around in his chest.

How likely was it that he would even get service in a place as re-mote as Huckleberry Hill?

With a lantern in one hand, and gloves and snowshoes in the other, he raced to the barn. Junior had laid a thick blanket under-neath the saddle.

"*Denki*, Junior. I'm sorry about the cell phone."

Junior waved away the apology. "She was gonna find out soon anyway. Sometimes I forget to turn the ringer off."

"Who do you call with that thing?"

The corner of Junior's lip twitched upward. "Lots of girls have them."

Gid tied his snowshoes to the saddle, shoved the gloves onto his hands, and mounted.

"It helps if you hold it high above your head," Junior said.

"What?"

"The cell reception isn't all that good out here. When I can't get a signal, I hold it over my head, and it sometimes works."

"How do you talk to anybody with the phone two feet above your ear?"

Junior grinned. "I put it on speaker."

Gid resisted the urge to roll his eyes. Junior had given him his phone. He would be grateful for that. But he wouldn't be happy until he'd found Dottie and brought her home.

By the time Gid turned up the lane to Huckleberry Hill, the snow fell so hard, he had trouble seeing three feet in front of his face, even with the lantern. He'd watched for Dottie the whole way, but nobody was out on the road tonight, not even the *Englischers* in their cars.

He'd noticed a few tracks at least a mile back already buried with new snow, but they had turned off onto a narrow road that led into the woods. Dottie would know not to take that way home.

The temperature dipped into the twenties when darkness fell. The cold didn't bother him. He had the gear to withstand it. But he had worried himself into a gut ache over Dottie. If she was outside in this, she'd be in deep trouble.

Holding his lantern aloft, he spurred Pete into a brisk walk, making sure not to push the horse too hard up the icy hill. He'd feel a whole lot better when he found Dottie safe and sound inside the house, sitting beside the fire and drinking hot cocoa with his grandparents.

He led Pete to the barn and tied him to a post. No use in the horse staying out in this any longer than he had to. Shielding his eyes from the snow pelting his face, he trudged up the porch steps and knocked on the door.

Mammi opened the door, squealed with delight, and ushered him into the kitchen. After the brisk air, the warmth nearly knocked him over and made his lungs feel heavy.

"Look, Felty, it's Gid. Just the boy we wanted," Anna said, her eyes a twinkly blue.

"I'm sorry I didn't tell you I was coming to Bonduel," Gid said, not wanting to spoil Dawdi's Christmas snowshoe surprise.

Dawdi and Cousin Beth sat at the table sipping something from a steaming mug. It was right where Gid had hoped to find Dottie.

Beth grinned. "Gid, how nice to see you."

Dawdi's eyes danced. "Well, hello, Gid. I'm surprised to see you, but somehow your *mammi* knew you would come. You picked quite a night for a visit. It's making down hard out there."

"Very hard. I almost can't see a thing."

"*Cum*," Anna said, nudging him farther into the room. "Stand by the woodstove and warm your hands. You look like Jack Frost with that layer of snow on your hat."

Gid didn't move. He wouldn't make himself comfortable until he knew Dottie was safe. "Is Dottie here?"

"*Ach, du lieva.*" Anna burst into an infectious smile. "You're looking for Dottie?"

"Is she here?"

"You just missed her. Well, I can't say you *just* missed her. She left about half an hour ago."

What was left of Gid's stomach plummeted to the floor. "Half an hour? Did she say where she was going?"

"I hope she went straight home in this storm," Beth said.

Fear set Gid's heart to pounding against his chest. Dottie was out there somewhere, and if he didn't find her soon, he didn't even want to think about what might happen.

"She hadn't arrived home yet when I left to come here. I came all the way from her house to see if I could track her down. I'm afraid she might be lost. I can't see a thing through that blizzard out there."

"Oh no," Anna said. "What do you think happened? Do you think she's okay?"

Gid closed his eyes and took a deep breath. "I hope so."

He took off his gloves and pulled Junior's phone from his coat pocket. "I'm going to call the police."

Anna covered her mouth with her hand. "The police? Is it that bad?"

"Maybe not, but I'm not going to wait to find out."

He turned Junior's phone on and dialed 911. The phone seemed to think about it for a minute and then blinked its rejection. *Call failed.*

Growling in frustration, he lifted the phone clear over his head and dialed again. *Call failed.* No good.

Ice ran through his veins as he tucked his coat collar around his neck. "I'm not getting any service. I'll ride down the hill and try again and see if I can pick up any sign of her. Maybe she took a wrong turn and couldn't find the way back."

"If anybody can find her, you can," Dawdi said. "Dig a snow cave if you can't see your way out of the storm."

"I will," said Gid, hoping it didn't come to that. If he was desperate enough to dig a snow cave, both he and Dottie would be in serious trouble indeed.

"Wait," Mammi said. She bustled to her closet and pulled out an emerald-green scarf. "Take this. It's made with lots of love. It will keep you extra warm."

"Thank you," Gid said. Mammi claimed her scarves had saved more than one life. Gid was never quite sure what she meant. "I'll come by tomorrow to take you . . . I'll visit tomorrow."

"Bring Dottie along," Mammi said, not grasping the gravity of the situation at hand. It was probably better that way.

Not wanting to waste one more minute, he bolted out the door without saying good-bye and ran for the barn. At least Pete had had a chance to get a drink and a little rest.

He coaxed Pete down the hill and onto the main road keeping a sharp lookout for any sign of Dottie and her sleigh. He tried the phone again, fearing he'd get the same result as before. He did.

As fast as he dared prod Pete to go, he headed in the direction of the path where he'd seen tracks earlier. Lord willing, he'd find Dottie at the end of those tracks.

A long, slow mile from Huckleberry Hill, Gid found the turnoff where he thought he had seen the tracks. He held the lantern at his side high enough to light his way but not so high that the light reflecting off the heavy snowfall blinded him. If there had been any tracks, they had been wiped clean by the snow and wind. He followed his gut and turned Pete down the lightly worn path. If Dottie had gone this way, she couldn't have gone far.

"Dottie," he called. The wind carried his voice away almost before it was out of his mouth. She wouldn't be able to hear him above the roar of the storm, and even if she could, he would never hear her answer back.

He tried the phone one more time with little hope. If it hadn't worked on Huckleberry Hill, chances were it wouldn't work in the dense woods.

The trees grew thicker the farther he ventured off the road. Gid let Pete choose the pace as the horse gingerly plowed his way through the deepening snow. Snowflakes accumulated in Gid's eyelashes and slithered down his neck despite Mammi's fuzzy green scarf. His nose and cheeks felt raw in the biting wind.

Please, Lord, don't let Dottie be out in this.

How far had he gone? Two, three miles? It was taking too long. He needed to find Dottie and he needed to find her now. And still, the snow fell in thick sheets.

He was just about to turn back when Pete nearly stumbled over an abandoned sleigh in the middle of the path. It was covered with snow, but its shape was easy enough to distinguish. His heart pounded even as a pit formed in his stomach.

It had to be Dottie's sleigh. Where was Dottie?

Gid slid off Pete and studied the ground. His lantern cast a ghostly light over the snow. The drifts seemed less smooth to his left. Had Dottie led her pony farther into the woods? Maybe she had been so disoriented that she hadn't known what direction she headed in.

Heavenly Father, please guide my steps.

Keeping his eyes glued to what looked like evidence of Dottie's trail, Gid walked his horse deeper into the woods. He couldn't see more than about four feet in front of him, but faint signs of footprints were enough to give him hope that he was going in the right direction.

A glint of something through the trees caught his eye. He put the lantern behind his back to smother its light. There it was, a tiny beacon up ahead. His heart jumped into his throat.

He trudged madly through the snow, pulling Pete behind him and keeping his gaze fixed on that light. He soon saw what he was headed toward. The dark shape of a hunter's cabin loomed in front of him with a tiny light shining in one of the windows.

He guided Pete around the cabin until he found a door. Without even thinking to knock, he shoved the door open and lifted his lantern. A pony stood inside the small room, where half the floor was covered with snow. The pony looked no worse for the wear, even though he had to be cold.

A dim flashlight sat on the windowsill of an open window, pointed out into the darkness. The battery was just about spent.

He dropped Pete's lead and stepped around the pony to another doorway, letting his light show the way. He could almost hear his clamoring heartbeat as he glimpsed a dark figure huddled in the corner. Holding his breath, he lifted the lantern higher and nearly passed out with relief.

"You came," she whispered.

CHAPTER 9

At first she wondered if he was an angel come to take her to heaven. She felt cold enough to be near death. Then the light illuminated his face.

Gid.

Gid. The boy she'd snapped at today. The boy who couldn't hum but who could make her feel all tingly inside just by looking at her. The boy who slept in snow caves and probably fought wolves with his bare hands.

"Dottie," he nearly shouted, his voice a mixture of panic and relief.

She was too weak to stand up. Her legs felt as if they were frozen to the cold dirt floor, and her arms wouldn't move properly.

He set his lantern on the floor next to the wall. With two giant steps, he was at her side. Enveloping her in a smothering bear hug, he pulled her to her feet. He held her firmly in his embrace as if he understood that she couldn't stand on her own. With his arms around her, it felt like a heat wave had just blown in. "Dottie, are you okay? Can you move your legs?"

"I . . . I don't think so."

Keeping a tight hold of her, he said, "Stamp your feet on the ground. Get the circulation moving."

She did as she was told and winced with pain as her half-frozen feet met with the rock-hard floor.

"I'm sorry," he said, pressing his cheek against hers. "I know it hurts. You're experiencing mild hypothermia. But don't stop moving."

Holding her arm, he unzipped his coat, pulled her closer, and wrapped her inside the coat with him. She sighed as his body heat engulfed her. His heavenly masculine scent filled her nose. Would Dat consider this inappropriate behavior? Should she step away? She couldn't step away. She couldn't even stand on her own.

"I can't feel my fingers. Will they have to cut them off?"

"Slip your mittens off and wrap your hands around my back. Inside my coat."

She took off her mittens and slid her ice-cold hands around him. It was freezing in here. How could he be radiating so much heat?

"Keep stamping," he said when she paused the savor his warmth. They must have looked like they were doing some strange dance together.

Dottie gasped with every step. Her feet felt like two chunks of ice, and frosty needles stabbed into her each time her sweatpants rubbed against her skin.

"Do you feel the circulation coming back into your legs?"

She nodded.

"Can you stand on your own? I need to build a fire."

The thought of Gid withdrawing his body heat made her want to cry. She bit her lip. "Maybe if I lean against the wall."

"Okay, I'm going to let go. As soon as I build a fire, I'll wrap you up again."

She reluctantly pulled her hands from behind his back and reached for the windowsill. She winced. The window was boarded up, but the sill was covered with a layer of ice.

"Here," he said, pulling off his gloves. "Put these on."

"Your hands will freeze."

He took her hands and slid his gloves onto them. "I'll wear your mittens. Once I get the fire going, neither of us will need them."

She shifted her weight stiffly and grasped the ledge as if it were a lifeline.

"Keep stamping," he said.

Stiffly, she stomped one foot and then the other. "I fell in the snow. My sweatpants are starting to freeze."

Alarm joined the concern already on his face. Bending over, he lifted the hem of her dress a few inches so he could get a better look. Grabbing a handful of the pants' fabric, he said, "These are soaked. They've got to come off."

"Come off?" The thought of exposing her legs to the frigid air made her throat constrict. "I can't."

"You're more likely to develop hypothermia when you're wet. Trust me. You'll feel warmer without them."

It took all her strength not to burst into tears. She was so cold. "Are you sure?"

"I'll bring Pete in while you take them off. Are your shoes wet too?"

Dottie nodded.

Gid stepped into the other room and took the leather jacket from Brownie's back. "Take your shoes and socks off and stand on this. It will be warmer than the bare floor."

Without another word, he stepped out of the room. While she slipped off her shoes, stockings, and sweatpants, she heard Gid coax his horse into the cabin and shut the door. With the snow blowing in the open window, it couldn't have been much warmer for the animals inside than it was outside.

She shivered as the frigid air pinched her exposed skin. The pain was nearly unbearable. Taking shallow breaths, she held on to the ledge, stood on the jacket, and tried to borrow some warmth from it. It didn't make her feel any better.

Gid reentered the room holding a pair of snowshoes in one hand and the lantern in the other. He glanced at her with immense anxiety etched into his features. "Here, sit down," he said, taking off his coat. She sat on the jacket, and he laid his coat across her legs. "Hang on. Just let me build a fire."

"You need your coat, Gid."

"I've got layers." He knelt down next to the fireplace and regarded the pile of logs. "We need some newspaper."

"Are you going to rub two sticks together?"

His lips twitched upward. "A good mountain man never leaves home without matches." He pointed to her bag sitting in the corner. "Do you have anything in there we could use for kindling?"

"I don't know."

He grabbed it from the floor and rifled through it as if his life depended on it. He found the plastic garbage bag and pulled the quilt out. "Dottie," he growled. "Why didn't you use this earlier?" She gasped as he tossed it to her. "Wrap it around your legs and then put my coat over the top of that. Layers."

Dottie squeezed the tears from her eyes. "It's Mamm's special quilt. I don't want it to get dirty. It will be ruined."

He pressed his lips into a rigid line and scolded her with his eyes. "I refuse to let you get frostbite."

Her heart sank as she looked at the lap quilt in her hand. All those months of carefully stitching the small strips of fabric together. She couldn't bear to get it dirty.

"Dottie, wrap that quilt around your legs." Now he sounded angry.

She wanted to resist him, but she knew he was right. And her feet were so cold. With a lump in her throat, she bundled Mamm's beautiful quilt around her legs and pulled Gid's coat over it.

He must not have liked the look on her face. Scooting next to her, he laid a gentle hand on her shoulder. "Quilts are made to keep people warm, Dottie." His smile was a little sad, and she could tell he truly felt bad about the quilt. "Your mamm would rather have you than the most beautiful quilt in the world." He brushed his cold fingers down her cheek. The cabin grew ten degrees warmer. "And so would I. You and all your toes."

She pulled her knees up to her chin, wrapped her arms around them, and curled her toes. They were stiff, but at least she could feel them. "I'd like to have all my toes for Christmas."

Satisfied, Gid nodded, went back to the fireplace with some urgency, and continued his search of her bag. He pulled out the special card she'd made for Mamm. He glanced at her guiltily. "Sorry, Dottie. I need something dry and flammable."

She nodded, not trusting her voice to remain steady. She'd spent an hour on that card. Was Gid determined to ruin everything?

She scrunched herself into a tighter ball and watched as Gid tore her beautiful card into strips and laid the scraps into a pile on the grate inside the fireplace. Tears ran down her face, but she didn't make a sound. It seemed ridiculous to be crying over something so small when a fire could save their lives.

Embarrassed to be caught crying, she blotted the tears from her face with Gid's large glove before taking it off and stuffing her hand into her coat pocket. She discovered a treasure. "Here's more paper if you need it."

She pulled out the dollar bills she had found in the leather jacket. Gid nodded and took them from her. He shredded them and put them in his pile. "Oh, wait," he said. "One more thing." He scooted to his coat she sat on, reached into the pocket, and pulled out a wadded-up piece of paper. His lips twisted wryly. "Ada's letter."

Dottie wouldn't have thought it possible to feel any warmth in her cheeks, but she felt herself blushing all the same.

Gid tore the letter into his pile. "We need kindling if we have any hope of catching the big stuff on fire." His hand went into her bag again.

He smiled, actually smiled, when he pulled out the yarn potholders Anna had given her. "Will I hurt Mammi's feelings if I burn these?"

"I think Anna would be pleased to know her potholders came in handy."

He formed three of the potholders into a little tent over the scraps of paper, money, and glittering paper stars. Then he formed a tent-like structure over that with four of the smaller pieces of wood. He turned to her and nodded reassuringly. "This is going to work."

"Lord willing, the chimney is clear."

"God is watching out for us. It will work." Yesterday, she'd found his overconfidence irritating. Today, she found it comforting. If Gid was sure, then she didn't need to doubt.

He took a match out of his snow pants' pocket and struck it against a brick. It caught fire, and he carefully poked it under the strips of paper. The paper flared into flame, and Dottie held her breath. If the potholders didn't catch fire, she didn't know what Gid would do.

He pressed his lips together and a line appeared between his brows. Gid was holding his breath too.

The potholders smoldered for a few seconds, and thick smoke curled out from underneath them as the flames from the burning paper lapped at the corners. Then, suddenly, there was a puff of air and the potholders burst into bright, welcome flame.

Dottie sighed in relief. Gid's grin took over his whole face. "I told you it would work. Never underestimate my many abilities."

"Like humming?"

He cocked an eyebrow. "Look into that fire and tell me how important my humming skills are now."

Gid threw the rest of the potholders onto the fire and watched as the flames danced merrily around the wood. When the smaller logs had taken hold, he threw a bigger one onto the fire. "That should be enough to warm us up. *Cum*, Dottie, scoot as close as you can."

She stood but couldn't straighten her back or her knees. Gid grabbed the jacket and the quilt and coat and moved them while Dottie, hunched over and shivering, shuffled closer. Gid folded up his coat and put it on the ground. "Sit on this instead or the floor will absorb too much of your heat."

When Dottie sat down, he laid the quilt over her legs and then tucked it underneath her. Dottie winced. Her log-cabin design already wore several smudges of dirt. Gid laid the jacket over her feet. This close to the fire, she felt much better already.

"Do we have enough wood?"

"Should last a few hours yet." Standing up straight, Gid pulled a cell phone out of his pocket.

"Where did you get that?" she asked.

"It's Junior's." He dialed a number and raised it over his head as if he were asking the teacher a question.

She heard it ring. Gid must have had it on speaker.

"Hello, Gid?" It was Aunt Elsie.

"Aunt Elsie," Gid said, the relief evident in his voice. "Tell Melvin I found Dottie, and she's okay."

"Oh, Gid, wonderful-*gute*. That is an answer to our prayers. We got so worried when we didn't hear from you. Are you staying at Anna and Felty's?"

"Aunt Elsie, I need you to call the police and tell them where we are."

"Hello? Hello, Gid? Are you there?"

Gid spoke louder. "I need you to call the police."

"Gid? I can't hear you," Aunt Elsie said before her voice cut off and the phone went dead.

Gid frowned. "A cell phone will only get you so far out here. But at least they know you're safe."

"I've never seen anyone talk on a phone that way before. Is it how *die youngie* are doing it these days?"

He chuckled in spite of himself and sat down next to her. "A tip from Junior. He said it was the only way I'd get reception if I got any at all. I've tried making a call on that thing seven times since I left my mammi's house." He warmed his hands near the flame. "At least we've got a fire. You won't freeze."

Without warning, he grabbed her canvas bag, turned it upside down, and dumped the rest of its contents onto the floor.

"What are you doing?"

"We're not out of the woods yet," Gid said, "Literally. I'm taking an inventory of our assets. Didn't you ever read *Hatchet*?"

"I don't even know what you're talking about."

There wasn't much in her canvas bag: the plastic garbage bag that used to hold her mamm's quilt, the small Ziploc bag for Mamm's Christmas card, and the two apples Felty had given her.

Gid laid them in front of him as if they were gold nuggets. He reached inside the pocket of his snow pants and pulled out a knife, a handful of matches, and a white handkerchief.

"We also have your mittens, a bucket, the lantern, and a tin cup," he said. "And my snowshoes." He rubbed his hand up and down her arm. "Are you feeling warmer?"

"*Jah*. It is getting better."

"Then I'm going to try to get us safely through the night. I don't think anybody is coming for us. They probably think we're staying with Mammi and Dawdi."

"We could try to make it home."

"Not in this weather."

Her heart thumped loudly in her chest. They were stuck in this frigid cabin for the rest of the night. A chill ran through her bones just thinking about it.

But then she remembered, and she could breathe again. Gid was here. He had strong hands, a quick mind, and a *gute* heart. He could take care of them both. She was safe.

He snatched the garbage bag and the bucket and went into the other room where Brownie and Pete stood silently, side by side, no doubt trying to share their body heat. Dottie leaned her head to the left to see what he was doing. He took the dead flashlight from the windowsill and put it and the bucket on the floor. Then he hung the garbage bag around the open window by stuffing the bag's edges into the small space between the window frame and the wall. He used the blade of his pocketknife to wedge the garbage bag deeply into the narrow slit all the way around the window.

He searched the floor and found several pebbles, which he stuffed tightly into the slits, effectively anchoring the garbage bag into place. The plastic blocked the wind and kept the snow outside.

"That was smart," she said.

She saw him grin by the light of the lantern. He quickly took off Pete's saddle, but left the blanket. Opening the door just wide enough to slip through, he picked up the bucket and went outside. He came back with a bucketful of snow that he set next to the fire. "The horses could use a drink," he said. He scooped some snow from the bucket with the tin cup. "Let this melt, and then you have a drink too."

He wouldn't stay still. After throwing another log on the fire, he cut one of the apples in half and fed it to the horses. He used one of his snowshoes as a clumsy broom to sweep up the pile of snow in the front room and push it out the door.

Dottie stayed close to the fire, flexing her fingers and toes and letting her body soak up all the warmth it would. She still wore her bonnet and *kapp* plus her coat and Gid's gloves, but she didn't think she'd feel truly warm ever again.

Gid went to the boarded-up window and took the scarf from around his neck.

"Is that one of Anna's?" Dottie asked.

He nodded. "I hope she doesn't mind." With his pocketknife, he sliced the scarf into six pieces. Bits of yarn rained on the floor.

He stuffed the pieces of scarf into the gaps in the boards, effectively sealing up any cracks where the wind wanted to sneak in.

By this time, the water in the bucket had melted to slush. He let Pete and Brownie have a drink and then went outside and filled it with snow again.

With the windows sealed and the fire crackling, their little shelter felt almost cozy. When he had refilled her tin cup with snow and watered the horses for a second time, Gid sat next to her on the floor. "How are your hands? How are your feet? Are they warm?"

"My feet will never be warm again," she said with a half smile. "But I'm sitting on a dirt floor in a shack with two horses in the next room. All things considered, I am toasty enough."

He held out his hand. "Let me see."

Hesitantly, she folded back Mamm's quilt and stuck out one of her feet. Gid wrapped it in his surprisingly warm hands. Taken aback, she tried to pull away.

"It's okay," he said, flashing his irresistibly cocky grin. "I don't bite."

"Boys don't usually touch my feet."

He chuckled. "Oh, well, girls touch my feet all the time. I've been told I have really nice feet."

She couldn't keep one side of her mouth from twitching upward. That boy was completely devoid of humility.

But she surely liked that smile.

She relaxed as he massaged up and down the bottom of her foot, being careful not to touch anything above her ankle. Even in these dire circumstances, the bishop would not approve. "Your foot feels like a popsicle."

"What flavor?"

He didn't reply, just grinned and rubbed until he was satisfied. He did the same with the other foot until Dottie knew that she wanted her feet rubbed every day for the rest of her life.

He sat back and unlaced his boots, laid them aside, and took off his stockings. Dottie caught her breath when his bare feet were exposed and she saw that one of his big toes sported a purple bruise. "You really do have a sore toe."

His eyes sparkled with firelight. "Ice-fishing accident." He held out one of his socks to her. "Here. Would wearing my socks be disgusting?"

"Um, yes."

"Can you put them on anyway? I'll feel better knowing your feet will be warmer."

"What about your feet?"

"I'll put my boots back on."

Dottie didn't mind wearing Gid's stockings. As a matter of fact, she didn't mind a lot of things about him. She slipped his long, wool socks onto her feet and immediately knew it was a good idea. "*Denki.* These are wonderful-*gute,*" she said. "But I feel bad taking your socks. You need warm feet too."

"You can consider my socks your first Christmas present."

"Oh," she said, slumping her shoulders. "Tonight is Christmas Eve." A sudden and profound feeling of loss filled her chest. "I'm missing it."

"I'm sorry."

She might not be in danger of freezing to death, but she was still sitting on a dirt floor in a shack with two horses in the next room while her family ate stollen and sang carols without her.

The thought of stollen was too much. Her composure disintegrated in a deluge of tears. She plucked off Gid's bulky gloves and buried her face in her hands.

Gid scooted closer and wrapped his arms around her. "It's okay," he said in his low, soothing voice. "It's going to be okay."

She leaned her head on his shoulder and bawled harder. His kindness only served to remind her how *deerich*—foolish—she had been. "I don't have anyone to blame but myself," she sobbed. "I was running late because I insisted on redoing poor Eva's cookies." She fingered a corner of Mamm's soiled Christmas quilt. "Then I spent all that time at Anna's house embroidering leaves onto this quilt that's completely ruined, and I wasted an hour on the card that is now a pile of ashes."

She felt him stiffen beside her. "I shouldn't have taken you on that sleigh ride. I messed up your whole schedule."

She lifted her chin and found his face within inches of hers. Ignoring the way her heart seemed to pause in its rhythm, she said, "But . . . I wanted to come."

"I practically dragged you kicking and screaming."

"But wasn't it wonderful-*gute* how happy Lou was?"

His expression relaxed. "It was wonderful-*gute* how happy I was."

This time her heart did jumping jacks. She should insist that he quit looking at her like that. She would die of a heart attack. "I'm sorry I snapped at you."

"I shouldn't have put my oar in the water when I don't really understand what you've been through this past year."

"Mamm spent last Christmas in the hospital. I wanted this Christmas to be nice for her."

Gid pulled her closer and nuzzled his chin on top of her head. "Do you think she'll be disappointed about the quilt?"

His embrace was uncommonly comforting, as if he had pulled her into his circle of protection.

She wiped the leftover tears from her face. "*Nae*. She would rather have me home safe than get a thousand special quilts for Christmas."

A load of coal seemed to settle on top of Dottie's chest, and she nearly growled out loud. "*Oy*, anyhow. I didn't lose track of time. I lost track of what's important. I worked so hard to give Mamm the perfect Christmas that I didn't realize how many feelings I was hurting or how much time I was spending away from home. All those hours spent working on her quilt could have been spent just being with her. My *mamm's* perfect Christmas isn't about *lebkuchen*. It's about being with the family." Tears stung her eyes again. She blinked rapidly to clear them away. "And I can't even give her that. I've messed up everything for everybody, even you. You could be at Onkel Joe's house, playing games with Junior and singing Christmas carols."

"Now why would I want to be there when I get to spend Christmas Eve with the prettiest girl in Bonduel?"

She nudged him with her elbow. "Ha," she said. "If it weren't so sad, I'd laugh."

"I'm not joking. Now that it's unlikely we'll freeze to death, we have every reason to celebrate."

She smirked. "Oh, really? What reasons?"

"Plenty of dry logs to burn and Anna's green scarf."

"I can celebrate that, I guess," she said.

"We have a spacious cabin with enough room for us and our horses."

Dottie thought of Brownie out in the blizzard. "*Jah*, thank you, Lord."

"And it's Christmas Eve. This is the night Jesus was born. That's the best thing to celebrate."

She nodded. "*Jah*, of course." She grabbed his hand and held on tight. "*Denki* for reminding me."

He cleared his throat. Maybe she shouldn't have touched his hand. He seemed a little discombobulated. "I'll be right back," he said.

With that, he stood up, taking his warmth with him. He grabbed the tin cup from the floor and walked into the room with the pony and the horse. He maneuvered around the animals and opened the door, letting a blast of cold air into the room. Dottie shivered. The snow had drifted three feet high just outside the door. He didn't have to go far to scoop some of the white stuff into the cup and slam the door as quickly as possible. He'd let in too much cold air as it was.

He came back to the fire and laid the cup at the edge of the coals. It didn't take long for the snow to melt. Sitting down, he slipped his hand into the pocket of his snow pants and pulled out a candy cane. "You gave me this last night," he said, a tease gleaming in his eyes. "I'm impressed at how big it is."

She grinned. "Any Christmas party worth attending serves extra-large candy canes, not those tiny ones they hand out at the bank."

Before unwrapping it, he crushed it into smaller pieces, then tore open the wrapper and let the shards of candy fall into the cup.

"What are you doing?" she asked.

"Just wait," he said. "It's all part of the Christmas Eve festivities."

When the water started steaming, he pulled the cup from the fire, using one of Dottie's red mittens as an oven mitt.

"Christmas peppermint tea?" he said, handing her the other mitten to use as a hot pad so she wouldn't burn her hands.

Dottie grinned uncontrollably and took a sip of Gid's peppermint tea. "Delicious," she said. "It tastes like Christmas morning."

She took another sip before handing it to him. He drank, and when he handed the cup back to her, his eyes danced and she saw something deep and tender there.

Warmth tingled to the very tips of her toes. Who needed a fire when she had Gid Stutzman around?

She and Gid shared the tea until it was gone. "The fire is wonderful-*gute*. I'm almost hot," Dottie said.

"Here," he said, getting up on one knee. "Take off your bonnet and coat. You don't want to sweat under there. That will actually make you colder."

She removed her bonnet, leaving her prayer covering in place. She folded the bonnet neatly and was about to stuff it in her pocket when she remembered the riches she had been carrying with her. She slipped her hand into her pocket and retrieved six Hershey's kisses. "Look what I found."

Gid bloomed into a smile that pushed the shadows back a bit. "Where did you get those?"

"Lou gave them to me as we were leaving. A Christmas gift."

Gid palmed the apple. "We've practically got a Christmas feast."

After laying the chocolate next to the apple, Dottie unzipped her coat, and Gid helped her slip it off her shoulders. She stuffed the bonnet in her pocket, and Gid hung her coat on the hook. He sat next to her and picked up a piece of chocolate. "Shall we eat?"

Dottie quirked one side of her mouth upward and took the chocolate from his fingers. "Not yet. I'm going to make you a fancy Christmas dessert."

He cocked an eyebrow. She was beginning to adore that self-assured, cheeky grin. "What else is in that pocket?"

She unwrapped the first chocolate kiss and plopped it into the cup.

"Wait," he said. "Save the foil and the little paper thing."

She looked at him sideways.

He shrugged as amusement flickered in his eyes. "This tiny piece of foil might save our lives."

She unwrapped the rest of the chocolates, carefully making a little pile of foil and paper next to her. All the chocolate went into the cup, and using a mitten, she held it close to the fire until the chocolate melted.

She held out her hand to Gid. "If I may trouble you for your pocketknife."

His grin grew wider as he pulled out his pocketknife and flipped the blade up. "Careful. It's sharp."

"Believe me, Gid Stutzman, I know how to handle a knife. I can chop a peck of green peppers for chowchow in about two minutes."

"Okay," he said, holding up his hands in surrender. "I just want you to know that I am really handy with a pocketknife. It takes a lot of skill."

"If you were any more arrogant, your head would swell bigger than this cabin and we wouldn't be able to fit inside."

He cupped his hands on the top of his head as if to keep it from exploding. "That sounds painful."

She giggled and carefully cut the little green apple into sixteen slices. "Here you go," she said, handing him some slices and putting the tin cup between them. "This is like caramel-dipped apples, except they're chocolate-dipped."

"Hey," he said. "I got ten pieces and you only got six. No fair."

"You built the fire for our little party, not to mention the fact that you saved my life. You deserve more."

"You cooked Christmas dinner for Lou and sacrificed your potholders to my fire. You deserve them just as much as I do."

She ignored his attempt to be gracious and dipped one of her apple slices into the chocolate. The silky melted chocolate combined with the crisp, tangy apple tasted better than the best batch of *lebkuchen* she'd ever made. It tasted like Christmas memories and Christmases yet to come. It tasted like being home safe with her family's arms securely around her.

"Are you okay?" Gid asked.

She sniffed back the tears as they pooled in her eyes. "It wonders me if Mary and Joseph felt like this. Alone and away from home, with no one to rely on but each other."

"And God."

The emotion welled inside her. "*Jah*. God is watching over us tonight."

He slid close and wrapped his arm around her. "Warm enough?"

She'd never felt so cozy. She gazed into his sky-blue eyes and nodded.

Smiling back, he tightened his arm around her and began to sing. "*Stille Nacht, heilige Nacht.*" "Silent Night" in German. He had such a rich tenor voice, as if all the herald angels joined with him.

"*Alles schläft; einsam wacht, Nur das traute hochheilige Paar.*" All are sleeping, alone watches only the close, most holy couple.

"*Holder Knabe im lockigen Haar.*" Blessed boy in curly hair.

"*Schlaf in himmlischer Ruh! Schlaf in himmlischer Ruh!*" Sleep in heavenly peace.

Although her voice wasn't near as angelic, she joined him on the second and third verses. Her heart ached to think of the lonely couple from Galilee. How forsaken they must have felt. In comparison, Dottie knew she had nothing to be sad about and every reason to rejoice.

When the last strains of their carol floated to the ceiling, Dottie thought her heart might overflow with gratitude. She was safe and warm. Gid had trekked through a blizzard to save her, and God had sent His Son to save them both.

Gid put another log on the fire, sat down, and grinned at her. "In eighth grade they asked me to recite the Christmas story for the school program because I was the best memorizer."

She rolled her eyes. Gid Stutzman, cocky and braggy.

"Do you want to hear it?"

"Of course," she said. "It's Christmas Eve."

Gid leaned in and pressed his lips to her forehead. She ignored the somersaults her head was doing. "*And it came to pass in those days, that there went out a decree from Caesar Augustus, that all the world should be taxed. And Joseph also went up from Galilee, unto the city of David, which is called Bethlehem to be taxed with Mary his espoused wife, being great with child. And she brought forth her firstborn son, and wrapped him in swaddling clothes, and laid him in a manger, because there was no room for them in the inn.*"

The fire crackled as Dottie nestled deeper into his embrace.

"*And there were in the same country shepherds abiding in the field, keeping watch over their flock by night, and lo the angel of the*

Lord came upon them, and they were sore afraid. And the angel said unto them, Fear not, for behold, I bring you good tidings of great joy, which shall be to all people. For unto you is born this day in the city of David a Savior, which is Christ the Lord. And this shall be a sign unto you. You shall find the babe wrapped in swaddling clothes, lying in a manger.

"*And it came to pass, the shepherds said one to another, Let us now go even unto Bethlehem, and see this thing which is come to pass, which the Lord hath made known unto us. And they came with haste and found Mary and Joseph and the babe lying in a manger.*"

The firelight danced on the contours of his face as he fell silent and stared into the flames.

One by one, Dottie picked up the foil squares that had been wrapped around the Kisses. She molded each of them into a tiny silver star and laid them in a line on the edge of the brick fireplace. "To remember the wise men who followed the star," she said.

"And found the Light of the World."

"Do you know 'In the Bleak Midwinter'?" she asked quietly.

"*Jah.*"

"It's my favorite."

Gid smiled. "Do you want me to hum it?"

"How about just singing?"

"I'm a wonderful-*gute* singer."

She shook her head indulgently and kissed him on the cheek. "That's one of the things I like about you."

He held his breath momentarily as he stared at her mouth. After a pause that seemed to last for hours, he began to sing. "*In the bleak midwinter, frosty wind made moan, Earth stood hard as iron, water like a stone. Snow had fallen, snow on snow, snow on snow, in the bleak midwinter, long ago.*"

A gust of wind rattled the boards on the window. Dottie shivered involuntarily.

"*What can I give Him, poor as I am? If I were a shepherd, I would bring a lamb; If I were a wise man, I would do my part. Yet what I can I give Him . . . give my heart.*"

She leaned her head back against him and savored his warmth. "Merry Christmas, Gid."

"Merry Christmas, Dottie."

He didn't take his eyes off her lips as he wrapped his arms all the way around her and pulled her close. Her heart pounded so hard in her chest that she thought her ribs might crack. He brought his lips down on hers and kissed her gently.

Slipping her arms around his neck, she pulled him closer. He obliged by tightening his arms around her. A sigh came from deep in her throat. It was a bright summer day, and she was sitting on the beach in the warm glow of the sun. He had such nice lips.

He pulled away, and she reluctantly let him go. A teasing smile played at those nice lips. "I'm sure glad I didn't go to Mexico," he murmured.

"Me too."

"It's because I'm such a *gute* kisser."

She cuffed him on the shoulder. "Do all the girls tell you that?"

He chuckled softly. "You know I'm kidding. You're the only girl I've ever kissed, Dottie." The embers of a powerful emotion glowed in his eyes. "And the only girl I ever want to kiss."

She felt as if she might burst with joy as her heart soared to the sky. "I'd like that."

His smile was as dazzling as the sun reflected off the snow. "This is the best Christmas ever."

The horse whinnied, sounding unusually close. They turned to see Pete watching over them, his head sticking from the doorway while his body stayed in the other room.

"I think Pete likes the Christmas story," Gid said, standing up and nudging his horse back the way he'd come. "I better get more snow in the bucket. They can drink even if we can't do anything about feeding them until morning." He took Dottie's coat and spread it out in front of the fire. "You should get some sleep yet. You've had quite a day."

"What about you?"

"Your *dat* wouldn't be so keen on us sleeping in the same room."

"You know he'll be grateful for what you've done."

Gid rubbed the back of his neck. "It doesn't matter. I won't get to sleep anyway. My head is so full of you."

The way he said it sent a tingle up her spine.

He squatted beside her and rubbed the back of his finger along her cheek. "I'll keep the fire burning so you'll stay warm, and I won't let Pete trample you."

She curled her lips. "*Denki.*"

"I promise no harm will come to you."

"I'm sure it won't. You are a *gute* camper."

"The best in the world," he said, cocking an eyebrow and coaxing her to laugh.

Dottie lay down, and Gid spread the quilt over her and kissed her forehead like a father might do when tucking his child into bed. *In the bleak midwinter, snow on snow on snow.* Jesus had come for her and every other poor sinner in this world. And He'd come on a night like this.

She closed her eyes knowing she wouldn't sleep a wink. Gid Stutzman had kissed her. That thought was enough to keep her awake and floating in the clouds for days.

Gid sensed the morning before he actually saw it. Dawn came softly, obscured by the plastic bag fastened around the window. He'd fed the last log to the fire two hours ago. Fearing they'd run out of heat before daylight, he'd reluctantly burned his snowshoes too. He'd made them out of birch wood. They'd burn hot and long. Once he saw Dottie safely home, he'd have to come back to the cabin with a new supply of wood. Whoever used this cabin next shouldn't be left without.

The wind had calmed sometime early this morning, and the snow had stopped falling before the sun peeked over the horizon. The silence felt comforting, as if the tempest had finally given up trying to tear down their shelter.

Pete and Brownie survived the night okay. They were hungry, but at least they'd been warm. He'd tend to them as soon as they got home. An extra bucket of oats for them both. It was a fitting Christmas present for a horse.

He gave in to the urge to gaze at Dottie while she slept, but only for a minute. Watching her like that made him feel as if he was invading her privacy. But he couldn't resist one look at that porcelain skin or those long, dark eyelashes that brushed against her cheeks when she closed her eyes. His gut tightened when he thought how much he loved her and how close he had come to losing her last night. He resolved never to let her out of his embrace again.

She stirred and pushed herself to a sitting position, smiling at him with the dazed look of recent sleep. "Good morning. You're still here."

"I thought of taking the horses and hightailing out of here after you fell asleep last night," he said. "But you were sleeping on my coat." He squatted next to her and rested his forearms on his knees. "Besides, I wanted to be the first to wish you merry Christmas."

He bent and kissed her. She kissed him right back. He felt that kiss clear to his toes.

"Merry Christmas to you too," she said.

They fell silent, just looking at each other and savoring the emotion between them. Every muscle in his body awakened with longing. She was so beautiful.

He wasn't even planning on doing it, and then his tongue kind of tripped ahead of him. "What I said last night, about not wanting to kiss another girl ever—I meant every word." He lowered his eyes and stared at the ground. "What would you think about marrying me?"

Her silence compelled him to look at her. She smiled with so much joy, his heart skipped out of the cabin, through the woods, and up the road.

"I think I would like that very much," she said.

Gid whooped loud enough to make the horses jump. Gathering her into his arms, he kissed her until he thought he might explode with happiness. He pulled away to catch his breath. "I should have picked a more romantic spot, but I figured that maybe since you were just waking up, you wouldn't be thinking all that clearly. So, later today when you come to your senses, just remember you already agreed to a wedding. No take-backs."

She playfully laced her fingers with his. "Same goes for you. When you're not lightheaded from lack of breakfast, don't change your mind."

He brushed his lips against hers. "I'm never going to change my mind."

"Me neither."

They shared one more blissfully wonderful kiss before Gid

stood up and put some distance between them. No more of that if he wanted to have any of his wits left for the journey home. "Much as I'd like to spend my Christmas Day kissing, I won't be comfortable until I get you safely back. Your *mamm* will be missing you."

"Do you think we can find our way to the road?"

He smiled. "I have a very good sense of direction. Probably the best sense of direction ever."

He loved making her laugh. "Before you get too big for your britches," she said, "may I remind you that you cannot hum to save your life. When you hum, the dogs run for cover."

He dropped his jaw in mock indignation. "One thing. I'm not good at one thing, and you can't let it go. Are you going to keep bringing that up after we marry?"

"Oh course. Somebody will need to keep you humble."

He paused as if deep in thought. "As long as you marry me, I can live with that. Very, very happily."

CHAPTER 10

There seemed to be quite a stir going on at Dottie's house when Dottie and Gid finally turned up her lane. Gid was on foot, leading Pete and Brownie, while Dottie rode on Pete's back. He'd insisted on Dottie's riding since she didn't have snowshoes and her feet still ached from last night's ordeal. Both animals trudged up the lane, no doubt hungry, but they'd fared well in the storm.

Every cloud had blown away, leaving the sky so blue it almost hurt to look at. The new snow sparkled in the sun. If Dottie hadn't been so weary, she might have considered it another perfect day for a sleigh ride.

After making sure she could make it on her own, Gid lifted Dottie from the horse to let her walk the rest of the way to the house while he led Pete and Brownie straight to the barn. Their well-being was even more important to him than his own weariness.

Puzzled by the crowd gathered in her front yard, Dottie hurried up the lane. Mamm, Dat, Aunt Elsie, and Uncle Joe stood in a circle with Junior, Mammi and Dawdi Helmuth, and several neighbors. Their voices were filled with agitation, though Dottie couldn't tell what they were saying.

Was all this for her? They must have figured out she and Gid were not where everybody thought they were.

"Dottie!" she heard Mamm yell.

When he caught sight of her, Dat sprinted down the lane as quickly as he could in the deep snow. He threw his arms out and lifted Dottie off the ground. "Thank goodness you're safe. Are you hurt? Where is Gid?"

With his arm protectively around her, he squeezed her tight as if making sure she was real and then led her toward the house.

"Dottie," Mamm said, enfolding her in the embrace Dottie had been waiting for all morning. "What happened? Anna and Felty arrived this morning and said you hadn't been with them last night. We were frantic. Gid called Elsie last night to say you were all right."

Dottie glanced at Anna, who looked more than a little relieved. "Sorry, Anna. I should have stayed at your house when the storm started." She hugged her *mamm*. "But I didn't want to miss Christmas Eve. I made you a quilt."

Mamm took Dottie's face in her hands. "You are more important than any quilt."

"I know. I figured that out."

"Did you get lost in the storm?" Junior asked.

"*Jah*, Brownie and I got stuck in the snow. Eva's sleigh is buried so deep we couldn't find it this morning. I found a hunter's shack, but I still would have frozen to death if Gid hadn't found me."

"Thanks be to God," Mamm said.

Anna nodded at Felty. "I knew you two were meant for each other. I just didn't expect your courtship to be quite so exciting."

"Gid built a fire, and we spent the night in the shack with the animals. When the storm blew out this morning, we came home."

"Where's Gid?" Dat asked. "We were just about to call the police and start a search."

"He's in the barn feeding Pete and Brownie. They haven't had anything to eat since yesterday afternoon."

"Junior," Endie Elsie said.

Junior and Onkel Joe were already jogging in that direction. "We'll take care of it," Junior said. Junior was a *gute* boy, even if he was a little annoying at times.

"Let's get you in the house," Mamm said. "You look like you could use a warm bath."

The neighbors wished Dottie well before climbing into their buggies or sleighs and going off to the Christmas celebrations that awaited them at their own homes.

Dottie furrowed her brow. "They all came to help look for me?"

Mamm nodded. "Christmas can wait when one of our own is in trouble."

Dottie's heart swelled at the thought of being so cherished by her community *and* by Gid Stutzman. She was the happiest girl in the world.

Gid came from the barn and smiled at her, but he looked worn out, like a spent candle. "Junior ordered me out of the barn and insisted that he and Uncle Joe would take care of the animals." He massaged the back of his neck. "That was nice of them. I don't know how much longer I'll be able to stand up straight."

An old maroon Cadillac rolled up the lane. Dottie caught her breath. "Is that Lou?"

Gid snapped his head around. "Lou? What's he doing here?"

Lou stopped his car in front of the house, and Gid and Dottie walked around to the driver's side of the car. Lou rolled down his window with a smile as wide as Lake Erie. "I heard you two were lost. I was going to volunteer to help find you, but I see I'm too late. I'm glad you're not dead."

"Oh, thank you," Dottie said. "We got stuck in the blizzard, but found a hunter's cabin to shelter in for the night."

Lou tapped on his steering wheel. "Well, you don't look any worse for the wear."

Gid took Dottie's hand and squeezed it. She smiled at him, and he nodded slightly. "Lou, we'd be very glad if you would have Christmas dinner with us. You haven't tasted anything until you've tasted Dottie's chocolate-dipped apples."

"I'd like to, for certain I would, but my son called last night and said they'd changed their plans. There's a cold front moving through Florida, so they're driving up this way to spend the week. They'll be here tonight at six-fifteen."

That explained the irrepressible smile. Dottie felt the emotion bubble up inside her. Lou would have his heart's desire for Christmas.

Gid seemed to have no reservations about holding her hand in plain sight of everybody as they watched Lou back his car down the lane. His handsome smile took over his whole face. "Lou gets his family, I get you, and we both get to keep our toes," he said. "This is the best Christmas ever."

Even without the perfect quilt or a shiny Christmas card. Even with burned *lebkuchen* and tinfoil stars. Dottie had her family, and she had Gid Stutzman's love. It truly was the best Christmas ever.

Anna crawled into bed and pressed her cold feet against Felty's legs. He nearly jumped out of his skin. "Banannie, your toes are like icicles."

"*Denki* for warming them up," Anna replied.

"Warming them up? Now I'll need a hot water bottle for both of us."

"Wasn't it a wonderful-*gute* Christmas Day? Because of us, two of our grandchildren got engaged."

Felty rolled over and studied Anna in the darkness. "Two? Tyler and Beth are engaged. Who else?"

"Dottie and Gid, of course."

"They had a scary night in the woods, but they're not engaged."

"Now, Felty. They most certainly are engaged. They haven't announced it yet, but we *mammis* have a sense about these things. There'll be wedding bells for sure this summer."

"If you say so, Annie. I've never known you to be wrong about anything."

"Thank you, Felty. You have to be very observant to be a matchmaker."

"But I still think our grandchildren are perfectly able to make their own matches. This matchmaking rigmarole is exhausting." To prove his point, Felty rolled over and sank into his puffy pillow. "Good night, Annie. And merry Christmas.

Anna sat up in bed and propped herself on her pillow. "I don't think it's exhausting. I think it's the most fun I've had in all my eighty-three years. Watching two people fall in love, have you ever had so much fun in your life?"

"Never," Felty mumbled, about to drift off to sleep.

"I've been thinking," Anna said, as if she still had her husband's full attention. "Since we are responsible for two engagements this Christmas, I think we should try for three next Christmas. Doesn't that sound like the best idea ever?"

Felty answered her with a loud snore.

She took it as a yes.

Look for the fifth Seasons of the Heart novel,
Harvest of Blessings, next February.

HARVEST OF BLESSINGS

CHARLOTTE HUBBARD

CHAPTER 1

"Welcome back to Willow Ridge, Nora. It's a pleasure doing business with you."

How weird is this? Sixteen years ago, Nora Landwehr had never imagined herself returning, much less accepting the keys to a prime property from the man who'd been the bishop when her father had sent her away. But this little Amish spot in the road had changed a lot. And so had she.

"Thanks, Hiram," Nora murmured. "I hope I've done the right thing."

"At least you've arrived while your parents are still alive—if you can call it that." His gaze followed the road toward where the Glick house stood a ways back from the county blacktop. "Mending fences in your situation will be much like opening Pandora's box. Once you raise the lid, all your secrets will swarm out like hornets, whether you're ready or not."

His choice of words made her wonder if she'd been wise to confide in Hiram Knepp . . . to even go through with this transaction. But it was too late for second guessing. As her gaze swept the panorama of Willow Ridge farmsteads, Nora was amazed at what she saw. From this hilltop perspective, Willow Ridge looked like an idyllic little town where nothing hostile or cruel could ever happen—like Mayberry, or Walton's Mountain. But appearances could be very deceiving. "So, does Tom Hostetler still live there where all those buggies are parked?"

"He does. He's the bishop now."

"This being Thursday . . . is that a wedding or a funeral?"

Beneath Hiram's short laugh, Nora imagined the *bwah-hah-hah-hah* of a melodrama villain. "As you probably realize," he replied wryly, "a wedding, in retrospect, might indeed be a funeral of sorts, depending upon how it all works out. Annie Mae's marrying Adam Wagler today."

Nora thought back . . . waaay back, to when Adam must've been about school-age and Annie Mae Knepp had been a toddler—

And you're not there to see your daughter marry, Hiram? She bit back her retort. Her realtor had hinted that Hiram had committed even more heinous sins than she had . . . and after all, her father hadn't attended *her* wedding, either. If Hiram had been run out of Willow Ridge, she and this man with the devilish black goatee had a lot in common.

Nora didn't want to go there.

She was looking for a way to move Hiram along, so she could figure out where her major pieces of furniture would fit before the moving van got here. And yet, if everyone in town was at the wedding, this would be a fine time to look around . . .

"I'll have my crew remove the Bishop's Ridge entryway sign tomorrow." Hiram's voice sliced through her thoughts. "That way you won't be living in my shadow."

Nora didn't miss the irony there. Every Amish colony lived in its bishop's shadow—and she sensed the cloud over Willow Ridge had gotten a whole lot darker of late, even if Hiram no longer resided here. "That'll be fine. Thanks again."

"What will you do with that big barn? I miss that more than the house."

Nora smiled. No need to tell this renegade everything, for who knew what he'd do with the information? "I have some ideas," she hedged. "Figured I'd live here a while before I committed to any of them."

Finally, Hiram was headed down the road in his classic, perfectly preserved black Cadillac. Nora closed her eyes as the summer breeze caressed her face. She'd really done it . . . spent her divorce settlement on this house and acreage with the huge barn, in the town where she'd probably be greeted with hatred and hostility as she stirred up old grudges like muck from the bottom of a farm pond.

But blood is thicker than water . . . isn't it?

Once the shock and accusations ran their course, Nora sincerely hoped to reconnect with her family. To ask forgiveness and make her peace while creating a purposeful, productive new life. Was she acting even more naïve and fanciful than when she'd believed *Englischer* Tanner Landwehr was her ticket to a storybook ending?

Nora glanced at her watch. Still an hour before the van was to arrive. She slid into her red Mercedes convertible to cruise town while she could still pass as an *Englisch* tourist—not that anyone would see her. Everyone from Willow Ridge and the nearby Plain settlements would be at Adam and Annie Mae's wedding.

Once on the county blacktop she turned left, away from town, and drove past a timbered mill with a picturesque water wheel. With its backdrop of river rocks, wildflowers, and majestic old trees shimmering in the breeze, the Mill at Willow Ridge was a scene straight out of a Thomas Kincaid painting.

Nora turned back toward town. Henry and Lydia Zook's home looked added-onto yet again, and Zook's Market had expanded as well. The white wooden structure sported a new blue metal roof that glimmered in the afternoon sunlight. A handwritten sign on the door proclaimed the store closed today for the Knepp-Wagler wedding.

Purposely not yet looking at her childhood home, Nora focused on the fine new house built on what had been the northeast corner of her father's farm. Across the road sat a building that housed the Sweet Seasons Bakery Café and a quilt shop—more new additions, although she recalled the blacksmith shop behind them, and the large white home down the lane, which had belonged to Jesse Lantz. From what she could tell on the Internet, Jesse had passed on and Miriam had opened a bustling business. Who could've guessed an Amish woman would have a website with delectable pictures of her meals and bakery specialties?

A little way down the road stood the Willow Ridge Clinic, with what appeared to be a horse-drawn medical wagon parked beside it. Yet more startling changes ... but as Nora headed down the gravel road on the left, the Brenneman Cabinet Shop looked the same as always. So did Reuben Riehl's place, and Tom Hostetler's dairy farm, where black and white cows grazed placidly in the pasture with the red barn in back of the tall white farmhouse. Dozens of black buggies were parked along the lane and around the side of the barn, yet the place looked as manicured as her former lawn in Ladue. Not so much as a scrap of paper or a missing shingle marred the Plain perfection of the scene.

The sound of an ancient hymn drifting out of Tom's windows compelled Nora to stop. She'd all but forgotten the German words, yet the power of hundreds of voices singing with one accord made her suck in her breath. She swallowed hard as the melody seeped into her soul, its slow, steady cadence slowing the beat of her heart.

Quickly swiping at tears, she drove on. Could she *really* go back to three-hour church services, hard wooden pew benches, and endless, droning sermons? She couldn't recall the last time she'd attended a worship service. You couldn't consider a quickie ceremony in a Vegas wedding chapel *worship*, after all.

Maybe you won't have to worry about sitting through church. You haven't been allowed back into the fellowship yet. Haven't been forgiven.

Nora drove around the large loop that passed the Kanagy place and then a few homes where the Schrocks and other Mennonite families lived. She rolled past the fork that led to Atlee and Lizzie Glick's place—she wasn't ready to go down *that* road yet—and followed the curve that meandered in front of the Waglers' house and then past her own new residence. Definitely the finest house in town.

But what shall it profit a man, if he shall gain the whole world and lose his own soul?

Nora let out a humorless laugh. Her father, ever the sanctimonious Preacher Gabe even among his immediate family, had often quoted that verse to chastise her for wanting new dresses or some doodad she'd seen at Zook's. The mere memory of his harsh discipline tightened her chest even after sixteen years of living in the English world. If that was her visceral reaction without even seeing him, how did she think she could face him in person? So much water had gone under that proverbial bridge that Gabriel Glick would never, *ever* cross it to see his errant, banished daughter.

Nora brought herself back into the present. The moving van hadn't yet arrived, so she pulled back onto the county highway where she'd begun her trip down memory lane. While everyone in town was at the wedding, she had the perfect chance to revisit her childhood home. To prepare herself for the ordeal she would soon face.

She pulled into the lane and parked behind the house . . . slipped into the back door, knowing it wouldn't be locked. Stood in the kitchen, which appeared smaller and shabbier than she recalled, as though it hadn't seen fresh paint since she'd left. How odd—and how sad—to stand in this hub of the house and not detect even a whiff of breakfast.

Nora moved on before she lost her nerve. She felt like an intruder—and she wanted to be long gone before anyone came home from the wedding. She peeked into the small downstairs room where she and her mother had sewn the family's clothes on an ancient treadle machine—

Nora gaped. On a twin bed lay a motionless female form, like a corpse laid out in a casket. Was this what Hiram had meant by implying her parents were barely alive? Did she dare approach, or would this woman pop up like a zombie from an old horror movie and leer at her with hollowed eyes and a toothless grin? Nora wanted to bolt, yet she felt compelled to at least look this woman—surely her mother—in the face. If Mamm was so far gone, why wasn't someone sitting with her? Or was she merely napping, too tired to attend the wedding?

Holding her breath, Nora slipped silently to the bedside. Even though the room felt stuffy in the July heat, a faded quilt covered her mother's shriveled form up to her chin. A *kapp* concealed all but the front of her white hair, so all Nora saw was a pallid face etched with wrinkles. The eyes were closed, and again Nora felt as though she was observing a stranger in a casket rather than looking at her own mother. Last time she'd seen Mamm, her face had been contorted with indignation as disgust hardened her piercing hazel eyes—

And suddenly those eyes were focused on her.

Nora froze, unable to look away. Not a muscle moved in her mother's face yet Mamm's gaze didn't waver—until her eyes widened with recognition. Or was it disbelief, or fear? Or an emotion Nora couldn't interpret without other facial cues?

She didn't stick around to figure that out. Hurrying from the airless room and back through the kitchen, Nora burst through the back door. She couldn't gulp air fast enough as she climbed into her car and sped down the lane. She felt as though she'd stared Death in the face and Death had stared right back. If she looked in the rearview mirror, would a skeleton in a cape dress and *kapp* be chasing after her?

Her tires squealed as she turned onto the hot blacktop and sped toward her new home. What a relief to see the moving van lumbering across the bridge by the mill! Nora made the turn onto Bishop's Ridge Road too fast and fishtailed in the gravel, righting herself just in time to steer up the driveway toward the house. She pulled around behind the huge barn—to be out of the movers' way, but also because she felt compelled to conceal her car.

Better get over that, she chided herself as she got out. *You live here now, whether the neighbors like it or not.*

She was approaching the house when a tall, broad-shouldered figure stepped out of the shade behind it. His straw hat, broadfall pants, and suspenders announced him as Plain, and there was no mistaking the fascination on his handsome face. Yet Nora hesitated. Had this stranger been roaming around in her house? *Note to self: call a locksmith.*

"Something I can help you with?" she asked breezily. Better to believe in basic Amish honesty than to accuse him of something he might not have done. It wasn't as if he could take anything from her empty house.

"Just coming over to meet my new neighbor," he replied in a resonant voice. "I'm Luke Hooley. That's my gristmill on the river."

If you'd like to visit Ice Mountain again, read on for a sample of
The Amish Bride of Ice Mountain, on sale now!

THE AMISH BRIDE OF ICE MOUNTAIN

KELLY LONG

PROLOGUE

Coudersport, Pa. 1894

The miner wielded the pick axe with ruthless precision, pausing only now and then to wipe his brow in the high summer heat. He was sure that he was mining the spot that the Cattaraugus Indian had indicated as the source of the silver ore he possessed. The rocks and dirt gave, and then he was through. The shine flashed against his eyes with a blast of cool air. He leaned into the hole, staring in amazement, as his dreams of silver gave way to a palatial display of summer ice...

Chapter 1

Present Day
Ice Mountain, Pennsylvania

Associate Professor of Amish Studies Jude Lyons squeezed his eyes shut in the bright light of the summer sun and pretended he hadn't heard what the girl said.

But the word rang indelibly through his mind . . . *dishonored.* He opened his eyes and stared down the wooden porch step into the serious young face of the Amish girl, Mary King. Her dark hair was neatly coiled beneath her *kapp*, displaying only a straight, white part, her hazel eyes were soulful, mournful, and the pale skin of her throat was even whiter than he remembered.

Say something, you idiot . . . his brain chided him. But he couldn't seem to get past the heated imagery that flashed through his memory—the day had been hot, the blueberry patch more than cool. And maybe he'd known somehow that their relationship would build to that sudden torrential burn of intense moments, but he stupidly hadn't considered the consequences. And he certainly hadn't imagined that Mary's older brother, Joseph, might have been observing from the forest.

Jude usually never let himself go physically, not even with his fiancée. The blood thrummed in his ears—Carol . . . what would he say to Carol about this? But of course he was overreacting. He needn't mention making out with Mary at all . . .

"My *daed* and *bruders* will be along shortly—to make sure you do the right thing."

Her melodic voice was calm, rich with decades of dialectal purity, but he blinked at her words.

"What?"

"I expect they'll take a while to rouse the bishop. He likes to sleep, you know."

He likes to sleep . . . Jude took a shaky step down to the flagstone nearest her and her small bare feet.

"Mary, I'm sorry. It was all a mistake . . . I'm due to be married in the fall. Are you sure Joseph saw . . ." He let his eyes drop to her shoulders, as if she'd bear the imprints of his fingertips somehow, but there was nothing visible between the covering of her apron and dress.

"You know you were the first man who ever kissed me like that or touched—"

"I know. I know," he broke in hastily, not wanting her to verify what he remembered all too well. Her innocence had been as palpable as his own heartbeat, her novice mouth returning his kisses with a tentative response that had made his throat burn.

"*Dat* wasn't happy what with you being an outsider and all, but he's willing to settle seeing that you're *schmart* in the head."

Jude thought of the endless hours of study, sleepless nights upon nights, now his doctorate work, and his almost-completed book about the Amish of Ice Mountain, Pennsylvania. He had plans of returning home and breaking away from his father's successful business and wealthy lifestyle and becoming a professor of Amish Studies. He told himself that there was no way he was going to be coerced into "doing the right thing" for kissing a willing girl in the broad light of day. But he should have known better. If there was anything that he'd learned from his study of this people, it was their inherent sense of old-fashioned honor. The Mountain Amish were also about a hundred years farther behind the times than other Amish both in values and circumstances, and he was in the middle of nowhere with not a single soul to speak in his defense.

He scrambled in desperation for an answer, an angle . . . "Mary, your dad isn't going to want you to leave the mountain and you'd have to if I . . . if we did anything hasty. You know I'm supposed to go back to Atlanta in two weeks."

"Metro Atlanta." She emphasized what he knew she had heard him say from time to time.

"Never mind," he muttered, but then another thought came to him. He peered into her eyes. "Mary, how old are you?" *And why in heaven's name have I not asked that before?*

"Eighteen—nineteen in October."

"Well, that's something . . ." She wasn't underage by his world's standards at least. At least—what the devil was he thinking? He owed her nothing. "I'm twenty-six," he offered in spite of himself.

"Way past marrying age," she observed.

"Yeah." *From your world's view.*

She glanced behind her as instinctively, he knew, as a doe. "Here they come."

Jude was suddenly more than nervous. He wanted to sink into the ground, dissolve, or at least run as the four men broke from the line of trees, their faces set like stone. And then he felt everything go black . . .

Please turn the page for an exciting sneak peek at
Jennifer Beckstrand's newest Huckleberry Hill romance
Huckleberry Christmas, now on sale wherever print
and ebooks are sold!

HUCKLEBERRY
CHRISTMAS

JENNIFER BECKSTRAND

CHAPTER 1

Crouched on her hands and knees, Anna Helmuth shined her flashlight into the darkest corner of the cellar, where old storage boxes and ancient furniture gathered dust.

"Felty, dear," she called, hoping her voice carried up the stairs, through the cellar door, and into the kitchen, where her husband was washing up the dishes.

He might not be able to hear her, but she could hear him singing at the top of his lungs. *"Each day I'll do a golden deed, by helping those who are in need."*

It was no use. Felty was in one of his singing moods, and Anna wouldn't be able to make him hear her. She grunted as she tried to get to her feet. Her left leg had fallen asleep, and she couldn't budge an inch. Not a single inch. She turned off the flashlight, stowed it in her apron pocket, and slowly pushed herself backward with her hands. Her knees creaked like a pair of rusty hinges as she shifted to a sitting position. Propping her hand on a sturdy cardboard box, she attempted to pull herself up. No use. Her hinter parts would not cooperate.

How had she gotten herself into this predicament? She was only eighty-two years old, for goodness sake, hardly an old lady. It must have been that extra biscuit with strawberry jam she'd eaten for breakfast.

She could still hear Felty singing. "*While going down life's weary road, I'll try to lift some trav'ler's load.*" Oh, how he loved that song!

If only he knew how badly his wife needed her load lifted at this very minute. "Felty, dear," she called again.

She might be forced to crawl up the stairs. Either that or she could take a lovely nap on the cellar floor, and Felty would notice her absence when supper didn't appear on the table.

Anna waited until he took a breath, then yelled as loudly as she could without straining her throat. "Felty, do you have Rhode Island?"

The refrain halted abruptly. Felty always attuned his ear to talk of license plates. Smiling at her cleverness, Anna heard him shuffle to the top of the stairs and open the cellar door. "Are you down there, Annie?"

"*Jah*, and I'm stuck. It wonders me if you could lend a hand."

Felty clomped down the steps and peered at her by the dim light from the small window.

"My knees gave out," Anna said.

Felty reached out both hands and, nearly toppling over himself, pulled Anna to her feet. Anna limped around the cellar, testing her legs for signs of arthritis. "Fit as a fiddle," she finally declared.

"Why was you sitting on the floor?" Felty asked.

"I was looking for the baby crib."

"That old crib? I chopped it up for firewood twenty years ago yet."

"Firewood?" Anna propped her hands on her hips. "Felty, that crib cradled our thirteen babies."

"And got mighty gute use. It was like to collapse with the next baby. So I burned it." Felty's eyes twinkled. "We ain't had a baby in this house for forty years, and unless you're thinking of bringing another one into the world, it was better as firewood."

"Now, Felty. We need the crib for our great-great-grandson Toby."

"Is he coming for a visit?"

"He and his mother are going to live with us. They'll be here tomorrow."

Felty massaged his forehead just above his right eyebrow. "Annie, what are you up to?"

"Amos has been gone over a year now, and it's time we found Beth a new husband."

"Beth told her mother she doesn't want a new husband."

"Well, that's silly. I'm sure her mother didn't believe that. Every girl wants a husband, and Beth has a son to consider."

Felty wrapped his arm around his wife of sixty-three years. "I lost a lot of sleep over your last match, Annie-banannie. The doctor says I need a nap every day."

Anna kissed Felty on the cheek. "I can't see how a budding romance will interrupt your daily nap."

Felty sighed in resignation. "Who is the lucky fellow destined for our great-granddaughter?"

"Do you remember Tyler Yoder?"

"Of course I remember him. Our grandson Aden stole his fiancée."

"Lily and Tyler were never right for each other. But Tyler and Beth are a match made in heaven."

"Made in heaven or in an Amish mammi's daydreams?"

"Now, Felty, every match we've ever made has been a success."

Felty grunted. "In spite of us, not because of us."

"Beth needs our help. She's obviously not very gute at picking her own husband."

Felty shook his finger. "Don't speak ill of the dead."

Anna turned around and started climbing the stairs. "I didn't say a word against Amos. It was more a criticism of Beth."

"Where are you going? I still haven't agreed to this."

"Seeing as Tyler hasn't set foot here since church five months ago, I've got to pay Aden a visit. I need an excuse to get Tyler to Huckleberry Hill. Aden still feels guilty about marrying Tyler's fiancée, and when I tell him I've found Tyler's match, he'll be eager to help."

"Annie, I don't think I can stand any more lovebirds disturbing my peace."

Anna stopped halfway up the stairs. "So, you admit they'll fall in love." She grinned. "We should buy a crib so the baby doesn't have to sleep in a box."

Felty chuckled softly and followed Anna up the stairs. "I slept in a bureau drawer until I turned three."

"What a lovely thought, Felty. I can imagine that you were an adorable baby, like Beth's son, Toby. Cute, lively, and in need of a father."

"Every child should have a father. Especially our only great-great-grandchild."

"I knew you'd come to see it my way."

Felty shook his head in resignation as he paused at the top of the stairs to catch his breath. "Did I hear you say something about Rhode Island?"